True Joy

By

Ophelia Mixon

Dedication

To my daughter, Sophie, whose life reminds me daily that dreams are worth holding onto. May you chase yours boldly and watch them unfold

Acknowledgment

I am deeply grateful to everyone who supported me throughout this writing journey. To my sister, Ericka—thank you for believing in this story long before I did. Your excitement over the storyline kept me writing when I questioned myself. To my sister, Touna—your encouragement reminded me that my message is something the world truly needs to hear. To my best friend, Tamika—no one has ever cheered me on the way you do. Thank you for always wanting my highest good.

To every voice, both large and small, and to every encounter that helped shape the pages of this book, I am sincerely grateful. And to every reader who picks up this book, I pray you triumph over every battle you face and discover a joy that is real, deep, and lasting.

About the Author

Ophelia Mixon is the author of True Joy, her debut novel. She is an educator and the founder of His Heart Ministries, a blog and devotional ministry that help others grow in their faith and purpose. Her daily devotions focus on spiritual growth and spreading the message of God's love and grace. Her greatest joy is being a mom. Through her writing, she hopes to encourage others that their story matters and that they can overcome any obstacle. She lives with her family in Augusta, GA, and enjoys cooking, drawing, creative writing, and knitting. You can learn more about her upcoming projects on her website.

Table of Contents

Chapter 1

"Will that be all, ma'am?" a sales associate asked, bringing Zola back from her thoughts. "Yes, thank you," she said as she handed the woman money to pay for the art supplies. Zola James, a single mother and divorcee, had purchased new art supplies for her new pottery class she was going to teach this Saturday. Zola moved to the town of Ridge Haven a few months ago with her daughter, Sophie. She had decided to move to the town because she believed it would be more efficient while getting her new store up and running. She had opened a new store in Ridge Haven in March and had been traveling back and forth. *A Messa Stuff* is her second arts and craft store, and Zola couldn't be prouder of its success. She had always dreamed of expanding her business. Zola worked very hard over the past five years building her business despite the turmoil she faced. Now her first store is running like a well-oiled machine, thanks to the help of her wonderful staff. She didn't know what she'd do without their faithfulness to her dream and vision for her business. Zola often found herself feeling so very grateful for her life and the people in it. If she were to be honest with herself, however, her move to Ridge Haven had a lot more to do with letting go of her past rather than a new store. Zola, now 40, divorced her ex-husband Jonathan Pendleton four years ago rather than the other way around. She suspected for a year that he was seeing someone else, but she believed that if she prayed hard enough, then God would save her marriage. It seemed like the harder she prayed about it; the worse things became between them. Jonnie had become cold and distant towards her, barely speaking to her unless he had to. At least in the beginning, when he was cheating, he was sweet. "Overly sweet", she thought, but back then, she was happy to receive his attention, even if it came from guilt. Towards the end of their marriage, Jonnie became a stranger to her, a man she didn't know. This man was a far cry from the kind, shy, and considerate young man she had met while in college. After college, Jonathan went to law school and began working for the same firm where he is now a partner. He worked really hard over the years to provide for their family, and she was always grateful for the kind of man he was. He'd always say, "My aunt taught me to love and cherish my wife and our children." "So much for that lesson," Zola thought as she turned into her driveway.

As she walked into her kitchen, she was greeted by her daughter's cat, Pencils. Her daughter Sophie had found the cat around the same time Zola and Jonnie were divorcing. Under normal circumstances, she would have taken the cat to a shelter, but she was so occupied with the craziness in her life that she told Sophie she could have it. She also felt a little guilty that her marriage was falling apart, and Sophie wasn't taking it well. Back then, there wasn't anything she wouldn't do to change that sad look in her baby girl's eyes. She wasn't exactly a cat person, but in the past four years, Pencils had grown on her. The orange tabby cat brushed up against her leg in an attempt to get her attention. She knelt and scratched his ear with one hand, "Ready to eat, son?", grabbing his food with the other. Once she took care of the cat, Zola walked through her country home, the one in which she had grown so fond of. The house was very old, and parts of the kitchen had the original exposed brick. She fell in love with the house at first sight although the house was a fixed upper. She worked to put her personal touch on it. This was the first house she had ever owned by herself, and she wanted this house to be a sanctuary for her and Sophie. "There's nothing like being in your own element," Zola thought as she walked through her den and out onto the back porch, she had recently turned into a sunroom, glazing it in. She walked through the room and outside to her studio. If this house didn't have so many of the other perks wanted, wraparound porch, individual food pantry, and huge walk-in closets, the studio would have been the sole reason she would have purchased the house.

Zola began unloading her art supplies on the shelf, putting them away as Sophie's latest artwork caught her eye. Sophie had set it in the studio for her mom to examine. Zola taught her daughter how to draw and paint in oil, acrylic, and watercolor as she was growing up, and Sophie had become a fantastic artist. Zola knew how difficult it could be to get started in the art world, so she always featured local artists in her craft shop to help them gain exposure. It was at least three years before she sold her first painting. In college, she majored in architecture, determined to follow her father's footsteps; however, Zola found herself enjoying drawing landscapes and painting them rather than building structures. Needless to say, this disappointed her father, "How are you going to make a living painting baby?" "Daddy, I will manage, I will become a waitress or work in retail if I have to, so that I can stay afloat, but I can't go into a career that I don't enjoy just so I can make lots of money. What kind of life is that?" she responded. Zola was a free spirit, and her father loved that about her, but that was also what scared him the most about her. She was his baby girl, and she was so very different from almost everyone he knew. He was proud of that fact, but Zola knew in a way it bothered him, mainly because he often felt like he couldn't connect with her. Zola's father was a very old-fashioned guy, and with his military background, he was very strict, but fair. Zola is the baby of two girls and one boy. She was so different from her siblings growing up. Her mom often told her that she reminded her of her great-grandmother, Zola, her namesake. She'd say, "You have your great-grandmother's name, and your personalities are so similar. You are so much like her; it's like having her with us all over again." Zola was always proud to hear her mom say that.

She thought Sophie's technique was getting much better. It was routine for her to leave her finished work in the studio for her mom to examine. Zola would determine whether or not it could go into the shop to be put on display. Zola was impressed with her daughter because she had already sold two paintings. She knew that this encouraged Sophie to paint much more. Art had become such a solace for Sophie since the divorce, and especially during. Sophie once shared with her that when she experienced emotions that she couldn't handle by talking it out, she would draw, and it would make her feel better. "It's like everything would disappear, the hurt and the anger I'm feeling would melt away into my pencil or my paintbrush," Sophie mentioned one day as the two sat on the couch with their sketch pads. Zola had no response; she just looked at her daughter in awe because she was astonished at the similarities they shared. She, too, felt this way about drawing and painting. These days, Sophie was in the studio more than ever, and she wondered if it was for the enjoyment or if something was brewing.

Zola walked back into the house just in time to hear the phone ringing. "Hey Chica," Tori, her oldest sister, said. "Hey, Tee. What's up?" "Not much, just checking up on you, making sure you and baby girl are settling in alright in your new spot." "Yes, we are fine, the store is finally up and running, and I've got my first pottery class this weekend," They talked a few moments more, catching up. "Glad to hear things are coming along, baby sis. Listen, I've got to run; a client is calling on another line. I've been trying to catch this big fish for six months, and we are about to close the deal. Catch you later, love you," Tori cried. "Alright, girlie," Zola said and hung up the phone. An advertising executive, Tori works for a huge marketing firm in Chicago. Tori had always been a strait-laced, pigeonhole kind of person. When she sets her eyes on what she wants or wants to accomplish, she goes after it. Tori majored in Marketing in college and went on to NYU to get her Master's in Business Administration. Her sister was very successful. Tori married the equally successful Timothy Collins. Tim and Tori were the most successful people Zola knew, and she was very proud of her sister. Tori had everything she could ever want, except one thing: a child. Zola knew that her sister deeply wanted children in her heart, but she gave up the idea because it didn't fit in she and Tim's "Path to Success". At first, she had announced to the family that she had no plans to have children. Tori admitted to her sister that her heart had changed, but Tim had still had not changed his mind about having children. Zola thought about her own success and while she didn't make the same amount of money Tori made, yet that is, Zola didn't measure success in dollars. She thought that success was a mindset. Zola taught Sophie that success was not always measured in major accomplishments, but it's those little feats that matter too. Tori's view of success has always been different from Zola's. Over the years, she would express her concerns for what direction she thought Zola's career was taking and believed she should do so much more. Zola also learned to let her sister's words roll off her back. When she hung up with her sister, she thought about her brother and how they had more in common. Richard or Richie, as he is called by friends and family, is a freelance writer. A number of years ago, Richard was very career-oriented, like Tori. He worked as a headhunter, recruiting employees for firms. Success was everything to him. For Richard, it was all about how much money he could make, and he had no qualms about stepping on as many people as he needed to get to that place, he calls success. Richard married Dominique Thomas, who was a travelling nurse at the time he met her. When Richard met Dominique, he fell hard and fast for her. She accidentally spilled her Mocha Latte on him when she was coming out of a coffee shop he was entering. He was on his way to pick up a client when he decided to stop in for a chai Latte. As he rushed in, she was rushing out, and they collided. Mumbling an expletive, he grabbed a handful of napkins. She profusely apologized, not really looking up at him. "Great, my tie is permanently stained." Dominique laughed nervously and replied, "I think it adds character. It was a little dull anyway." Richard looked down at the woman who had just insulted his tie and looked into a pair of the most beautiful hazel eyes. "I'll be happy to pay for the dry cleaning," she said, pulling out her checkbook. She waited for him to respond, but he just stared at her. Feeling a little uncomfortable, she asked him, "Hey, are you alright?" Her question broke him out of his reverie, and he spoke up, "No, that's alright, but I will take your telephone number." They were married within six months of that accidental meeting. Dominique stopped traveling and found a more sedentary position in a hospital. Dominique and Richie couldn't have been more different, but he loved it. Dominique is a very simple person, but she appreciates everything in life. Besides Maranda, Dominique was the most positive person Zola knew. She knew how to find the beauty in everything. She has a way of making people feel genuinely loved. Richie had met many women with the same drive as he had, but things never worked out. "I just didn't feel fulfilled, Zo." Richie once expressed his feelings about Dominique to his sister. "Dominique is changing me in ways I didn't know were possible for someone like me. I'm beginning to think that making lots of money and driving expensive cars is not what truly matters in life," He explained to Zola. He confessed that he had always dreamed of becoming a writer. Much to their parents' dismay, Richie quit his job to work from home as a freelance writer. They blamed Dominque for the change in their son. Richard Sr. had the same concern for his son that he had for Zola when she announced that she was going to become an artist. "How can you quit your job and sit at home all day with a home and a wife to support? So, your wife is going to take care of the house now? I didn't raise my son to have his wife take care of him." Richard Sr. argued when Richie called his parents and told them about the decision he had made. "Is Dominique behind this change, son?" Lila James, their mother, asked. "Ma, not directly. She has inspired me a bit, but she had nothing to do with my decision to switch careers. Things are different for me now, and yes, I do give credit to her, but they are good changes, Ma," Richie said, attempting to comfort his mother. He went on to say, "Don't worry. We are not destitute. You know I've been saving for years. Tell Pop we've been planning this for a year now." Zola knew that it would take their parents a while to get used to her brother's decision, but eventually they did.

Zola's parents, Richard and Lila James, were very traditional. They wanted the best for their children, but they had their own idea of what the "best" was. Often, Zola felt like the odd girl out because she had ideas about life that her parents and siblings didn't often share, but when Richie switched careers, she was elated. "Finally, I don't feel so alone, Richie." Richard laughed, "Zo, don't get me wrong, you are weird, but I understand what you were saying all these years now." Ignoring his remark, Zola smiled because she gave that small part of herself, the one that always questioned whether or not she was making the right decisions or if everyone was right about her being in over her head by making such huge changes in her life, permission to be silent. Like Zola, Richard realized that his parents' idea about how life should be lived was totally different from his, and that was certainly alright with him. Of course, Tori thought Richie had lost his mind right along with their baby sister. When thinking about her family, Zola has always felt that these simple ideas are what divide the members of her family.

The phone rang once more, startling Zola a bit. "Hey Zo, what time are we meeting tonight?" said Veronica, one of Zola's best friends from college. "Hey, Ronnie, we are meeting at seven. Remember to pick up the wine," Zola replied. "I won't! That only happened one time, and now a sista can't live it down," cried Veronica with an exasperated sigh. "Nope, sure can't. That reminds me, I have to go pick up the cake from the bakery here in town. I hear the cakes are better than *Simply Sweets,* so I ordered the cake for Kha'ren's birthday," Zola said. "Alright then, you know how I am about my sugar. This cake better be up to par, Zo," warned Veronica. "It is girl! I had an éclair from there, and it was… mouthwatering." I ordered a cake from there because I knew you ladies would enjoy it." Zola sighed. "Alright, alright, before I go, Eric will be coming back into town on Monday night, and he said that he had something very important to talk about," said Veronica with a worried tone. "You know, most women would have that worried tone because they are hoping that their man will propose. You, on the other hand, are afraid that he will." Zola said, frowning. "Girl, I know he is a wonderful man, but you know I'm scared to commit," Ronnie spoke sadly. "Besides, you are one to talk, Zo. You haven't been on a date since you and Jonnie divorced. So, if we are going to talk about commitment phobes, you need to look no further than your own nose." Veronica said in an indignant tone. Zola grew quiet as she digested her friend's statement. For a moment, she thought Ronnie might have been right, but she spent the last four years of her life putting things in order and in the right perspective. She didn't feel as though she was running away from men as Veronica had been since Brian broke off their engagement eight years earlier. Veronica had been unable to fully commit to anyone for fear of being hurt. Her relationships have lasted no more than four or five months. She walked away from three promising relationships, claiming the problems were with the men. She would find things not to like about them. However, Zola knew that the problem indeed lay with her friend. "Zo? You there?" Veronica questioned. "Yes, girl. Listen, I'll begin dating when I'm ready. You cannot compare our situations, and you know it," Zola said with a sigh. "Ok, fine, but you know I have reason to feel the way I feel. We can talk about this tonight, though. Right now, I'm leaving the office so I can head to the wine shop," Veronica said hurriedly. "Ok, see you later on," Zola replied as she opened her refrigerator and pulled out a water bottle. She hung up the phone and then added her favorite flavor.

Zola had at least two hours before she had to meet the girls, so she decided to go for a run. While driving through town the other day, she spotted a nice park just north of her store. She figured this would be a good time to try it out. After her divorce, Zola lost self-confidence and figured that part of the reason Jonnie left was because of her body. She always had a petite figure, but was never skinny by any means. She figured that she was plump in all of the right places. When they divorced, she took to exercising more and eating healthier. She steadily lost the weight and liked how her new physique made her feel. She still didn't consider herself skinny, but she was pleased that she was more proportioned than she used to be. When she gained a healthier perspective on working out and living a healthy lifestyle, she realized Jonnie didn't leave her because of her body. After that realization, she just worked out because she enjoyed it. She discovered that one of her favorite things to do was to run, which surprised even her because she had never been much of a runner. Zola was still baffled at the interests, hobbies, and habits she picked up with Jonnie out of her life. She loved him with everything in her, but now she was coming into her own without him. There was an obvious change in her, and she thought it was absolutely fabulous.

Zola walked into the bustling bakery, and the aroma hit her nose immediately. The bakery smelled so delightful that it made her mouth water. She smelled fresh pastries, fruit, and coffee. "No wonder this place is popular," Zola thought to herself as she stood in line to pick up the cake. "May I help you?" a young girl said. Zola looked up and met the emerald eyes of an adorable, shy young lady. She wasn't sure why, but her heart felt a little softened as she observed the girl's demeanor. "Yes, I would like to pick up a cake. It's in the name of Zola James," Zola said with a smile. "Yes, ma'am, you are Zola James! I was going through the tickets earlier, and I noticed your name. I really like it. It is a little different," the young girl said with a smile. "Yes, well, I'm named after my great-grandmother. Apparently, I have her personality too. At least that's what I've heard since I was little," Zola said, reaching for the ticket the girl handed. "That's really cool. I'm Alexandria, but everyone calls me Alex," the girl said, extending a hand to Zola. Zola grabbed the girl's hand and shook it quickly. Alex told Zola that her cake would be out momentarily. She pulled a seat out to sit when someone said, "Excuse me, ma'am. Are you the one who owns that new shop on 4th? Zola looked up at the stranger and said, "Yes, yes, I am. Is there anything I can help you with?" A woman who looked to be in her late twenties said, "Yes, I hear that you will be teaching a pottery class this Saturday. Do I register, or can I just drop in?" Zola explained to the woman that she could register online or drop by the store to register in person. After she finished talking to the woman, Alex walked up to her and said, "I saw a flyer about the classes earlier today. Can I come too?" Zola said, "Sure, you can. Just drop by the store and register tomorrow, or you can do it online. As a matter of fact, here is my cell phone number," Zola scribbled the number down on her ticket for the young girl as a man with a husky voice said, "Is there a Mrs. James here?" "I am Ms. James," Zola said, raising her hand. "Ms. James, I'm sorry, but there was a problem with your chocolate cake. We will be glad to offer you a specialty cake from our list," he said, handing her a list of cakes. Zola took the list and asked, "Just what kind of problem did you have with my cake?" Looking embarrassed, the man said, "Ms. James, we've just discovered that one of our cashiers got your cake mixed up with another order and sold your cake. Now we can give you one of our specialty cakes. The specialty cakes are baked fresh daily, and you can choose any one of them, at no extra charge, of course. Zola glanced at her watch and decided to try one of the specialty cakes. She chose the Strawberry Cream cake with buttercream frosting. She asked the man, "Can you please add, 'Happy Birthday Kha'ren?" That's spelled, K-H-A-'R-E-N." The man obliged and disappeared into the kitchen. As the doors swung open and closed, Zola looked up and spotted Nicolas. He too looked up, and their eyes met for a second or two, long enough for the door to completely close.

The young girl's voice grabbed Zola's attention. "Soooooo what time is the class on Saturday?" Zola explained to the girl that the class began at 12:30. When the doors swung open again, a tall man wearing a black bandana with the same emerald eyes appeared before her. Zola's breath hitched as she looked into the man's eyes. He looked at her, eyes piercing as if he could see straight through to her soul. "I believe this belongs to you, Ms. James," the man said with a smile that made Zola's heart melt. She was almost speechless. "Good Lord, this man is handsome," she thought to herself before answering him. Zola smiled at the man and thanked him, and walked away as quickly as she could. She didn't ever remember responding to a man's presence in this way. She had come across different types of men in her life, but none who looked like this guy. From his broad shoulders to his silky voice, Zola was attracted to it all. She was a little taken aback by this because for four years, she never gave herself time to think of men. Sure, she'd seen handsome men, but none that had the effect that this man seemed to have had on her. She felt a little silly because she was acting like a teenager. She hurried out the door because the last thing she wanted to do was look like a fool in front of this man, whoever he was.

Chapter 2

The new owners of her old house were closing in three weeks, but until then, Zola had so much she needed to do. She still had a great deal of packing left, and there was furniture that she needed to sell. Veronica suggested that she have a yard sale, which was a great idea. While going through the attic, she ran across some of Jonnie's things and decided that she'd call him to give him a chance to collect them. Zola would at least give him an opportunity before she sold everything. She got the house in the divorce settlement, so everything in the house now belonged to her. As she pulled in the driveway, Zola realized that this would be the last time she would get together with her girlfriends in this house. She became a little teary-eyed as she thought about all of the conversations they had had over the years in this house. Were it not for her friends and family, she doesn't know how she would have gotten through the divorce or life afterwards. As she put the key in the door, Maranda Collier, another one of her best friends from college, pulled in the driveway. As the two women embraced, Zola felt a nudge between them. "I see baby Collier still likes the sound of Aunt Zola's voice," giggled Maranda as she rubbed her swollen belly. Maranda was happily married for six years and pregnant with her first child. Zola always enjoyed being around Maranda. Her presence always made Zola feel at ease. No matter what the situation was, Maranda had the right word to say. She was the eternal optimist and had a way of lighting up any room she entered. Over the years, when she was feeling down, Zola would pick up the phone and call her friend, and she would cheer her up. It wasn't until three years ago that Zola realized that all of the optimism that Maranda possessed was, in fact, faith. She and her husband, Michael, were trying to conceive. Only when Maranda went to the OBGYN did she learn that she had cysts on her ovaries. After an examination and a few tests, she was diagnosed with ovarian cancer. From the moment Maranda found out, Zola never once saw the light go out in her friend's eyes. She stayed so strong, and when anyone would begin to cry, she would say, "This is my storm, not yours. I can't be strong for both you and me." Immediately, that would put things into perspective for people. To Zola, Maranda exemplified strength and courage. She admired her friend so much for how she handled life with such grace and elegance. No matter how hard things were, she never lost her zeal for life. Zola shared this observation with Maranda over two years ago, and Maranda said, "I could say the same about you, my friend. You have had some very difficult experiences these past few years, and now I see you standing so strong. I am proud. There's a light that radiates from you, and it draws people." Zola couldn't help but tear up because it meant so much to hear those words from Maranda. She's usually saying something like this to Maranda. "My sweet friend, I have had the privilege of walking with you and observing your life's transitions, and I see how you have handled things. You have encouraged me to stand strong through this cancer. I'm determined to live and have children one day soon." Maranda continued with tears in her eyes. Zola remembered that crisp autumn day clearly. Maranda wore the most beautiful brown sweater that Michael had gotten her and a matching head scarf that her mother-in-law had made for her. Even in the midst of sickness, Zola thought her friend looked regal. Maybe it was her inner strength; she wasn't sure, but she certainly had something.

Zola believed then and now, in fact, that the inner condition of a person shows on the outside so powerfully. For this reason, she knew that she couldn't wallow in her self-pity after the divorce. She knew that Sophie would be there watching every move that she made. "Come on in, Maranda, and put your feet up, sweetheart. I have to go back to the car to get the bags." Zola said as she hung their coats up in the foyer. "Don't mind if I do. I've been on my feet most of the day, cleaning my classroom for the fall break. Please grab the food out of the car." Maranda sighed as she plopped down on the comfy leather sofa. Zola turned and said, "Maranda, you weren't supposed to make anything. I've taken care of the food. It's a special occasion." Maranda sighed and hunched her shoulders. Just then, Veronica and Kha'ren came walking through the door. Zola said, "Welcome, ladies. Please make yourselves at home; you all know where everything goes," as she began walking to the door to grab the cake and other items in her and Maranda's cars.

As the women assembled in the living room, they ate, talked, and laughed about everything. There was an ease between the four of them, a secure love that existed only as a result of true friendship. The four of them had all met in college, and although they all lived in different parts of the country for a while, they found themselves all living within thirty minutes of each other now. Zola was convinced that distance did not hinder real and genuine friendship. Even when they hadn't spoken for some time, she found that with each of the women, their conversation picked up as though they had spoken the day before. She loved her friends dearly and felt very fortunate that they were in her life. "Ok, dessert is in order," Zola said excitedly. It was Kha'ren's 39th birthday, and she really didn't like celebrating her birthday. She definitely did not like birthday parties. If no one said anything about it, Kha'ren would work right through her birthday. None of the women could quite understand why Kha'ren did not like celebrations, but they made it a point to celebrate her anyway. They knew she needed it. Although she'd make a fuss, no one missed that gleam in her eyes when she was being celebrated. Zola thought that out of all of her friends, Kha'ren was the toughest nut to crack. She'd always preferred to do things the hard way. She always saw life as a challenge to conquer, even if there weren't any real challenges. Kha'ren had her own practice as a civil rights attorney. She actually met Kha'ren through her ex-husband, Jonathan. Kha'ren and Jonathan were study partners while in law school, and Kha'ren would come over to the apartment that Zola shared with Jonathan. After they'd study, Kha'ren and Zola would end up talking for at least an hour afterwards. After a while, they would make plans to meet for lunch or to go shopping. Eventually, Zola introduced her to Veronica and Maranda, and the women kind of became a foursome. "Ok, so now back to you, Veronica," said Zola, pouring another glass of wine. "Eric will be back in town next week, and he says he wants to talk to you. Do you really think he is going to propose?" Zola asked before taking a sip of wine. "I guess he is. Things have been pretty good between us. Of course, we've had our ups and downs, but it seems like the logical step to take. We've been together for almost a year. I have met his family, and he's met mine. I've accompanied him to his family functions, and we all hit it off. What else could he have to discuss other than taking our relationship to another level?" said Veronica. Maranda raised her eyebrows at Veronica and asked, "Ronnie, are you seriously ready to take things to the next level with Eric? I mean, he is a good guy, and he treats you great, but if you are not ready, then you need to tell him." Veronica sighed, "I know, Randi. I care a lot for Eric; more than that, I love him. When I think of a future with him, I get so excited, but then that deep fear kicks in, and the walls go up." Kha'ren gave Veronica an annoyed look. "Ronnie, what are you afraid of? Your breakup with Brian happened so long ago. Why are you still carrying that around? Even you should know that not all men are the same." "I know that not all men are the same, Kha'ren, but the hurt from that one is still painful, and there's nothing wrong with being cautious. You would understand some of my pain if you put yourself out there in the first place, but you don't. You are perfectly content being closed off in your own world, so please don't lecture me about this subject because you wouldn't have a clue as to where I am coming from and how I feel." Kha'ren was taken aback by Veronica's statement. Shaking her head, she said, "Touchy touchy. I see I have struck a nerve, ladies." Rolling her eyes, Veronica said, "Whatever." Zola and Maranda were used to Kha'ren and Veronica going on like this. They loved each other, but they bickered about almost everything. They weren't afraid to tell hard truths to each other. This was something Zola loved about them, but she didn't exactly agree with the way they gave those truths. Zola was in favor of a much softer approach. That is why she said, "Ok, ok. Ronnie, I am worried about you. Eric is a great guy, and you don't have to convince me that you love him because it's written all over you. However, I am scared for you, sweetheart. I'm scared that you are going to unintentionally push this man away." Ronnie looked at Zola and asked, "Just how would I do that?" "Well, you play tug-of-war with his heart. One day, the two of you are close, and then the next, you hold him at arm's length. Eric strikes me as the type who is ready to settle down and move into the next stage of his life with his soulmate. He isn't, nor is any good man for that matter, checking for a woman who is fickle." Veronica sighed as tears welled in her eyes. "I don't mean to be, Zo. I don't know what to do. I am so scared to give my whole heart. I am so scared that Eric will leave me once I give him everything." Maranda chimed in and said, "Ronnie, you are so busy looking back that you cannot see the blessing that God's placed in front of you." Putting a hand on Veronica's shoulder, Kha'ren said, "Veronica, if Brian ended the relationship, then obviously it wasn't meant to be. God is trying to bless you, but you can't let go of your past hurt in order to embrace your future. Let's face it, you will never see how awesome a person Eric is because you can't fully see his heart. All you see is Brian and whoever in your past has hurt you. You have blinders on, and you use the pain they've caused as a protection mechanism to keep people away. Now I know I haven't been in a lot of relationships, but I know what I plainly see in you. Once you ask God to heal those wounds and take all of those people out of your heart, then and only then will you see Eric as God intends you to see him. Truth be told, you don't have a whole lot of room in your heart for Eric because you are carrying around so many other unnecessary people. These people should no longer be a part of you. They don't deserve residence in your heart, Ronnie." Kha'ren encouraged her friend. As Zola listened intently to Kha'ren, she wondered what had happened in Kha'ren's own life that enabled her to speak so eloquently on Veronica's situation when it clearly was meant for her as well.

Zola thought about how truly blessed it was to have been able to connect with such wonderful women. As she watched these ladies, she thought of all the things they'd been through over the years, and she had to smile. They all have truly seen some very dark days, but they were able to emerge as strong and determined women. The rest of the night was spent celebrating Kha'ren. Zola brought out the cake she'd gotten from the bakery earlier, with the candle numbers three and nine lit up. Although she acted indifferent, Kha'ren's friends knew she secretly enjoyed being celebrated by them. Veronica pulled a wrapped painting out from behind Zola's leather couch. In unison, Veronica, Zola, and Miranda yelled, "Happy Birthday!" Kha'ren picked up the gift-wrapped painting and began to rip it open, and gasped. "Oh my! This is that Joshua Coven painting!" she excitedly exclaimed. Maranda said, "This is the painting you said you loved so much when we were at that museum two months ago." Kha'ren just stared at the painting as tears welled in her eyes. She loved this particular artist, and after she saw the painting in the museum, she decided that she was going to purchase it. Of course, that meant watching her pennies, but this would be her birthday gift to herself. Imagine her surprise when she opened the wrapping and saw the same painting. Kha'ren looked at the women she had come to think of as sisters, and fat tears began to fall down her cheeks. They gathered around her, hugging her from all sides. "I'm so speechless," Kha'ren mumbled into Zola's shoulder. "Well, that's a first," Veronica spat out sarcastically. She didn't like emotional moments like this to linger for very long, so she always lightened the mood. The women began to laugh, wiping away Kha'ren's tears. "Well, if you think this gift was a tearjerker, the second part is sure to send you into a frenzy," Veronica said with a sly smile. Kha'ren narrowed her eyes on her friend. Zola motioned for Maranda to hand her the envelope as she spoke, "Joshua Coven is going to be in town on the 12th of next month, giving art lessons, and you will be one of his students." Kha'ren's eyebrows almost reached her hairline as her eyes widened with excitement. "You got me art lessons with Joshua Coven?" Kha'ren asked, unable to control her tears. For years, Zola had been attempting to teach her friends how to paint, and the only one who ever seemed to show any interest was Kha'ren. She knew that Kha'ren would enjoy going to the art exhibits with her. However, she didn't realize that Kha'ren was truly an art lover. When Kha'ren's friends heard her raving about the painting, they knew what they would get her for her birthday. "We know that you are very busy, but we want you to take some time out for yourself and do this," Maranda mentioned, smiling at Kha'ren. Since she started her own practice six years ago, Kha'ren had become more of a workaholic than she was before. It was undeniable, though, that she really enjoyed her work and felt fulfilled. Her friends felt that she focused way too much on her career and not enough on her personal life. This was their way of easing her into something different.

After the women had cleaned and left, Zola locked up and headed upstairs. This had been a long day, and she decided that a hot bath was in order. Just then, her cell phone began ringing. "Hey, Mama! How was your night?" a sweet voice heard on the other end said. "Hi, baby. It was great, a little emotional, but your aunt Kha'ren really loved her gifts," Zola said. "Good. She deserves it. I picked her gift up today when Daddy took me to the mall," Sophie said as she pulled her hair out of a long ponytail. "How did your evening go with your father? Did he pick you up on time after school?" Zola asked her. "Yes, Mama, he picked me up on time today, and I had a good time." Sophie rolled her eyes. She thought her mom could be so overprotective at times. "Elizabeth was not with Daddy when he picked me up, and she wasn't with us all evening," Sophie said matter-of-factly. Raising one eyebrow, Zola said, "Elizabeth wasn't with your dad? Did he say where she was?" "He didn't mention her at all today, Mama. I'm not sad about it, though, because it was good to have him all to myself today. We are going zip-lining tomorrow afternoon. He told me that we could do whatever I wanted to do for the next two days," Sophie said with excitement in her voice. Zola was curious as to what had gotten into her ex-husband. Is he going zip-lining tomorrow? He hadn't done anything like that in years. Since he became a partner, he focused on his work, and everything else, including his wife and child, took a back seat. To top it all off, Elizabeth was not with them today. She always accompanied him when he came to pick up Sophie. For some unknown reason, she was insecure about Zola's barely existing relationship with her Jonathan. "I have to make sure she doesn't get her hooks back into my man." Sophie overheard Elizabeth saying in a telephone conversation. When she mentioned it to her mom, Zola chuckled to herself, knowing that Elizabeth had no real worries in that area. She did not want Jonathan back. He was her past, and she was looking forward to a bright future with endless possibilities. "Well, keep me posted, baby. Call me tomorrow and let me know how your day went. I am going to take a long bath and get into bed. I've got a long day tomorrow. I love you." Zola said around a yawn. "Alright, Mama, love you too," and she hung up the phone.

Zola walked towards the bathroom that she had fallen in love with. Two years ago, she renovated it by separating the bathtub and shower. The counter now had one sink instead of his, and hers sinks that they had put in when she and Jonny first married. She now had a glass-encased stand-alone shower with gold-trimmed jets coming out of the wall. After a long day of working, she wanted to truly feel pampered when she got home in the evenings. That is also why she installed her huge claw tub. She wished that she could take the entire bathroom with her. This truly was her favorite part of the house. Zola might not have been able to take the bathroom, but she decided that she was taking her tub. She ran the water and put in her essential oils. As the water ran in the tub, she ran downstairs to make some chamomile tea. She thought that would be better than a glass of wine tonight, although she found that wine was just as relaxing. Zola stepped into the hot water and allowed the day to fade away and closed her eyes, and sank into the tub. When she closed her eyes, they popped back open, and she sat up. The face she saw when she closed her eyes was the man from the bakery. "Whoa!" she thought as she slid back down in the tub. He was still there when she closed her eyes once more. Since her divorce, Zola has met some very handsome eligible men, but none caught her attention as this man did. She tried her hardest not to think of him tonight while with her friends, but she couldn't help it. She couldn't get those emerald eyes and his silky voice out of her head. Zola

wasn't sure what was stirring inside her, but she knew it had been
several years since she felt it.

Chapter 3

It had been a long, tiresome day for Nick, and unfortunately, it was far from over. He still had a meeting with his lawyer about becoming the sole proprietor of the bakery. His wife, Karmen, oversaw the business side. Now that she was gone, it was important that the paperwork said so. After five years, he still could not believe that she was gone. Nicolas Gallo met Karmen Morales when they were students at The Cooking Institute. He thought she was so beautiful with her caramel skin and chocolate brown eyes. The moment she smiled, the room lit up. It took him two weeks to work up the nerve to speak to her. Usually, he was more coordinated and confident around women, but around her, he never knew just what to say or how to form a sentence. One winter day, he walked into their Candies and Confectionery class and spotted her. She wore a teal green sweater with blue jeans that accentuated her curves just right. From her beautiful brown eyes and pouty lips to the curvature of her hips, Nicolas was mesmerized. When she looked up and smiled, he swore his heart skipped a beat. He made sure he worked near her, and on that day, he decided that he was going to talk to her. Nicolas said, "Hi, how are you? My name is Nicolas Gallo." Karmen greeted him with the sweetest smile and said, "My name is Karmen Morales." For the next week, Nicolas found ways to strike up conversations with her until he was confident enough to ask her out on a date. He believed he was already half in love with her by their third conversation, but by their date, he was certain that he was absolutely and irrevocably in love with Karmen Morales. After almost a year of dating, Nicolas proposed. They got married within eight months and were happily married for the next sixteen years. They both worked to build their careers. They worked so hard that they barely saw each other. Then one night, lying in bed, Karmen came up with the idea of opening a bakery in the town of Ridge Haven. They invested their entire savings in their bakery. They eventually became very successful and were well known for their cakes and pastries. In those sixteen years, she gave him three beautiful daughters, Adrienne, April, and Alexandra, oldest to youngest in that order. Karmen and Nicolas lived a rather happy life. Nicolas fell more in love with his wife with each passing day, and he looked forward to spending a long and happy life with her while raising their three daughters. The day he found out that his wife had leukemia is still very fresh in his mind. They had been working some very hard, long days and were in desperate need of some rest and relaxation. As hard as he worked, he knew that Karmen worked harder, taking care of the business side of the bakery and coming home and taking care of the girls. They shared in the carpools, dance, piano recitals, and sports games as much as they could, but Karmen did the bulk of things like that. Nicolas could never understand how she did it all. She worked so hard to keep their family together and never complained, never grumbled. She kissed boo-boos and calmed fears. To sum it all up, his daughters' whole lives' happiness was wrapped in this dynamic woman. He decided that he was going to take her on a vacation. They didn't get to go on a honeymoon because they could not afford it. Working so hard over the years to build their careers and then their business, they still didn't get an opportunity to go on one. Nicolas was determined that he was going to change that. He planned a trip to St. Martin for a two-week vacation for the two of them. The night he planned on surprising her with the tickets was the night she told him she had leukemia, and he felt like the wind was knocked out of him. He remembered putting everything in order. Since it was the summer, the kids would be with his parents, and he informed his managers at the bakery of his plans and had everything ready to go. The only thing left to do was tell Karmen. It was late afternoon when she arrived home with April and Adrienne. Both girls had dance practice. Alex was dropped off at the bakery by the neighbor across the street because Karmen had a doctor's appointment. She had been feeling sick for a few weeks, but they weren't alarmed because feelings of being sick would come and go. Nicolas convinced her to go see a doctor. What he didn't realize was that when she first went, the doctors told her that she needed to have a biopsy. Karmen was scheduled to get one, and the results had finally come back, so she was called back to the doctor that day for her results. He noticed that she wasn't acting like herself the entire evening. While in bed, Karmen turned to him and said, "Baby, I am sick." "That's why you went to the doctor, silly," Nicolas said, smiling as he touched her nose. Then she gave him a look that he couldn't quite describe, and then just like that, he understood. She was sick. Karmen explained that she was diagnosed with leukemia. He held her as they cried together the entire night. A week later, he took her back to the oncologist, and they were told that she was stage three. For the next few months, she received aggressive rounds of chemotherapy and then radiation. They received great support from family and friends, but what surprised them the most was the support from the community. People donated money, cooked meals, mowed their lawn, and took the girls to their practices when Karmen was too weak, and Nicolas just couldn't afford to take any more time away from the business. Neighbors pitched in to take care of the daily, mundane things that made his children's lives as normal as possible. He owed a debt of gratitude to the town of Ridge Haven.

Then one day, Karmen got the call that the cancer was in remission. The doctor explained that she would have to come back for more testing, but his team was confident that it was all gone. Finally, Nicolas felt as though he could breathe again. For the better part of the year, Nick felt like he walked around holding his breath because he was never sure how things would turn out. He always hated the unknown, and not being an overly spiritual person, the extent of his prayers was at night with his little girls and saying grace before a meal. Now that the cancer had been gone, the heaviness finally went away. She steadily regained her strength, but she didn't go back to her life as usual. Karmen expressed to him that while she was sick, she began to see things differently. She felt like they worked entirely too hard, and they weren't really enjoying life with their children. She convinced him to cut back and give more responsibility to the employees in the bakery. He obliged her because he knew that her sickness had changed her. She was a much calmer person. She slowed down for life and valued what it had to offer her. Karmen paid attention. She began to see the world around her in a different light, and she became a better mother. That last part is what she said. Nicolas didn't think she could become a better mom than she already was to their girls. He took her on that vacation that he had been planning, and it was there that he felt he was truly getting to know his wife for the first time. There was no doubt that she was different, and she shared with him that while she was going through that difficult time, she felt like giving up. She never told him, but she was so exhausted with life. She loved him, and she loved the girls, but all of it was taking a toll on her, and then finding out that she had cancer was the topping on the cake. Sure, when she first found out, she wanted to fight and beat it and get back to her life. However, as the months went by and things became harder and she became weaker, she didn't know if she had any fight left. Then one day, while at the Cancer Center, she walked into a room by accident. Apparently, it was a support group of some sort because the people were sitting in a circle. As she was about to open her mouth to apologize and excuse herself, a woman who, Karmen guessed, was the facilitator invited her to join them. Karmen told

Nicolas that she almost said no, but something deep inside her urged her to stay. Karmen grew up going to church, and though she didn't go as much as she did when she was younger, she still held on to faith. Throughout the years, this faith had gotten her through many situations. She sat down and listened as the woman leading the group began to talk. "This journey that you all are on is very difficult. I want each of you to understand that you are in the right place at the right time. I know that it doesn't seem fair to be sick, but you and your family will get through this time. I want to encourage all of you to understand that you are stronger than you think you are. You have inner strength and are a fighter on the inside. Even if you don't feel strong, you should know that in your weaknesses, God is made strong. God will carry you through this; keep your faith intact," said the woman with the sweetest and warmest smile. Karmen had ever seen. Karmen explained to Nicolas that there was something about the woman that just drew her. She had an aura or an inner light that made her want to stay in her presence. She didn't intend to stay for the entire group session, but she had to meet this woman who had such a positive effect on people. When the group was done, Karmen walked up to the woman and extended her hand. "Hi. My name is Karmen Gallo." The woman gave her a bright smile and said, "My name is Maranda. I'm glad you stopped by today." Karmen told her that she had walked in by accident, but she felt a strong urge to stay. Maranda said, "That's so wonderful, Karmen. I truly hope that this session answered whatever questions you have about what you're going through and gave you encouragement to push forward." "It's amazing. Honestly, I was tired of chemo and radiation, and I was really beginning to give up. I feel a bit stronger now. I know that I am surrounded by loving people all the time, especially my husband, who has been so wonderful during this time, but I feel so alone," replied Karmen. Miranda told Karmen that it was great that she had all of the support; however, she had to be whole on the inside first. Karmen explained to Nicolas that Maranda helped her to understand that her attitude and mindset were an integral part of her experience on this journey. She told him that after that meeting, she continued to go back, and she found that the more she went, the stronger she felt. In addition to that, she told Nicolas how different she began to feel. She felt like there was a hunger or something, but she wasn't quite sure what it was. As a result of several conversations, Karmen began to look at life from a totally different perspective. Her faith was growing stronger. As his wife talked to him during the vacation, Nicolas began to look at her in a new light. He didn't know it was possible to fall in love with the same person all over again, but he did. She had such a glow about her, and she possessed such faith that he never knew she had. Nicolas wondered why Karmen never told him about the meetings. He asked her one day, and she replied, "It was my journey, Nick," and she left it at that. He didn't press her or ask any more about it. His wife had become different, but in a wonderful way. His feelings for his wife had grown deeper on their vacation. Unfortunately, that would be the final vacation he took with her.

Ten months after their vacation on a fall October day, Karmen and Nicolas had found out that the cancer was back, and it had come back more aggressive. The doctors explained that she could go through chemo and radiation again, but the cancer had metastasized, spreading throughout her body. The treatments would only give her a little more time with her family. That meant that it wouldn't get all the cancer, and it was inevitable that Karmen wouldn't beat it this time. Later that night, Nicolas held Karmen as they discussed the options the doctor had given them. "We can fight this thing, darling. Just go through the chemo and radiation, and you'll see. Doctors have told several cancer patients that they've had days to months to live, and they lived for years." Nicolas said with desperation in his voice. Karmen's eyes welled with tears as she watched her husband reach for any kind of hope he could, even if it meant lying to himself. She finally spoke and said, "Nick, I don't want chemo or radiation. I don't want aggressive treatments. I want to spend the days that I have left with you and the girls. The time I have left belongs to us." He just stared at her in disbelief. He couldn't believe that she was not willing to fight. How could she just give up so easily on their life together? How could she give up on him? He wasn't ready to let her go or accept that she was going to leave him. How could she leave him alone to face this life without her? After a long silence, Nicolas said, "I don't like this, Karmen. I want you to fight, but I know I can't make you. With sad eyes that made him want to hold her forever, she said, "Nicolas, I can't go through all that again. I don't want to spend my last days on this earth so focused on beating cancer that I stop living in the right here and now with you and the girls. I love you, sweetheart; you are every beat of my heart, but I am so tired." She went on to say, "I have made my peace with this. I'm not giving up on you or the girls." With tears rolling down her face, she explained, "I don't have a whole lot of time left, so I'm just going to love you with everything that I have and impart as much of me into the girls while I have the chance." Nicolas's feelings hadn't changed on the subject that night, but he knew that his wife's mind was settled on the matter. There was something in her words that told him that she was not giving up nor had she lost her faith; she was accepting what it is. She just wanted to be there for them if she could.

Chapter 4

Karmen did just what she said she wanted to do. She stopped working in the bakery, although she kept up with the books. A few months later, she trained their manager, Tounya, with the books because she was getting too weak to do them. She made videos and wrote journals and letters to the girls and him. He found the letters she wrote to him after she had died. She literally gave herself to her family with the little time she had left. Thanksgiving was a grand event that year. All his family and hers got together, and they celebrated her life. She had such a wonderful time. Although he hid it, he cried the entire day. He didn't know how he was going to face the next Thanksgiving without Karmen. That Christmas was a very intimate and special time with the two of them and the girls. He rented a cabin in the mountains, and the five of them spent their Christmas vacation there. Karmen was so very happy. The following spring, he lost her. All the well-wishes and condolences did nothing to ease the ache he felt in his heart. Adrienne, his oldest daughter, had a difficult time dealing with her mother's death. She was just so angry and distant after Karmen died. Nicolas constantly worried about his daughters, but he worried about Adrienne the most. She had become depressed; her grades dropped, and she was acting out in school. The daughter he knew had become a different person. "Hurting people usually hurt other people, son." Nicolas's mom explained to him as he was discussing the change in Adrienne. "Mom, my little girl is gone, and I want her back. "I don't know what else to do," he replied to his mom. Reaching out for him, his mom said, "Sweetheart, she is just acting out right now. She's not gone. She is angry, and she is hurt that her mother is no longer here. Her life has changed in ways unimaginable, and right now she is just sore about it." His mom held him as he wept in her arms. He wept for his children, their lives, and for himself. Nicolas didn't have a clue as to how he was going to raise their three girls without their mom. "Son, you must take it one day at a time. If you must take it moment by moment, then that is fine as well. Whatever you do, you must move on. Grieve in the way you must, but don't let it consume your life, honey." Elena Gallo said. He was so appreciative of his mom; no one could make him feel better like her. He tried to take her advice. There were some highs and lows over the past five years. They all tried to live, and at some point, a new normal began to take shape in their lives. Somehow, over the years, they all began to believe that allowing yourself to feel emotions meant that you weren't moving on fast enough. This thought was conceived by Nicolas. It had become so much easier to avoid, and he taught his girls to do it as well. "Son, you must allow yourselves to grieve." Nicolas's mom explained to him. "Mom, we've felt the pain, but at some point, we need to stop crying. Don't you think?" He responded. The pain of losing his wife and his children losing their mother was devastating, and it felt like they were all drowning in it. He didn't want to feel it anymore, and he didn't want his girls to feel it either. So, they "didn't." When they got into a rhythm of daily schedules and responsibilities, he took it as a positive thing. He didn't realize that he was virtually freezing their emotions and pain. It all became the backdrop of their lives. Karmen had always urged him to spend more time with them, and that's what he did. He hired extra help in the bakery so he could be home with them every night at a decent hour. Most weekends, he worked, but as they all grew older, they began working in the bakery with him, so he still saw them. Nicolas made sure that they vacationed every year; this was one of the suggestions Karmen made to him in one of her letters to him. They took some very adventurous vacations. They went SCUBA diving and zip-lining, hiked in the Grand Canyon, and went on several cruises. One thing that the girls wanted to do, but he forbade, was skydiving. The girls teased him, saying that he was afraid of heights. He never admitted it, but they were right. Nicolas went out of his way to make sure his girls had a great life. At some point in the ninth grade, Adrienne came around and eventually ended up finishing high school, graduating at the top of her class. Her hard work earned her an academic scholarship to college. He was so proud of her and her accomplishments. She has always been a humanitarian at heart. In her senior year, she developed this fund for young girls who lost their mom and wanted to further their education. She works diligently with that scholarship program even away at college. She is in her second year, and she is going abroad for the summer to do volunteer work in Costa Rica. Adrienne wanted to study abroad for a semester, but he was unsure if he was ready to let her go for that length of time. April and Alex are getting along just fine as well. April is now a senior in high school, and she is a true athlete. She plays volleyball and softball. Scouts have been to her games for both sports. Nicolas makes sure not to miss any games. Alex is in the tenth grade now and is a true daddy's girl. She thinks it's her mission in life to take care of him. She is so protective of him that it scares him. She cooks for him and April; she makes sure everything in the house is clean and neat for when he gets home. Elena believes that she clings to him like that because she's afraid she'll lose him. She fusses over his eating habits and makes sure he eats in the morning. Though he was proud of his girls and loved his life, he had begun to feel lonely. Over the years, his best friend Billy had tried to get him to date, but Nicolas felt that there were more important things he needed to focus on. He was not ready to date, and to be honest, he wasn't sure that any woman would measure up to his Karmen. "You've got to stop comparing every woman you meet to Karmen, man." Billy said while at Tommy's Bar and Grill one night after work. When Nick didn't say anything, Billy went on to say, "It's been a while since Karmen passed, and it's time you got out there on the dating scene. I think she would want you to be happy, Nick." Nick just looked at his friend and said, "Look, I'm not ready. Drop it." Billy dropped it, but Nicolas knew that his friend was worried about him. For the past five years, Nicolas's life was so filled with raising the girls, their activities, and building his business that he didn't have time to be lonely. Now the business was great, and the girls were in a good place; Nicolas found himself with nothing or no one to take care of. There are days when he longs for someone to talk to. Although his life had been busy, he spent a lot of time alone. He wanted companionship, but he hadn't come across a woman he was interested in—that is, until he locked eyes with one of the most breathtakingly beautiful women he's ever seen, since Karmen, of course. When the doors swung open, he looked up and spotted her. Usually, he didn't come out of the back to give customers their orders unless there was a serious problem, but he had to get a closer look at this woman. She was so pretty with her caramel skin, dark shoulder-length hair, and beautiful, soulful eyes. Even looking at her, Nicolas could tell that there was a story behind those eyes. She wore a brown sweater that accented her skin very well and denim jeans that accentuated her curves quite nicely. As she spoke, he listened to the sound of her voice, and he knew he wanted to hear it again and again. He hadn't had this kind of response to a woman since he was younger. He was prepared to make conversation with her as he approached the counter, but his mouth went dry, and he didn't know what to say. She made him nervous. He couldn't believe she had this kind of effect on him. He was grateful that Alex was standing there because if she hadn't, he would have made a complete fool of himself in that awkward moment. After she left, Alex stared at him and shook her head. She told him that she wanted to register for the women's art class this Saturday. "Zola

James is her name, Daddy, and she is holding a pottery class this Saturday, and I want to register," she said with pleading eyes. "Zola James, huh?" he said. She replied, "Yes, Dad, she owns that new craft store called *A Messa Stuff.* Can I register, Dad, please?" Nicolas happily obliged his daughter. Any opportunity he got to see her again, he would jump at it. Nicolas's phone rang just as he was getting into his truck. "What's up, man? What's going on?" his friend Billy said. Billy called him earlier in the day and said he wanted to meet for a beer tonight. Nicolas had a feeling that he was about to ask his girlfriend, Krista, to marry him. He liked seeing his friend happy. For so long, his friend had been a ladies' man. Billy was set on staying single and having fun, but one day, he met Krista. She came strolling into his bookstore, and as he said, he just had to talk to her. Billy described her as simply amazing. Nicolas chuckles when he thinks about the two of them because she is not the type of woman Billy usually dates. Billy's women are tall and very thin with long flowing hair. Krista was nothing of the sort. She was not tall, and she was very curvy. As far as her hair was concerned, it was long but in locs. Billy loved everything about this woman. Nicolas thought it was so amazing how people have their own ideas about how their ideal mate should look and act, but they usually end up falling in love with someone who is nothing like they imagined. This is the case with Billy and Krista. She is nothing like the women he usually dated or the type of woman he'd always pictured, but he fell in love with this shy, short, eccentric fourth-grade teacher. "Nothing much, man, just dropping off some paperwork. You still want to meet for that beer tonight?" Nicolas replied. Sounding a little off, Billy said, "Yeah. I'm starving. I'm heading across town right now. See you in ten.

Chapter 5

Nicolas watched his best friend stroll into Tommy's Bar and Grill. He wondered if he should tell him about this Zola James he wanted to see more of. Well, there really wasn't anything to tell just yet; he hadn't even said anything to her. He couldn't believe she made him nervous. He was prepared to carry on a coherent conversation with her, but when he stood in front of her, he was lost for words. She had such quiet elegance about her. There was a confidence about her that attracted him, and— "What's going on, dude? What's up with that dreamy look?" Billy jokingly punched Nicolas in the arm. "What? Shut up," a frowning Nicolas said. The two men ordered wing platters and beers and watched the 49ers game on the wide screen. Pulling a black box out of his pocket, Billy said, "I'm going to ask Krista to marry me." Nicolas looked at his friend and high-fived him. "I knew it! You were acting weird, dude." Billy chuckled, replying, "I know, man. I'm making dinner for her tomorrow at my place, and I'm going to ask her then." Nicolas looked at his friend in absolute amazement. "You? Cook? Where is my best friend, and what have you done with him?" Nicolas laughed. Billy narrowed his eyes on his friend and said, "Ha ha, very funny, man." With a serious face, Nicolas said, "Congrats, dude. I hope that everything works out for you guys. Krista is good for you." "Thanks, man. I want the same for you. You deserve to be happy just like this." Billy replied in a matter-of-fact tone. Nicolas thought of the woman he saw today and smiled. Billy's eyes widen when he realizes that his friend had, in fact, met a woman. "You met someone, didn't you?" "I saw one of the most beautiful women today in the bakery. I looked up from the back as the doors were swinging open and spotted her. For a brief second, we shared a look. I had to get a closer look and maybe strike up a conversation, but when I got in front of her, I couldn't say anything," Nicolas said. Looking confused, Billy asked, "What do you mean you couldn't say anything?" Nicolas, looking a little embarrassed, said, "She made me nervous. I didn't know what I was going to say, but I wanted to get a conversation going. When I looked in her eyes, all my words left me. Alex, thankfully, was standing next to me and had already been carrying on a conversation with the woman." Before he took a sip of his beer, Billy simply said, "Wow, Nick." Shaking his head, Nicolas replied, "Wow is right, dude. I can't believe I was at a loss for words. Man, she is beautiful. Her skin looked so smooth and soft, I just wanted to reach out and touch her. Her name is Zola James, and she opened a new shop here in Ridge Haven." He went on to say, "Alex is registering for a pottery class she is teaching this Saturday." Billy was seriously intrigued by the woman who could make his longtime friend act like a complete idiot. He decided that he liked her already. "So, are you going to ask her out?" Billy asked, popping a boneless wing in his mouth. "I don't even know if she is seeing someone. I didn't see a ring, but you still never know," replied Nicolas. Nicolas planned on taking Alex to the pottery class on Saturday in hopes of seeing her again. He didn't want to seem too obvious, but he didn't want to seem disinterested. "I'm going to take Alex to the class on Saturday, and I will talk to her then," Nicolas mentioned more to himself than to Billy. "Ok, good, that's a start. Look, I think you should go for it. If it turns out she is interested, you owe it to yourself to see where it goes." Billy encouraged Nicolas.

When Nicolas arrived home that night, April and Alex had already gone to bed. Not feeling particularly sleepy, Nicolas plopped in front of the television in the den and mindlessly flipped the channels as his mind began to wander. He thought of Karmen and how much he missed her and how she'd feel about his interest in another woman. Although he kept himself busy over the years raising his daughters, Nicolas secretly felt that he'd be cheating on Karmen if he began dating other women. Of course, Karmen was no longer with him, but to him, it had always felt as though he'd be disrespecting what they had together. Lately, however, he'd been feeling differently. He knew Karmen loved him and the girls, and she'd want nothing more than for them to be happy. His thoughts then drifted to her, Zola. Nick couldn't get this woman out of his mind. He wondered who she really was. What were her interests, hobbies, and goals? Did she have children? Was she married? He certainly hoped that the last part wasn't true. He thought of asking around about her in town, but he didn't want to start any gossip. With Ridge Haven, as small as it is, rumors were easily started. The last thing he needed was for word to get back to her that he'd been asking about her. He had settled on waiting until Saturday.

Friday morning was busy like any other time at home and at the bakery. At home, Alex made sure everyone was up and at it. Surprising, Nicolas and Alex both, April cooked breakfast. "What? I'm in a good mood," she simply said when she noticed the puzzling looks everyone gave her. The normal hustle and bustle at the bakery pleased Nicolas when he walked in this morning. He had been thinking about opening a new location for a few months now, but was unsure whether he should. He had been pouring over the books with his accountant for months, and on paper, it could certainly be done. The busyness of the bakery had really boosted his confidence in the new business venture. He hadn't told anyone about it because he wasn't sure if he was going to go through with it. However, the better the bakery does, the better the idea of opening a second location. Nicolas had a long day ahead, and he was working on a new recipe and needed to time it just right to put it out by next week. He believed that Ridge Haven really appreciated the authentic taste of the recipes he and his bakers produced. Every dessert made in *Confectioner's Corner* is authentic and tasty. Most of the desserts sold there, he and Karmen spent hours perfecting. Nicolas took pride in everything that he baked because baking is his passion, and he couldn't imagine doing anything else in his life. If he decided to open a new bakery, he would have a meeting with his managers to make the announcement once he had a location. Meanwhile, he would spend most of the day working on his new dessert.

After hours of baking, Nicolas decided that he needed some fresh air, so he decided to take a run. Although he runs with Alex every morning, he takes his lunch runs in Henry Park. He figured today would be a good day to clear his mind. Running usually did that for him. Lately, Nicolas's mind had been going a mile a minute. He ran home to change into some sweats and grabbed a bottle of water. Nicolas always liked this park because the city built a special track for runners. As he began stretching, he looked and saw a familiar figure running off in the distance. He knew it was her immediately. He watched as she ran the trail of the track that brought her closer to where he was standing. Zola had purple leggings with a matching halter sports bra-type thing. Her running outfit gave him an awesome view of all her curves. Boy, did he like her curves. Her hair was pulled up in a messy ponytail, which revealed her shoulders and neck. She had earbuds in her ears, so she wasn't paying much attention to her surroundings, which was good for him because he was staring with inappropriate intensity. He eventually turned away because he didn't want to get caught ogling this woman. He finished his stretches and joined her on the track. From where he started, Zola was running behind him. He didn't want to run too fast because he wanted her to catch up with him.

Chapter 6

Zola had decided to run during her break today to clear her mind. There was so much she needed to do with the house before it closed. Although she was able to do everything, she wanted this past year, moving and open her new store, it had all been exhausting. There was always so much to do, and she hadn't had a moment to herself in a long time. What bothered her the most was that she hadn't been able to finish her painting. She's been working on it since May, and it is now October. With everything going on, she hadn't had the time to work on it. This really bothered her. She thought about shutting the world out for a weekend so she could concentrate on her art. She knew she really needed a vacation, but that was just out of the question right now. Zola needed Sabbath, however. Running was a bit of a compromise for her. When she looked up, she saw him, the man from the bakery. Even from afar, she could make out his physique, one that she wouldn't mind seeing every single day. He entered the track ahead of her, and she watched him from behind. As her thoughts began to settle on him, she began to wonder about his interests, hobbies, and family. She knew he at least had a daughter, Alex. She was a sweet young lady and eager to learn about pottery. She didn't know much else about him, though. She wanted to talk to him, but didn't want to seem desperate. She was so terrible at this. She was not on the dating scene and had no clue as to how to approach a man. For all she knew, he could be married. Well, she was sure he was probably at least dating someone. No one that handsome is sitting home alone on any given Friday night. Just like that, Zola had talked herself out of approaching Nick. When she realized that she was catching up with him, she tried to slow down. She wanted to completely avoid making a fool out of herself today. As slowly as she ran, she still seemed to be gaining on him. "Wait, is he slowing down?" Zola thought to herself. She brushed it off. He probably hadn't even seen her. When she realized that it was inevitable that they would eventually run beside each other, she was prepared to give him a nod and keep running. "Ah, excuse me. How are you, Ms. James?" A deep voice pulled her out of her reverie. A little startled, Zola looked up and saw those beautiful green eyes. "Hi. I'm doing well. How are you?" Zola answered. She was nervous at this moment. She was hoping that she'd see him again, but she didn't expect to see him today while running, and she looked a mess. "I'm doing alright. I wanted to go for a run this afternoon before getting back to work," he said. Zola smiled, "Me too. I discovered this park the other day. I like to run to clear my head." "I do the same. I find it really relaxing, and any stress I'm feeling, I can just take it all out on this asphalt." Nicolas told her. She didn't say anything, so he took that as a sign to keep talking because he didn't want her to leave yet. "So, do you live in Ridge Haven? I know that you are new to the area because this is a small town compared to the surrounding areas, and everyone knows each other." Zola looked at him and replied, "Yes, I live here now. We moved here officially during the summer, right before school started, but I am back and forth a lot between this store and my other one. We moved here from Rose Creek." "Yes, that's right. Alexandra told me that you own the new craft store. So, you own another store?" Nicolas looked curiously at her. Zola said, "Yes, I've always wanted to have several stores. I thought it was a great idea to move here since the new store is here. My other business is doing fantastic, and now most of my focus is on this new store." "Fantastic, huh?" Nicolas said, smiling down at her. He extended his hand to her. "My name is Nicolas Gallo, but you can call me Nick." She took his hand and said, "My name is Zola James." "I am very pleased to make your acquaintance, Ms. Zola. So how are you enjoying Ridge Haven?" Nick asked, pleased that he could create sentences with all the thoughts floating in his head about her. "This is a nice town. Everyone here seems to be very friendly. I am trying to get my daughter to give it a chance, but she is still upset that we moved here and she had to leave her friends." "Oh, you have children?" Nick asked, wondering how old they were. Zola nodded, saying, "Yes, I have one daughter, Sophie. She is in the tenth grade." "Alexandra is in the tenth grade. Maybe they have met," he mentioned. "Perhaps they have. It would be nice if Sophie made friends. She hadn't talked about meeting anyone new yet. She seems to be doing fine, but I still worry whether this was a good move for both of us," Zola said. He noticed the crease in her eyebrows as she spoke about her daughter. He could tell that she was worried about her. Nick decided that he'd talk to Alex tonight when he got home about introducing her to Sophie. "If they don't know each other, they will meet tomorrow because Sophie will be helping me teach the pottery class." Zola mentioned it to him. Nick studied her for a moment and asked, "So are you an artist?" Zola smiled widely and replied, "Yes, I am. I've been painting since I was in college." She went on to say, "I majored in architecture and design in college just like my dad, but I realized that I loved drawing landscapes and painting those more than I enjoyed designing buildings." Nick nodded and asked, "So your father is an architect?" Zola nodded and went on to explain that her dad had been designing structures her entire life. She also told him about her dad's feelings about her being an artist and how Sophie has the same passion for the arts. "Opening my store was a way to get my work out, but also to showcase other artists. I remember how hard it was in the beginning to get my artwork out there, but I finally did it. It took me three years for any of my paintings to sell, but Sophie has already sold four, and she's not even sixteen yet." Nick was truly amazed. They talked briefly about their lives before it was time for both to go back to work.

Nick enjoyed talking to Zola and didn't want their conversation to end. "Zola would you be available for coffee this evening?" Nick asked. With the most adorable smile that he'd ever seen, she took his number and told him that she'd get back with him.

"She'll get back with you. What does that mean?" Billy asked, giving him a baffled look. Billy had stopped by the bakery later that day to pick up some chocolate-covered strawberries for his night with Krista. "I don't know what that means, Billy. I was hoping that you would tell me; I thought you'd be more familiar with this kind of thing." "Get back with you" is simply what it means; she'll get back with you, boss," Jessie, an employee in her mid-twenties, interjected. "If you are talking about the woman you were staring at the other day, she probably meant just what I said. She doesn't strike me as the type to play games and send mixed messages," Jessie also said. Nick looked down at Jessie, who was cleaning the cake display cases, and asked her, "Just how do you know who I'm talking about, Jessie?" "Well, when that woman came in the other day, I noticed that you came out with her cake. Sir, it's rare that you bring customers their orders, and since I was on my break, I decided to watch you to see how that little scene was going to play out." Jessie looked at her boss and sighed, "Epic fail, Mr. Nick." Nick frowned at her and started to respond, but she cut him off. "She must have affected you in some way, Mr. Nick, because it looked like you didn't know what to say to her." "Thanks for the observation, Jessie." Nick continued frowning at Jessie. Nick thought Jessie was a sweet young lady, but at some point, in her young life, she will need to tame her tongue and mind her own business. There isn't a thing she misses in this bakery, he thought to himself. "Listen to the lady, Nick." A smiling Billy said. "I didn't mean to offend Mr. Nick; it's just that I happened to have seen that incident play out the other day. It grabbed my interest because, for the past two and a half years, I've been working here, I've never seen you react that way to any woman who has walked through the door. I think it's kind of cute." Jessie giggled. Nick shook his head and smiled. She really is a nice kid, and he knows she means well. "Look, don't read so much into what she said. You did say she was a business owner like yourself, so she could be just as busy as you are. After all, you don't really know what she had planned this evening. Just relax, man, and let things happen; she'll call," Billy assured him.

Three hours later, Nick's phone rang, and when he answered it, he heard a familiar voice on the other end. "Nick? How are you? This is Zola James from the park this afternoon." Nick smiled as the memory of his run with Zola came flooding back to him. "I'm doing pretty good, Zola. How are you?" Nick said, "I am doing great. How are you doing?" She replied, "I'm doing quite well, Nick. I was calling to see if you were still interested in coffee later." Nick smiled widely at the thought of being able to see her again. "Sure, we can still meet. I'm getting out of here around six." Nick said, walking back to his office for privacy. "Ok, that's great. Where would you like to meet?" Zola said, shifting the cordless phone to her other ear. She had been sitting in front of her computer all morning making orders for the shop. This is her least favorite thing about owning a business. She always hated the mundane responsibilities. "Can you meet here at the bakery around seven?" Nick asked Zola as he thought of a special recipe he'd like to try out on her. Shuffling the paperwork on her desk, Zola replied, "Sure. I will see you then." Just then, she received another call and hung up with Nick.

"Hi, sweetheart. How are you? Are you and your dad enjoying yourselves? Zola said in a cheery voice. "Hey, Mom. We had a great time. Daddy is so cool! Sophie said with excitement in her voice. Zola's eyebrows crawled to her hairline when she heard

Sophie talk about her dad. "He is? How is your daddy so cool?" Zola asked her daughter with curiosity in her voice.

"Mama, I can't really explain it. He just seems so relaxed. I was surprised but happy. I had him all to myself, and he laughed. Daddy was definitely different." Sophie explained to her mom, while she packed her clothes into her suitcase to come home the next day. She and Jonathan were planning a mini vacation. This is the first vacation she has taken with him since her parents divorced. She wanted to spend more time with her father, but he was always so busy with work, and then when he met Elizabeth, he really disappeared. Sure, she would spend parts of the summer with him and weekends, but she didn't feel as though she had her dad's full attention until now. Sophie was excited yet a little surprised to learn that Elizabeth would not be joining them on their vacation in a few weeks. She missed her mom this week, but it was nice to finally have her dad all to herself. Her mother interrupted her thoughts, "Well, I'm so happy that you enjoyed yourself with your dad, sweetie. I'm glad you're getting to know that side of him. Your dad used to be that kind of person years ago." Sophie smiled at what her mom said. "Mom, I'll talk to you more about it when I get home tomorrow morning. Daddy is calling in, and I think he is pulling up outside. We're going to dinner." Zola smiled at the contentment in her daughter's voice. "Ok, baby, please call me before you go to bed tonight.

Zola was very happy that her daughter was having such a good time. She was starting to rethink her decision to move because Sophie had taken it so hard. There had been a lot of changes in her life these past few years, and Zola knew Sophie hadn't taken it well. She had spent much more time on her artwork, and usually that was an indicator that something was going on with her. This is one of the reasons why she had given Jonnie the go-ahead when he approached her with the idea of Sophie going on a mini vacation with him in a few weeks. At least for the moment, Zola could breathe a sigh of relief. As she started working on the paperwork on her desk, her manager, Quinn, walked into her office. "Hey, it's ten minutes to six. I've started closing the front." Zola looked at the time on her computer and smiled. She began putting her paperwork away as she looked up and said, "Ok, I'll be up in a moment." She thought of Nick and began to feel butterflies in her stomach. She still could not believe how nervous she was. "This is truly out of character for me." Zola chuckled as she got up and walked towards the front of the store. Her staff was busy at work as she looked around, pleased at the sight before her. The second store has really come together in the last six months. She dreamed of branching out for years and starting classes, but never thought she would be able to do it. It only took her a divorce and some self-confidence to do it.

Zola checked her makeup in the mirror before she got out of the SUV. Nick told her to meet him at the bakery after work, but it looked like it was closed and everyone was gone for the day. She hesitated as she walked towards the front door. Suddenly, she saw that familiar handsome face of his as he neared the door and unlocked it for her. "Good evening. It's nice to see you again." Nick said as he took her coat. He turned to walk around the counter, and she followed him. Although it was dusk, there was still some light in the bakery, and she could easily take a peek at his form. Gosh, this is a good-looking man. Everything about him was appealing to her, from his walk to his silky voice. This unnerved her a little bit because she couldn't remember responding this way to a man before. "Here we are," he said as he gestured to a little table adorned with silk table linen and purple roses in a vase. The aroma of fresh pastries and cakes wafted through the air. As Zola inhaled, she realized that she was hungry. She certainly hoped her stomach did not betray her. "I hope you are hungry because I have been working on a new pastry recipe, and I want you to try it. I hope you like it; you will be the first person to ever taste it." Nick mentioned as he pulled the pastry out of the industrial-size refrigerator. He further explained, "It's a strawberry rose pastry. It's a flaky pastry with infused flavors of strawberries and roses. I've been trying to get both flavors to shine because the strawberry can overpower the rose." He set the pastry down in front of her and walked over to the counter to pick up the coffee carafe. Nick finally sat down and set the pastries down on the table. "Wow, this looks delicious, Nick. It smells so delicious here. I can't believe I am the first person to taste your new pastry creation." Zola said, smiling, as he pushed it closer to her. "Thank you very much. I wanted to invite you for coffee, but I wanted to make it a little more memorable. How do you take your coffee?" Nick asked her. Zola studied an assortment of creamers for a second and pointed to the French Vanilla. He handed the creamer to her, allowing her to measure the amount that she wanted in her coffee. Zola picked up the fork and cut into a piece of the pastry, and tasted it. She immediately closed her eyes and sighed, "My god, this is delicious." He studied her as she enjoyed the first bite of the pastry and realized that she had that look that all chefs looked for when people tasted their creations for the first time: pure, unadulterated satisfaction. He began to wonder what it would feel like to satisfy her in other ways. Before he got any deeper in his thoughts, he replied, "I see you like it?" She opened her eyes and sheepishly smiled, "Yes, I guess I do. Sorry, I got carried away. This is out of this world. I hope you are planning to put it on the menu. People would fall in love with this dessert." He smiled and loved that she enjoyed his pastry. "That is the plan." He looked at her curiously and began to ask qualifying questions about her. She began to carefully answer each of his questions. He found that she had just turned 40 and had been divorced for almost five years now. Though he knew she had a daughter, she told him more about her. He asked her more about her business. He discovered that she was born and raised in Rose Creek, which is where her other business resided. He learned that her true passion was art, and that intrigued him. She loved to paint and believed it was great to be able to share that passion with her daughter. "I sold a painting just a few months ago, and I have been invited to do an exhibit in two months at the McCarthy Museum. I guess I got the love of art from my dad." As she talked about her family, divorce, and her business, Nick tuned in as if he were watching a movie. He wanted to be very attentive to her. The more he heard, the more he liked this woman. Not only was she beautiful, but she was creative, different, and free. Nick wasn't sure why these qualities attracted him so much, but her aura was infectious. As she spoke, Nick sensed such ease and confidence about her. He loved that she was present in her life, enjoying every moment. This reminded him of Karmen. There was a command about her presence. She was very pleasant and peaceful, and Nick knew that this was the kind of woman he could spend a lot of time with. He hoped he would anyway.

When it came time for her to ask him about himself, he told Zola about his girls, Karmen, the business, and his family. He talked about how he met Karmen and the life they had built together. He only spoke a little about their experience with her getting sick. Zola gave an attentive ear as Nick talked about his life. She noticed how he talked about his daughters with such devotion and pride. She could tell he had a great relationship with them. When he started talking about his late wife, Zola noted a hint of sadness in his voice. It also didn't go unnoticed that he avoided much talk about her. So, Zola didn't press him to talk more about her. She could tell that there was an ache there. Nick's healing may not be one hundred percent, and who is to say how long it takes to get over the death of a spouse? This was an area in which she had no expertise. She listened as he talked about the town and the people in it. She could tell that Nick truly enjoyed his life and was humbled by his success. He seemed to be a passionate and caring man. He focused on her while she spoke. He made her feel as though he really wanted to know her, as she mattered. Zola had forgotten what that was like, coming from a man. Jonnie stopped being attentive years before their divorce. Nick and Zola enjoyed each other's company. "I'm hungry. Would you like to grab a bite to eat with me?" Nick asked Zola. "Sure," replied Zola. They left the bakery and headed to Marianne's, a locally owned bistro not far from downtown Ridge Haven. Nick knew they were taking a chance on a Friday evening, but they went anyway. Nick wasn't surprised to see them crowded. They both agreed that they wanted to eat at a place less noisy and crowded. They tried three other places, and they were either crowded or had a long wait time. Finally, Zola said, "Nick, if you don't mind, I can make us some dinner. I'm getting kind of hungry, and I don't think we are going to find any place quiet and empty on a Friday night." She could not believe she had invited him over. Where this gumption came from, she did not know, but she was more than intrigued by it. "That will work. I mean, are you sure? You don't have to go through all that trouble," Nick said, silently praying that she wouldn't resend her offer. "No, it's absolutely fine. Sophie doesn't come back from her father's house until the morning, so my house is empty." Zola told Nick. Besides, she was truly ravenous, and she wasn't ready for her time with him to end just yet.

Chapter 7

Nick examined Zola's house as he pulled into the driveway. The changes that she had made to the old Wellington Farmhouse were amazing. He couldn't imagine anyone wanting to live in that old house, much less buy it. However, knowing what he now knew about Zola, she was just the person to do it. He observed the choice in colors and fabrics used. This woman was truly amazing. She intrigued him in more ways than one. Her creativity and style attracted him, and he was anxious to know more about her. As he followed Zola into the kitchen, he watched her from behind. She began speaking, but he couldn't quite make out what she was saying because he was admiring her physique. From head to toe, for Nick, this woman was perfection. He liked the way her hips swayed when she walked. His eyes followed the shape of her shoulders, and he imagined what it would be like to run his fingers through her shoulder-length hair. Zola was a very beautiful woman, and he had come across attractive women since Karmen, but no one else had managed to keep his attention like her.

"Do you like salmon?" Zola asked Nick as she pulled the fish out of the refrigerator. Nick shook his head yes as he looked around the floor plan of the house. Zola had really done a wonderful job with this old farmhouse. She opened up the dining room and living area to make it one big living space. She had an eye for design. Nick said, "I love what you have done with this house, Zola. It's so beautiful here. You have brought life to this old place." Zola smiled widely and thanked Nick for the compliment. "I really tried to put our personal touch on this house. This is the first home that I owned all by myself, and I want to make it special for both Sophie and me. I'm not finished; it's still a work in progress." Zola placed two pieces of salmon in the grill pan before going on, "I can give you a tour later if you'd like." Nick shook his head. "That would be great." As she moved around the kitchen preparing their meal, Nick studied this woman. She was so different from any woman he had ever met. There was something about her that drew him and made him want to know her. He loved the calm and peace about her. He believed that this was what drew him the most. In the little time he'd spent around her, he felt so at ease in her presence. He wasn't quite sure how to explain that.

Zola could not believe that she was making dinner for Nicolas. She couldn't believe the words came out of her mouth when she suggested that they come back to her house to eat. What was she thinking? Was she crazy? She didn't know this man very well, and here she is inviting him to her empty house. She thought it was out of her character, but she didn't feel regret. Something about Nick made her feel at ease. She really didn't want the night to end. She wanted to continue to spend time with him. He was a charming man, not to mention gorgeous. She tried her hardest not to imagine what it would be like to kiss him, but she could not get that thought out of her mind. Zola had been content being by herself since her divorce. She put all of her focus on Sophie and building a new life for both of them; she hadn't thought about dating. Her friends encouraged her to date and even offered to set her up, but she always turned down their offers, stating that she wasn't ready. Now here she was acting like some teenager, smiling like an idiot around a man she hardly even knew. What's worse is that she invited him to her house. Zola smiled as she blended the ingredients for the sauce for their salmon fillets. Zola seared the salmon in her grill pan and made some basil butter to accompany it, and roasted asparagus with parmesan.

Nick began walking towards Zola. When he finally reached her, he realized that he stood a good two feet over her. He wanted to see what ingredients she was using to make the house smell so delicious. "Is there anything that I can do to help?" He asked. "Sure, you can get the wine out of the wine chiller. There's only one bottle in there. I just got the chiller a few days ago." Nick grabbed the bottle of wine, and Zola handed him the bottle opener. She fixed their plates, and he poured the wine. With the lights low and candle lit, Zola and Nick sat across from each other eating in silence. Nick's mind raced, trying to find something to say to fill the silence. "This is very delicious, Zola. It's nice to get a meal like this and not have to whip it up myself." Nick said, savoring every bite. Zola looked up and smiled. "I appreciate that. It's nice to cook for someone. Sophie doesn't like for me to fuss over her much, and so she insists on making her own food most days. I tell her that it's never a bother, but she is so very protective. Then again, there are those days when she wants her mom's cooking. She seems to believe that she has to look out for me." Nick looked at her intently and replied, "My girls are the same way. They feel they have to take care of me, but I remind them that it's the other way around. Take Alex, for instance; she makes sure everyone in the house is up and together in the morning. She even insists on cooking most mornings before she goes to school." Zola looked at Nick with compassion in her eyes and replied, "Nick, you can't blame them; they see what you've been through these past few years. "I believe Sophie's the same way, Zola," Nick mentioned. Our children have witnessed our heartache, and they want to take care of us in their own way. She agreed.

They talked for at least an hour and a half after their dinner, and the plates were cleared. "Well, I guess I'd better go. I'm sure you have an early day tomorrow." Nick said. He did not really want to leave. He could have stayed and talked to her all night. He couldn't get enough of talking to her. "Ok, you are right. Well, before you go, let me give the tour." Zola said, getting up from the table. Zola gave Nick a very quick tour of the house, starting with the den and ending in the art studio out back. Nick especially loved the backyard. "I could hang out here and sleep under the stars. You are giving me some ideas," Nick said. He followed her to the front door. "Well, this has truly been a pleasure, Ms. James," Nick said. "The pleasure is all mine, Mr. Gallo." Zola blushed. As she reached for the door to open, Nick turned, caressed her face, and kissed her lips lightly. It took a couple of seconds to register to Zola that he was, in fact, kissing her. This handsome green-eyed man was standing at her front door, kissing her. Her lips began to move against his, and before she knew it, she was sliding her arms around his neck, and the kiss was deepening. "Oh my god! What am I doing? I need to stop!" screamed Zola in her head, but her body would not respond to her thoughts. Instead, it responded in a whole different way. She knew she should stop this kiss before it led to something she definitely wasn't ready for, emotionally that is. Physically, she was more than ready. It had been five years since she'd been with any man. Reluctantly, she broke off the kiss. "I should go," Nick said with an exasperated sigh. "Yes, that might be a good idea," Zola said, noting how fast her heart was racing. Nick leaned down and kissed her on the cheek before walking out the door. Zola watched him drive out of sight. When she closed the door, she leaned against it for fear that she'd fall. Her legs felt like putty. She hadn't been kissed like that in—well, ever. She and Jonathan shared moments over the years, especially when they were younger, but never like that. No one had ever kissed her like that. In that kiss, she felt several different things—beautiful, sexy, nervous—but most of all, wanted. She felt like this man truly wanted her, but not just for her body. She was having a difficult time wrapping her mind around what had just happened. She did not imagine that a simple coffee invitation would turn into dinner and then the most passionate kiss of her life.

As Nick drove home, thoughts of Zola whirled around in his head. From her conversation to the smell of her hair to the way her lips felt, Nick liked everything about Zola. He'd never felt this way before, and it started to unnerve him. For years, women had come in and out of his bakery, and none had an effect on him, but Zola was a totally different story. From the moment he looked her in the eyes at the bakery, he wanted to kiss her. The opportunity didn't actually present itself at her house; he created it. He just could not imagine walking away from her tonight and not kissing her. Nick then began to question himself. "Did I come on too strong? Did I scare her away?" He certainly hoped that none of it was true. The last thing he wanted was to come on too strong and scare her away. It had been a while since he was in the game, but he didn't think that he could be that rusty that he'd send her running. Nick quickly dismissed those thoughts and began revisiting the events of the day. It had been a very long time since he spent time with a woman besides Karmen. He hadn't dated anyone seriously since her passing. He went out on a few dates here and there, but those were only set up by friends and family. He wasn't interested. Truth be told, Nick wasn't ready, and more than that, he felt that he would be unfaithful to Karmen. Familiar guilty feelings crept up again. Something about Zola made him feel different, though. She has a great personality to fit. Nick thought she was beautiful on the inside and out. Nick had come to appreciate this type of woman as he grew older.

While talking to Zola, Nick noted a lot of vulnerability, and he would never take advantage of that. He sensed that she had gone through a lot in her life, and she had to make some huge changes to get where she is today. He hoped that one day she would trust him enough to share all of her journey with him. He knew all too well about vulnerability. Karmen had been gone for quite some time, and he still has some bad days. There were days when he missed Karmen so much that he could hardly breathe. He learned, though, that he could not linger in that place for long. He had grieved her death, and he didn't want to constantly relive those moments. He knew that she would not want that for him or their girls. She would want him to move forward with his life. For the first time, he entertained the idea of another woman in his life, but he didn't want to get ahead of himself. For now, he'd just take it one day at a time.

That night, Zola fell asleep thinking about her evening with Nick. She had such a great time with him. She couldn't completely identify the emotions she felt when she was with him. She and Jonnie had been married for a long time; heck, they'd even known each other for longer than that, and he never affected her this way. When she saw Nick for the first time, he made her feel anxious and nervous, but in a good way. When she saw him in the park this afternoon, her racing heart had as much to do with him as running. She felt the same way when they met for coffee. Zola only hoped that her face didn't betray the way she felt inside when she was around him.

She woke up abruptly to the sound of her alarm clock and sat up and looked around the room. The sun peeked through her curtains, lighting up the entire room. Zola loved waking up to natural light. This is why she insisted on lighter curtains and light colors on her walls in her bedroom. As she rolled out of bed, she heard a noise in the front part of the house. Panicky, Zola looked around her room for an object to protect herself from the possible intruder. Suddenly, she heard a familiar laugh. "Jonnie?" Zola thought to herself. She thought she was hearing things, but then she heard him laugh again. Yes, that was definitely her ex-husband in her house at seven o'clock in the morning. She grabbed her robe and walked to the front of the house to see her daughter and her ex-husband making breakfast in her kitchen. Sophie looked up, "Good morning, Mama! I've missed you so much." Zola returned her daughter's embrace. "When did you get here? Why didn't you wake me up?" Sophie giggled at her mom's exasperated sigh, "Well, we got here an hour and a half ago. I saw you sleeping so peacefully, and I decided not to wake you. I wanted to make breakfast before we left, so I invited Daddy to eat with us." Sophie said, flipping a pancake on the griddle. Zola looked from Sophie to Jonnie and said, "You couldn't have called to let me know that you guys were on the way." Jonnie gave Zola a hard stare for a few seconds, and his features softened. "We did call Zo, but you didn't answer. When we finally got here, we realized why. You were conked out." "Wait. You were in my bedroom?" Zola asked Jonathan, raising her eyebrows. "Ma, he only peeked in because I was giving Daddy a tour of the house. He's never been here, remember?" Sophie said, rolling her eyes in her head at her mother's overdramatizing. Zola turned on the coffee maker and walked back to her room. She could not believe that her ex-husband was in her house right now, the house that she did not invite him into. As she brushed her teeth, she could not figure out why she was so annoyed by his presence. It might have something to do with the fact that after their divorce, she created a new life, and this was the first property that belonged to her and not both of them. She wasn't ready for him to be a part of this life, this new life she created that was all her own. Yet, there he was, grinning like an idiot in her kitchen, making breakfast with their daughter. "Ok, Zola, pull it together. Sophie looks very happy, and you don't want to mess this up," she said, hoping that this pep talk would make her feel better. Zola changed into yoga pants and a shirt and walked back to the kitchen. "You're just in time, Ma." Sophie smiled while fixing a plate for her dad. "Zola, I know that seeing me in your kitchen this morning might be a shock. I have not been one of your favorite people for a while, but Sophie and I have had the greatest time together this week. When she asked for me to tour your home, I couldn't say no," Jonathan said. Zola looked at Jonathan with a strained smile. "It's alright, Jonathan; you are welcome here." He gave her a sly smile, knowing that she didn't mean a word of it.

For the next hour, Sophie and Jonathan filled Zola in on their time together. Zola loved the spark in her daughter's eyes. She looked happy talking about her time with her father. This is the happiest she's been since their new move. Jonathan looked equally as happy. There was an obvious difference about him, but she couldn't put her finger on it. He seemed more at ease, and his countenance was lighter. Normally, Jonathan's an intense person, but he was a very different man sitting in front of her this morning. Zola was grateful to him for not putting anything else before their daughter so she could have a great week. They haven't sat around the kitchen table since Sophie was a very little girl, and she had the same smile then that she does now at fifteen. "So, I hear you are teaching a pottery class over here this afternoon," Jonathan said to Zola. "Oh yeah, the pottery class. I have to get ready." Sophie said, jumping up from the table. Zola looked at Jonathan and said, "Yep. This is my first class. I hope it is as popular here as it is in Rose Creek. I have about fifteen people scheduled to attend the class today." That's good, right?" Jonathan asked, sounding hopeful. "Yes, it is actually. I hope that they keep their interest." Zola replied. Shaking his head and studying her, Jonathan said, "So how are things going with the second store?" Zola gave him an astonishing look and answered, "Coming along well. A little better than I expected. Apparently, there isn't much in the way of arts and crafts in this town. So, I don't really have any competition." Jonathan gave Zola a look that she couldn't quite explain or understand, but it made her a little uncomfortable. He just looked at her with an odd intensity. She looked away and looked again, but he just kept looking. "Jonnie, what is going on with you?" Zola finally asked him. With a confused look, he replied, "What do you mean?" She frowned and said, "Well, let's see. First, you don't include Elizabeth in your week with Sophie. Second, you are not tense and serious like you usually are. Third, I find you in my kitchen this morning cooking breakfast with our daughter." When he didn't respond, she went on to say, "Two months ago, I couldn't get you to come to the house to get the things you say you wanted because you wouldn't make time. Every conversation we've had since our divorce has been strained, and now you are asking me about my life like we are old friends. This is a little puzzling, to say the least." "Things aren't the same for me anymore, Zo," Jonathan simply said. He offered no other explanation besides that. He gave nothing to explain his weird behavior, nothing to explain why Elizabeth wasn't around to ruin their daughter's quality time with him by attempting to compete for his attention. He didn't explain why he was in her house, now talking to her as if they were friends. "Things aren't the same?" Zola asked. "Jonathan, how are things different for you?" she asked him. He finished off the rest of his juice and said, "They just are, Zo. This house is absolutely beautiful. Only you could take an old farmhouse and transform it into something so lovely. You are a true artist." His compliment nearly floored her. She had to admit, he always supported her being an artist, but he never seemed very interested in that part of her life. He didn't seem to care about her creativity over the years. He never paid attention to anything new she did in the house they shared in Rose Creek. For the most part, he was only interested in things that involved them together, not anything that made her a person outside of him and Sophie. Now that he was acknowledging her, she didn't know how to receive it. "Thank you" was all Zola could muster up. "Before I forget, I'll come this week and gather my things from the house." Jonathan said. "I only have a few things left there. We can meet at the house on Wednesday when I'm back in the area," Zola replied. She got up and began cleaning up the kitchen and stacking the dishes in the dishwasher. "Let me help you with that." Jonathan said to her, grabbing a glass out of her hand. She wiped down the countertops as he stacked the dishes in the sink. They cleaned in silence, and as she turned toward the sink, Jonathan grabbed her arm and pulled her into a tight hug. She wasn't sure why, but she sank into his hug. She hugged him back, surprising herself by wanting to. "You are truly remarkable, Zola James," Jonathan said. He released her a little and looked down at her with his same uncomfortable look as before. She didn't know what to do in his arms, but she knew she had to get away from him quickly because his behavior was really confusing her. Just then, her phone rang. She pulled away from him to answer the phone. "He—Hello?" "Hi Zee. Are you alright? Your voice sounds shaky." Maranda said in a perky tone. "I'm fine, dear. What's up?" Zola replied. "Well, I was wondering when you were coming back to Rose Creek. I wanted you to come over and help me move some things around in the house." Maranda answered. Zola knew that meant they needed to talk. "I'll be in Rose Creek on Wednesday morning. I just need to check on things in the store and gather the rest of my belongings out of the house. I should be finished by at least two. I'll come over then. Is everything alright?" Zola said. "I'm alright, I just needed your help. Two is fine; I'll cook," Maranda replied. As they were hanging up, Sophie walked in, pulling her hair up in a messy bun and tying her apron around her waist. "Listen, ladies, I'm going to get going," Jonathan said. "Aww, Daddy, are you sure you can't stay longer? I wanted to show you my latest piece," Sophie said, looking sad. She knew her dad could never resist "the look." "Ok, I'll have a look at your piece, and then I've got to get on the road. You guys have a long day ahead, and I've a couple of appointments later today." Sophie's father replied. Zola chimed in, "While you guys are outside, I'm going to get ready." Zola quickly walked off before she could get roped into the three of them spending more time together. When she reached her room, Zola sat on the edge of her bed and tried to figure out what had just happened between her and Jonnie. She was curious to know what was going on with her ex-husband and what prompted the change in his behavior and attitude. She showered and got herself ready for the day. As she looked in the mirror, she thought about the time she spent with Nick. Zola blushed again. That seemed to happen when she was around him or when she thought of him. She could not remember the last time she felt like this. The thought of seeing him today made her smile. For the first time in five years, she considered what her life would be like with a man in it. For so long, she had put the idea of a relationship out of her mind. She had so many other things she needed to focus on, including creating a new life, helping Sophie deal with the divorce, and starting a new business. As she thought about it, she didn't have the time to put into a relationship. However, if she were perfectly honest, Zola was afraid to start a new relationship. Things were certainly different now than they were five years ago. She was a different woman then. All those years she put her soul into her work and being a mother, and today she is stronger. There was a time when she never thought she would smile again. Now, she can't stop grinning.

Chapter 8

By the time she was ready to go, to her relief, Jonnie had left. She found Sophie out in the studio working on her newest piece. "Sweetie, today you will meet a young lady named Alexandra. She goes to your school, and I think it would be nice if you guys became friends." Zola mentioned that she was wrapping her painting to hang in the store. "Why should we be friends?" Sophie asked her mom, stopping to look back. "Well, Sophie, I don't hear you talking about any new friends here, and she seemed like a nice young lady. Her father owns the bakery, *Confectioner's Corner*, in town, and I met her there." Sophie gave her mom a weary look, "Mama, I am fine. I'm not starving for friends, and I am not lonely. The girls here are different from the girls back at home, but I am adjusting." Sophie went on to say, "Besides, there are a few girls I talk to here and there." Zola gave her daughter a concerned look. "Well, will you give her a chance for me?" Sophie looked back again, "Alright." They reached the shop an hour before the pottery class started. Sophie went into the back to set up while her mom hung her new painting up in the store. She wasn't sure why her mom thought that her life would be so much better if she had a lot of friends. As far as Sophie was concerned, she was fine with the friends she already had. She would give this girl a chance for her mom's sake, but she suspected that this Alexandra would turn out to be like all the other girls in her school, total flakes. "I wish she would just accept that I am a loner and that doesn't make me sad or depressed. It just means that I enjoy being by myself." Sophie once shared with her Aunt Ronnie some time ago. "Sophie, honey, your mom is just worried about you and your adjustment to moving to a new area. You didn't take your parents' divorce very well, and I don't think she wants you to feel like that again with this new move. She knows that this is a big adjustment for you," replied Veronica. Sophie thought about that conversation, and because of her aunt's words and the promise she made to her mom, she decided to give Alexandra a chance.

"Daddy, you are not dressed yet," Alexandra said to her father, who was sitting in the rocking chair on their back porch, reading the paper. Every Saturday morning, Nick sat on the back porch and read the Haven Chronicle while sipping his herbal tea. This Saturday wasn't any different, except Alexandra had her first pottery lesson today. They still had an hour to kill before it was time to be there. An hour before, he would see Zola again. He could have easily gotten April to take her and go on with the rest of his peaceful morning, but he had to see her again. As Nick thought about Zola, his stomach started to churn, and his palms got sweaty. He hadn't managed to feel this way since he first met Karmen. He anticipated the time he'd see Zola again, and that got him getting up so he could get ready. "What do I wear?" Nick thought. He couldn't believe he was mulling over what he was going to wear. He needed to get a hold of himself. He remembered being a lot smoother when it came to the ladies. "Daddy, I'm going to Kara's in a few, and later on we are going to the mall in Parson Hills," April yelled out from the other side of her father's bedroom door. Nick rushed to the door, "Wait, when are you leaving?" April jumped back, surprised as her father's door suddenly opened. She should have known he was going to have a hundred questions about where she was going and what she was doing, and who she was with for today. "I'm leaving in an hour or so, Dad, and I'm going to Kara's house. Before you ask, Kara is going to drive, but her brother, Daniel, is going with us." April replied. She might as well tell him all of her plans because he was going to give her the third degree after the first question. Her father can be so overprotective at times. This always annoyed April because she would be eighteen in six months, and it was time that her father stopped smothering her.

Ever since their mom died, her father could be a bit overbearing. She knew he meant well, but it was still annoying nonetheless.

"April, be safe and keep your phone on," Nick replied to her with a worried look. He knew he was overprotective when it came to his daughters, but as far as he was concerned, they were still his little girls. It didn't matter to him that Adrienne would be studying abroad and April would be graduating this year, and Alexandria would be a junior in high school next year. They were growing up too fast for him. Nicholas wasn't looking forward to the day when all of his daughters were grown up. He quickly pushed those thoughts out of his mind so that he could finish getting ready. As he walked downstairs, he was greeted by a smiling Alexandria holding his coat and scarf. "Let's go, let's go, Dad, class starts in twenty minutes." Alex, I doubt that we'd be late since it's only a few miles away." Nick said, smiling at his daughter's enthusiasm. "Hey, are you just dropping me off, or are you staying for the class? Wait, did you register too?" Alex asked as her thoughts went a mile a minute. Nick hadn't exactly thought about whether or not he was going to stay; he was just excited about seeing Zola again. "I'm not entirely sure, sweetheart. I suppose if there is room, I will pay for a slot." Nick replied. He talked to her about becoming friends with Zola's daughter, Sophie. "She's new in town, and it would be nice if you were friendly to her. Maybe you two could hang out or do whatever it is teenage girls your age do these days." Nick said. Alex thought for a moment, "I didn't realize Ms. Zola had any children. Well, if she is as cool as her mom, then we'll be fast friends."

Chapter 9

On their way to the class, they stopped by the bakery and picked up some pastries, and Nick got a cup of coffee for Zola. He wished now that he had paid closer attention to how much creamer and sugar she put in her coffee last night, but he was just glad to be with her. When they arrived at the store, people had already started walking in for the class. As he examined the crowd, he noticed the variety of women. There were younger women of Alex's age and much older. "Small towns," he thought to himself. He knew that most of the women who showed up today came out of pure curiosity, and then others were downright nosy. He was glad to see them anyway because Zola was very excited about this class. "I'm hoping to get a class going a few times a month," Zola said to him while in the bakery. He was immediately impressed when he walked into the store. She had an assortment of items in her store. She said she had a little bit of everything, and that was definitely true. Her store catered to any kind of artist. What caught his eye was the art. Zola did mention something about showcasing artists. "This artwork is amazing," he said to himself just as a young woman walked up. "Yes, I especially like this one," she said, pointing to the painting of the little girl holding a candle. "I think the owner painted this one. A lot of her artwork is in here, too." Nick raised an eyebrow. "Really?" He really wanted to see her work. He didn't know much about art, but he sensed that her artwork was an expression of who she truly was. "Excuse me, everyone," a light voice spoke up. "If you could make your way toward the back and find a station, we will get started shortly." Nick looked up and saw a young girl who looked to be about sixteen years old with dark hair and hazel eyes. She had fair skin, high cheekbones, and thick brows. She looked vaguely familiar, which meant she must be Zola's daughter. She was just as beautiful as her mother, Nick thought to himself. "Hey Alex, that's the young lady I was telling you about," he said. Alex looked up and squinted. "She looks a little familiar, but that's because I've probably seen her at school before." As they made their way in, he spotted Zola toward the back of the room. She looked so beautiful with her hair pulled back in a ponytail. She was so beautiful with her chestnut brown skin. Her apron was covering fitted jeans that hugged her hips, and she was wearing a red turtleneck. Blushing, he quickly shifted his gaze as she turned around and looked up. When he looked again, he spotted her walking in their direction. Alex's face immediately lit up. "Hi, Ms. Zola, I'm so excited about class today." Zola smiled at the teenager and said, "I'm glad you came, and you brought your dad with you." Alex's expression changed. "Well, he's not registered, but if you have room, he'd be glad to pay." Zola laughed, "It's alright, my dear. I think we could squeeze your dad in and give you the two for the price of one deal." Alex relaxed as her mind registered Zola's comment. "Hey, Alexandria, I would like you to meet my daughter, Sophie," Zola said, gesturing for Sophie to come over. Sophie strolled over with a look of uncertainty. Nick could tell she was only doing this for her mother. As Sophie approached, Alex immediately extended her arm. "Hi, my name is Alexandria, but everyone calls me Alex." Sophie smiled. "My name is Sophie. It's nice to meet you. My mom told me about you, and she thought we could work together, so I set up a station for you over here." Sophie said, pointing over her shoulder. "That's great, thanks," Alex said as the two girls walked off.

"Hi, beautiful. How are you doing?" Zola heard Nick say something, but she was a little too caught up in his beautiful green eyes to hear exactly what he said. "I'm sorry, what did you say?" Zola shook her head. Nick smiled. "I said, 'Hi, beautiful.'" A blush crept across Zola's face. She said, "Oh, hi." Nick knew he made her nervous, and he tried to hide his satisfaction. "It's good to see you again. I had a great time with you last night," Nick said. A smiling Zola said, "Me too. I had a very lovely time getting to know you." Nick handed her the coffee and pastries. "I wasn't entirely sure how you took your coffee, so I just brought you an assortment of creamers and lots of sugar packets," Nick said, smiling down at Zola. "She's such a pretty lady," he thought to himself. "Thank you very much," Zola replied. She looked in the bag and realized that it was the same pastry he had let her try last night. Her smile grew wider. "Thank you so much for this," she said, holding up the bag. "I've been thinking about this pastry all morning." Nick stumbled back and put his hand over his chest. "You thought about the pastry and not the chef? I'm hurt." Zola looked up at him and said, "Of course, I've even been thinking about the chef; I just didn't want to seem obvious." She went on to say, "Why don't we finish this conversation after class before we create an audience? Everyone is already seated. Why don't you sit here, and we can get started?" He nodded in compliance, and the class started.

Zola was so nervous she didn't know how she was going to conduct the class. She knew that she'd see him today, but she did not imagine that he'd be staying the entire time. She began the class by explaining the tools that they'd be working with, making sure not to look in his direction. She could feel him looking at her as she moved about the room, talking. When the class began to work on their own, she and Sophie walked around and assisted them. When she stopped at his station, she noticed that he'd always need her help. She had begun to think that he was coming up with excuses to get her over there so she could put her hands over his as his creation began to take shape. At some point, Zola looked back at Alexandria and Sophie, and they were getting along so very well. It was nice to see her daughter smiling and laughing. She was beginning to think that Sophie was too serious. She blamed herself because of all of the changes that took place in her young life, but she still wanted Sophie to enjoy life as a teenager. Since they'd moved, all she'd focused on was her artwork. While she loved her zeal for art, she still wanted her to enjoy being a teenager. She wanted her to make friends in Ridge Haven and do the type of things she did in Rose Creek. To see her now, Zola felt like a weight had begun to lift.

When the class was over, Sophie and Alexandria came walking up to Zola. "Hey Mom, can I go over to Alex's house tonight to watch a movie?" Sophie asked enthusiastically. Zola was taken aback at her daughter's question. Usually, it took her daughter time to warm up to a new friend. "You can go only if it is alright with her father," Zola replied, looking up at Nick as he joined them. "Daddy, can Sophie come over tonight and watch a movie?" Alex asked her father with the sweetest smile. He looked from the girls to Zola. Finally, Zola said, "I told them that it would be alright with me if it was alright with you." Nick thought about the idea for a moment and then answered yes. The girls squealed with delight. They walked off giggling and talking about the kinds of movies they'd like to see, leaving Zola and Nick alone again. By the time the girls walked out of the room, everyone else in the class had cleared out. Nick looked down at Zola, and she felt her face going hot. "I've got to do better with this." Zola thought to herself. "Well, I bet—

Nick's lips brushed against Zola's, catching her off guard, and then he deepened the kiss. She wrapped her arms around him, rubbing the back of his neck. "He's such a good kisser," she thought to herself. Before she could get lost in the kiss, he pulled away and whispered, "See you tonight." He walked out of the room, leaving her staggering. She felt like a teenager. She was definitely not used to this feeling, the feeling of being wanted. Insecurity immediately set in, making her wonder if Nicolas Gallo might be too good to be true. Zola began to think of all the things that could be wrong with Nick. "Maybe he is a womanizer or a control freak. Something has got to be wrong because no one is that great." If she were honest with herself, pieces of her past marriage and the rejection she felt from Jonathan were beginning to surface. She intentionally began thinking about something else. "Mom, you were right." Sophie walked up to her and hugged her. "I really like Alex, and I'm looking forward to being friends with her. I didn't think I would make friends here because everyone here is so different, but you were right. If I don't give people a chance, I'll never know what could happen." Sophie said. Zola returned her daughter's hug. She felt more at peace now that Sophie was becoming more acclimated to living in Ridge Haven. She and Sophie needed a change in pace and scenery. Initially, she questioned her decision to pack up her life and move to a new city, but now she realized it was best for them both. In Ridge Haven, Zola felt like her life was her own, not remnants of the life that Jonnie left behind. Although she created a new life after the divorce, she constantly felt like she was picking up the pieces. Living in Ridge Haven gave her different feelings, of wholeness and completion, and above all, accomplishment.

The rest of the day had gone by rather quickly as the store had been very busy. Zola had gotten calls from potential students requesting to join the next pottery class. Zola had scheduled another in a couple of weeks. As they travelled home, Alex called Sophie, and movie night somehow turned into a sleepover. When they got home, Sophie scurried to her room to pack a bag. Zola walked into her room. "You don't want dinner first?" Sophie looked up at her mom with an exasperated teenage sigh. "No, Mama, we're going to order out." Sophie's excitement made Zola smile. She was very happy for her daughter. Forty-five minutes later, they were ringing the Gallo doorbell. Zola knew Sophie was excited, but she was also excited to see Nick again. She had butterflies in her stomach as he opened the door; his beautiful green eyes landed on hers. He smiled and said, "Come on in, ladies." Just as they walked in, Alex came dashing down the stairs. "Hey Sophie, come on up; I'm getting everything ready for tonight." When she reached the top stair, she turned around and yelled, "Hi, Ms. Zola, I loved the class today." The girls had left Zola and Nick alone again. Standing in the foyer, she looked around at what seemed to be the living room straight ahead, and just to her right, she could see the dining room. The stairs were to her left, and next to the stairs was a closed door; she was not sure what it led to. "I'll be happy to give you a tour if you'd like," Nick mentioned, grabbing Zola's attention. "Sure, I like the layout of your home." Zola smiled. As they walked out of the foyer and into the living room, Zola noticed that each room had a specific color. Most homes have rooms that are the same color, but each room in Nick's house is a totally different color, which gives each room a different feel when you walk in. The living room was red, with a blue couch and red and blue pillows. The coffee table was glass with red trimming. All of the artwork had some hues of red and blue in it. The dining room was a teal green, and everything that accented the table was teal and gold, which matched perfectly. As Nick led her through the dining room, they walked through the pantry to get to the kitchen, which was black and gray. The island in the middle of the kitchen held the sink and the dishwasher with black marble countertops. All appliances were black, and the backsplash was some design of black and grey. She really liked Nick's house. "The girls and I changed everything in here a few years back," Nick finally said. He went on to say, "Everything in here reminded us of Karmen, and we needed a change. We, of course, weren't trying to erase her from our memories, but this house began to feel like a memorial to her." Zola gave Nick a concerned look. "Nick, you don't have to explain anything to me. I've never experienced losing a spouse, but a divorce feels like a death, and in order to completely move on, you have to make some changes in your life." She gave him a knowing smile, and Nick relaxed, glad that she understood. He finished giving her the tour. There were three bedrooms upstairs with two full bathrooms. Downstairs, just outside the living room, was the sunroom and grilling porch. That room with the closed door by the staircase was Nick's room. "So, what do you think?" Nick asked Zola. "I think your house is absolutely beautiful, Nick; the layout is rather unique." Nick replied, "Thanks. The girls and I worked really hard to make this a new home to go along with our new life." Nick gave Zola a questioning look. "So, Zola, what are your plans for the evening?" "Actually, I was just going to go home, cook dinner, and work on a project that I wanted to finish." "I don't want to take you away from your project, but I was wondering if you would like to join me for dinner? The girls can order pizza, but I wanted to cook a meal for you." Zola replied, "Sure, I'd love to stay for dinner. Maybe we could cook together." Nick thought about it after a moment. Any kind of time with Zola would be great, so cooking together would be lovely. "Cooking together sounds like a plan."

"Wow, this looks delicious," Zola said as she sat at the table across from Nick. She looked across the table at the food they had prepared together: tossed salad, shrimp Sicilian, and veal parmesan. Zola has a wonderful time cooking with Nick. She thought of the things shared with him, from her previous marriage and her relationship with her sister to the relationships she has with her friends. She felt so comfortable talking to him. "Eat up; you are going to love dessert," Nick retorted. Zola's eyes lit up. "Dessert? I love your desserts, Nick." Nicholas looked at the woman across from him and realized that a vaguely familiar emotion was welling up inside of him. Zola was a breath of fresh air for him. Since Karmen, Nick had dated a little, but none of them were memorable. The women he dated either wanted too much too fast, or they simply weren't his type. He had always been the type of guy to take things slowly in a developing relationship. Before he took things to any kind of level with a woman, he wanted to be certain that it was right. He needed to be extra careful because of his daughters. However, looking across the table at the woman whose smile was so beautiful that it lit up the entire room, he wasn't sure which way was up or down. He knew the right thing, the sensible thing, was to slow down and take his time, but his emotions were telling him differently. Nick had never met a woman like Zola before. She was beautiful, confident, and passionate, and her eyes held so much depth. He knew there was so much behind those pretty brown eyes of hers, and he wondered if she would allow him to see just what was there. They ate their dinner and laughed and talked. Zola has discovered that while Nick ran out to the store, he stopped by his bakery and picked up some chocolate truffles. She loved the time she was spending with Nick, which had begun to worry her. After five years of not dating, she didn't want to jump into the first potential relationship with a man. She had Sophie to think of, and she had her heart to think about as well, but with Nick, she wanted to jump headfirst.

When they finished dinner and dessert, Nick took her to his favorite place, which was his backyard patio. After a long day's work, he came home and spent hours there. This area was his sanctuary, and he surprised himself when he suggested that they go there. "This is nice," Zola mentioned, sitting next to Nick on the patio swing. For a few minutes, they sat in silence, and then Nick spoke up, "Zola, I've really enjoyed spending time with you. If you would allow me to, I would love to spend more time getting to know you." Zola looked up at Nick's tender expression and replied, "I'd love that. It has been a pleasure getting to know you as well, Nick." Then she cuddled up next to him and lay her head on his shoulder.

"So, you cooked dinner with this Nicolas? Why is this the first time I'm hearing about him?" Maranda spat out as she ladled soup into their bowls. Zola smiled. "Calm down, Maranda. I haven't said anything about him because, for one, it's all very new, and two, I didn't want to jinx anything. I didn't want to build him up to you all, and then he turned out to be not at all what I've expected." Zola retorted, taking the bowls from Maranda and setting them on the table. "Well, are you two dating now or like an item?" asked Maranda with an arched eyebrow. Frowning at her friend, "No, Randi, it's only just begun. We are merely getting to know each other. We have not talked about dating each other. Nick and I are just enjoying each other's company right now." That's really all they were doing, Zola thought as she poured the drinks. All she knew was that she enjoyed his company and he was the most compassionate man she'd ever known. "Maranda, girl, he is so attentive and charming. When he looks at me, it's a little unnerving because he looks as though he can see my soul." Zola retorted with a dreamy look in her eyes. Maranda studied her friend across the table for a while. For as long as she's known Zola, she's never seen her respond like this to any man. That's saying something about this Nick guy because Zola had been married to Jonathan for most of their friendship.

"Wow. Any man that can put that kind of look on my best friend's face is alright in my book." Maranda smiled as she began eating. "When do we get to meet him? I know! I'll have the two of you over for dinner. It'll be great." Maranda squealed. Zola dropped her spoon. "Absolutely not! Not right now, Randi. I'm not ready for him to meet anyone yet, and I'm sure he's not ready for that either. So why don't you just reel that excitement back in for now?" Pouting, Maranda said, "Fine, but you can't hide him forever, Zo." "So, what did you need my help with, Randi?" Zola asked, happy to change the subject. "Well, I was wondering if you could attend some Lamaze classes with me when they start. The dates are set, but Mike has some ministering dates out of town. He wanted to change them, but I wouldn't let him," Maranda responded. Maranda's husband was a pastor, and he frequently went away on speaking engagements. Zola loved Maranda and Mike, or "M and M," as she called them. They got her through the most difficult times in her life after she and Jonnie divorced. Zola recalled spending several evenings at their home with Sophie, sometimes staying overnight. She would watch how they interacted with each other and saw the love and affection they showed each other. That was how a marriage should have been, not what she had with Jonnie. What they had was cold and empty. Zola never really considered getting married again, but she did know that at some point in her life, she was going to date again. Based on her observations of Maranda and Mike, she knew what she was willing to tolerate and what she wasn't from a man. "Of course, I will do it, Randi. Think nothing of it. Besides, that's my niece or nephew I'm waiting to meet." Zola replied to Maranda's request. Maranda wanted to know the sex of the baby, but Mike insisted on being surprised. This life bubbling inside of her dear friend is a miracle. The doctors told Maranda that she would never be able to conceive a child and that they should consider adoption. Maranda and Mike never lost faith or hope. She admires both of them for their determination and courage to still believe in what seemed impossible since three doctors told them that they would never be able to conceive.

"Thanks, honey. We really appreciate it." Maranda beamed. Zola was truly happy to be there for her friend. There wasn't much she felt she could do to repay her for being there and walking her through the most difficult times in her life. "Hey, have you spoken with Veronica?" Maranda asked Zola. "I know Eric came home yesterday, but I've not heard anything from Ronnie. I actually tried to call her this morning when I was at the shop, but she is not picking up." Zola replied. "I tried to call her as well, but I got no answer, and Kha'ren said she hadn't heard from her either," Maranda said. After observing the twist of emotion on her friend's face, Zola said, "Let's not jump to conclusions and get too concerned right now. We know that Veronica loves Eric just as much as he loves her, and hopefully she has not pushed him away." Zola tried to console her friend, but honestly, she wasn't sure what had happened between Veronica and Eric. She knew her friend was very destructive when it came to relationships. She was just as worried as Maranda, but she was better at hiding it. Getting up from the table, Maranda said, "Let's go see for ourselves."

The women arrived at Veronica's office, Miller and Associates. Veronica Miller was the founder of her own accounting firm. She's been running it successfully at the helm for seven years, and her friends couldn't be prouder of her. They loved how savvy and resilient she was in the business world, but in her personal world, the girl could use some help. Good afternoon, ladies, "Ms. Miller is not taking any visitors today," Mrs. Wallace, Ronnie's executive assistant, motioned, stopping them from entering the office. Maranda smiled sweetly at Mrs. Wallace, removing her hand, and said, "We figured she wasn't taking any visitors today, but we're not visitors; we're family. Maranda walked past Mrs. Wallace with Zola in tow as Mrs. Wallace reached for her phone to inform Veronica that the two intruders were coming into her office. Veronica removed her glasses and looked up as her interrupting friends entered. "Why haven't you been answering your phone, Veronica?" Maranda asked. Veronica rolled her eyes and sighed, "I've been busy today, Randi, no big deal." "We know Eric came back into town last night, and you two were going to talk. We've all called you, but you haven't returned any of our calls. Zola chimed in. "Wow. "What great observations, Sherlock," Veronica said sarcastically. "Uh oh, you two broke up." Zola said, ignoring her friend's sarcasm. She knew that something was brewing and that Ronnie wasn't ready to deal with it yet. "As a matter of fact, he left me last night. He said he couldn't stay with a woman who always kept him at arm's length." Veronica replied. Putting her glasses back on and looking back at her screen she said, "I guess the joke is really on me. I thought he was going to propose, and I was going to say yes because I was finally ready to put it all on the line. I imagined that he had this wonderful speech prepared about how much he loved me and how he couldn't imagine his life without me, and I was going to tell him how much I loved him and that he was the only man I was ever able to be myself with and that I felt secure with him. However, the conversation went the total opposite." Veronica went on to say. With tears welling up in her eyes, Zola asked, "Did you tell him that you loved him and that you were willing to commit?" Veronica said, "Humph, no. I wasn't going to look like I was begging him after he said that he was leaving me." "Veronica, you would not have been begging the man; you would have been putting yourself out there for the man you love," Maranda begged. "Well, what's done is done, and it's over now. I'm not going to dwell on it. Don't worry, counselor, I'm going to deal with my emotions, but I'm not going to wallow. Veronica said, hugging her shoulders. "I'm not suggesting that you dwell on it, Maranda, but you can certainly drop this act. You know as well as we do that this affects you more than you put on." Maranda said, getting annoyed with her friend's nonchalant attitude. "Look, Maranda, we can all have perfect relationships like you and Mike, ok? All of this is pretty cute coming from a woman who has the perfect husband and, in a few months, will have the perfect family." Veronica replied. "That's not fair at all, Veronica. You know no relationship is perfect, but it takes work. However, you have to take ownership of your relationship not working out. You did keep that man at arm's length while he did nothing but love you. We warned you not to do that and admit your true feelings for him. He needed to know that." Maranda said, raising her voice. Veronica stood up, looking angrily at Maranda, "Well, aren't we just the experts these days? That's why I didn't answer anyone's calls because I didn't feel like hearing this garbage about it being my fault. Maranda, don't you know I own up to my part in my relationship breaking up? I won't have you come into my office telling me how I should handle myself. I am not one of your parishioners. You don't have to try and fix me. I'm not in denial about anything in my life. I suggest you take your— "Ok, ok," Zola said. "Emotions are high, and we should go before you two say things you don't mean." Veronica sat down. "That might be for the best." Maranda waddled out of Veronica's office, fighting to hold back her tears. Zola turned back before leaving. "I'm going to call you tonight, girl. Please pick up the phone."

When her friends left, Veronica threw her paperweight across the room. She looked at the time on her phone. "Good, I've got to get the out of here." "Mrs. Wallace, I'm not going to be in the office for the next couple of days; please forward all my accounts and calls to Marc and Benjamin," Veronica said to her assistant as she was walking out of her office. Marc Stowe and Benjamin Sloane were associates in her firm. She knew she could count on them to handle her business while she was out. Veronica arrived home and plopped down on her couch. For a long time, she sat in silence, replaying the conversation she and Eric had last night. She had been so happy to see him. After all these years, she was finally ready to give her whole heart to a man since Brian. She was all prepared to tell him until she realized that the engagement speech was actually a breakup speech. What was she supposed to do then? She couldn't look like a sad puppy as he was walking out the door. She had too much pride for that. Before she realized it, fat tears began to pour down her cheeks. She picked up the phone. "Can you please come over?"

Thirty minutes later, her doorbell rang. She opened the door, and on the other side stood Kha'ren with two pints of her favorite Strawberry Cheesecake ice cream. "I brought reinforcements," Kha'ren said with a weak smile. "Thanks, girl," Veronica said, gesturing for Kha'ren to come in. She told Kha'ren everything that happened, including the altercation between her and Miranda in her office earlier that day. "Dang, girl," Kha'ren said. "All you can muster up is dang Kha'ren?" Veronica asked her friend. "Ronnie, you already know I'm not about to sugarcoat anything for you. I love you, girl, but you have to deal with your issues before you are alone for the rest of your life." Kha'ren went on to say, "I know you don't want that, so stop letting your past and that pride of yours get in the way of anything healthy for you." Veronica dug into her ice cream and ate in silence. Finally, she said, "You know what? Miranda said the same thing to me today. Why do you think I could take this from you and not from her?" Kha'ren looked at her friend. "Because you are not used to Randi being raw with you. She told you what you needed to hear and not what you wanted to hear today. Plus, you are jealous." Veronica almost choked on her ice cream. "Jealous? Why would I be jealous of Maranda?" Kha'ren rolled her eyes at her friend. "Please don't go there with me, Ronnie. Randi has the life you want. She has a husband who is devoted to her, and they are about to have a baby to make their family complete. That's exactly what you want. You are so shell-shocked from your disastrous relationship with Brian that you anticipate the worst in every relationship, so you do something to break it up before you get hurt. However, at the core, you want someone who is devoted to you, and you want to be a mother." As she looked over, she saw tears meeting under her friend's cheek and hugged her. "I can tell you this because I want the same thing. We are a lot alike, Randi; that's why we bicker so much. I tell you like it is, and you do the same for me. Well, it's time for you to dig deep, my dear sister, and find out what is at the root of all this self-sabotage because I believe it goes far deeper than Brian. You cannot continue to go through life like this. You have to face your pain and get healing. Buried pain is still alive. Kha'ren said to her friend, hugging her tighter. By this time, Veronica was sobbing in K'ha'ren's arms.

The phone rang, startling both women. "That's Zo; she said she was going to call me tonight." Kha'ren reached over and looked at the caller ID. "It sure is. Do you want me to answer it?" Kha'ren asked. When Veronica nodded, Kha'ren pressed the button. "Hey Zo." "Oh, good, I'm so glad you are there. How is she?" Zola asked with worry in her voice. Kha'ren sighed, "Not too good, but she will be. I'm putting you on speaker." "Hey, Ronnie, sweetie. Are you alright, boo?" Veronica pitifully said, "Not really, Zo. Tell Maranda I'm sorry." Zola said, "No, you can tell her yourself; she is here too." "Randi, I'm sorry for my behavior today. I was out of line," Veronica said. Maranda said, "Veronica, on both sides, emotions were running high. Let's move past it. We're sisters, and not every moment is going to be pleasant with family. I love you, girl." "Ladies, listen. I am so grateful for all three of you. Thank you for being true friends and telling me the truth even when I don't want to hear it. There are a lot of issues that I need to work through, and it's time that I start to deal with them instead of burying them and using them as an excuse for my destructive behavior," Veronica said. The women talked for an hour more and then made plans to come together in Ridge Haven the following week because they hadn't seen Zola's new house since she remodeled it. That night, Veronica vowed to get rid of her negative way of thinking about herself and feeling sorry for herself for losing. She finally learned to be thankful for the things and people she already had in her life. For the first time, Veronica felt hopeful.

"Hey, baby, I'm almost home. Do you want me to stop and get dinner?" Zola asked her daughter. "No, Mama, I made spaghetti for dinner. I'm just draining the pasta now." Sophie replied. Zola could hear the smile in her daughter's voice. "Great, I'll be there soon; I can't wait to taste it," Zola said. Just as they hung up, Zola's phone rang. She didn't recognize the number, but thinking it might be business, she answered the phone. "Good evening, Ms. James," a familiar voice spoke over the car intercom. Zola knew immediately that the voice belonged to Nick. "I hope you don't mind that I called." Nick said in a hopeful tone. Smiling, Zola said, "Hi Nick. No, it's not a problem at all. I almost didn't answer from this unknown number." She didn't want to give away her excitement over his call. "I'm calling from the business line at the bakery. How was your day? Nick asked her, kicking himself for not planning out what he was going to say. Zola paused for a few seconds, thinking about the events of the day and how they were emotionally draining, but simply said, "Not too bad. How was yours?" Nick sighed, "My day was very busy, especially in the morning. I was lucky to be able to get a run in today. I was hoping to see you out there today." "Oh, you were hoping to see me?" Zola flirted. Nick blushed. "Well, yes, I was." He went on, "Since I didn't see you today, I took a chance and decided to call you." Zola responded, "Wow, I'm glad you did. Part of my day was emotionally draining, to be honest, and talking to you is a great way to get my mind off it." Nick said, "Well, let me try and lighten the mood altogether by asking you out on a date."

Zola said, "I'd love to go out with you, Nick." She thought to herself, "This really is a way to end the day." Nick and Zola spoke until she reached her house. Before they ended the conversation, they discussed meeting the next day at the park for a run.

When Zola entered the house, she immediately smelled the aroma of garlic bread. She walked to the kitchen and spotted her daughter looking all grown up, cooking dinner. She began thinking of the times she rushed home to cook dinner for Sophie after her divorce. She thought about how difficult it was to balance life as a newly single businesswoman and, more importantly, as a single mother. Zola had remembered how terrified she had been when the realization hit her that she would be doing everything alone. She thought of raising Sophie, paying bills, growing a new business, and all those other things that she and Jonathan did together. At that moment, observing her soon-to-be sixteen-year-old daughter, she realized that she managed to do it. Zola had learned so much about herself as a person during those days. She thought, "Hey, Mama, see, I cooked." Sophie beamed. Sophie wasn't big on cooking, and most days they would eat out because of their schedules. Smiling back, Zola replied, "I see, honey. I can't wait to eat." After Zola had gone to her room, put her bags down, and washed up for dinner, she came back to the kitchen to see if she could assist in anything, but her daughter had done everything. She had already set the table, put the food on the table, fixed the drinks, and was sitting and waiting for her mom to join her. As they began to eat, she asked Sophie what brought on her change of heart to cook. Sophie explained to her mom that Alex had inspired her.

"Alex and I talked a whole lot that night of the sleepover. She talked about how much she does for her dad and the time they spend together. We both shared our stories, but for some reason, she inspired me," Sophie told her mother. "That's great, Sophie. See, I told you meeting new people would be a great idea. Alex is a sweet young lady, and I think she is a great influence." Zola said to her daughter. "Mom, I want to tell you how much I appreciate you and everything that you have done for me and everything that you do now. I know things were really hard for you when I was younger, after you and Daddy divorced. You always made sure I was alright, and you were always strong and brave for me, even when I knew you were hurting. Even now, you push me to be a better artist, and you take time with me to teach me art techniques when you have your own projects to finish." Sophie said with a watery smile. Zola had been so proud of the young woman that her daughter was becoming. She realized then that these are the days and conversations you don't get to see when you are going through so much turmoil in life. That's why it's worth it just to fight through all of the circumstances in life, for moments just like these. The two talked and ate, and even cleaned the dishes together. Shortly after Sophie had received a call from one of her friends from Rose Creek, and went to her room. Zola, sitting on the edge of her bed, lay back and allowed the events of the day to wash over her. The one thing that always lifted her spirits and calmed her was painting. She still had three pieces she wanted to complete for her exhibition, so she went out to her studio.

Glass of wine in hand, Zola examined the latest project she had been working on for a month. As she painted, she began to think about the conversation she had with Sophie over dinner, and she was inspired. Her next painting will represent her relationship with Sophie. She began thinking about the project, and before she knew it, she was grabbing her sketchpad. When Zola looked up at the clock, it was one-thirty in the morning. The hours always rolled by when she painted like this. She would put her phone on vibrate and shut out the world and focus on nothing but her art. She looked down at her phone and had a missed call from Miranda and a text from Nick. She would return Maranda's call tomorrow, but she would open Nick's text now. It read, "Zola, I can't stop thinking about you." Zola smiled. She texted him back, "Hi Nick, I know it's late, but I just got your text. I've been working in the studio all night. I've been thinking about you, too. I'll call you later in the morning."

Nick's alarm went off at seven o'clock. He felt like hitting the snooze button and rolling over, but he knew Alex would be in to wake him. So, he sat up on the bed and looked around his room. On mornings like this, he missed Karmen. She would jump right up when the alarm went off, and he would wrap his arms around her, beckoning her to stay and lie next to him just a few minutes longer. She would try to get up again, and he would just hold her tighter, nuzzling the back of her neck. She would say, "Babe, the girls have to get up for school." He would respond by saying, "Just a few more minutes, Kay." She would give in because she loved when he called her Kay and said, "You drive a hard bargain, Nicky. I tell you what. Let me get the girls up and going, and I'll meet you back here in ten minutes." She did just that, and when she would come back, he'd be there waiting on her with open arms. They would spend the next hour or so cuddling and talking. As Nick thought about it, he realized he really missed those mornings. He missed being able to hold the one he loved on days like this. Just as he was putting his phone down, he saw a text message. The message was from Zola, who told him that she would call him this morning. Nick smiled as he thought of Zola. Since his wife died, he hadn't thought about a woman this much. Nick liked everything about Zola: her smile, those beautiful brown eyes, her soft skin, and the curve of her hips. Most of all, he liked how he felt when he was with her. She made him feel alive. He was becoming increasingly desperate to escape the monotony of his life. His daughters were getting older now, and he wanted to experience something different in his life. Nick knew that after his wife died, the thing his children needed the most was consistency and stability, so he gave it to them. Now he needed a change, something fresh and new. As he thought of Zola, he thought that she might be the biggest change he was craving after all.

Showered and shaved after his jog with Alex, Nick made himself some tea and sat on his back patio. He was enjoying the peaceful fall morning when his phone began to ring and Zola's name popped up on his screen. "Good morning, beautiful." Nick said, smiling. Blushing, Zola replied, "Hello." "I got your text this morning. Did you get enough rest? It looks like you were up pretty late," Nick said. "Well, not a whole lot, but I'm not going in today. There are some things that I need to take care of around here today. I will, however, stop by for some pastries and coffee, and I was hoping to see a certain baker this morning." Zola replied. With a smile in his voice, Nick said, "That can definitely be arranged. What time will you be dropping by?" "Around 9:30," Zola answered while attempting to put her robe on. They hung up, and Zola knocked on Sophie's door so that she could wake up and get ready for school. When she didn't get an answer, she opened the door to discover that Sophie was not in her room. Zola headed out to their art studio and found her daughter putting some finishing touches on her latest piece. "Good morning, sweetheart. How long have you been up?" Sophie looked back at her mother. "Good morning, Mama. I've been up for about an hour so far. I see you were working last night." Sophie gestured towards the three pieces of artwork that had been sitting on the easels and floor. "Yes, I had so many ideas flowing through my head last night, and I also wanted to get these done before I have to meet with Mr. Cromley about the exhibit next week. I wanted to make sure that I had new pieces to show him." Zola replied. Mr. Cromley was the curator for the

Crimson Art Museum. Zola had been working with him to get the exhibit set up just the way she wanted it. She had enough artwork to show, but she wanted to showcase these particular pieces. "They are beautiful and unique. These paintings are very different, but I love them," Sophie said. Zola hugged her daughter, thanked her, and ushered her off to the house to get ready for school.

After she dropped Sophie off, she stopped by her shop to gather some paperwork and to inform her manager, Kristie, that she would be working from home. Just as she was climbing into her car, her phone rang. As she answered, Nick said, "Hey, beautiful, would you like to have breakfast with me this morning? I mean, I know that you have a full plate today, but I thought I would ask anyway. Zola considered her morning, and normally, she didn't deviate from her plans for the day. Over the years, she rarely allowed anything to get in the way of the plans she set for the day. Among the many things she's had to learn since her divorce was time management and discipline; however, today she was going to make an exception. "Sure, I'd love to," Zola replied with a smile. "Ok, good. Can you meet me at this address around 10:30?" Nick asked her. Zola scribbled down the number. She did not recognize the address but looked forward to enjoying her time with Nick today.

Upon entering her farmhouse, Zola's phone rang. "Hello?" Zola answered, holding the receiver to her left ear. "Good morning, daughter, who never comes to visit her mom since she's moved away. " Zola's mother, Lila, said. "Hey, Mama. Now you know it's not like that." Zola replied with an exasperated sigh. "Oh yeah, then how is it?" Lila responded. "Mama, you know how hectic things have been lately. You know what's been on my plate these days," Zola said. "Alright, neglect your mother," her mom said, laying it on thick. Zola rolled her eyes in her head because her mother often did this when she was missing her children. She also knew that it meant that something was up with her mom. "Are you alright, Ma?" Zola asked in a concerned tone. "As a matter of fact, I am fine, sweetheart, but I would like for you to set aside some time and come to the house because I need to talk to you," Lila responded. "Ok, I'm off today, so I can come later this evening," said Zola. "No, don't come for dinner; I don't want to talk when your dad is around," her mom said. Zola's eyebrows lifted. "Since when don't you want to talk around Daddy?" Her mom sighed, "Since I want to have a conversation with you without him around." Zola didn't press her mom any further. It was obviously important to her. "Well then, let's meet for an early dinner, say around 4 pm," Zola said to her mom. "That will work. Call me later with the details." Lila answered. They hung up, and Zola sat on the edge of her bed, wondering what was up with her mother. She decided that before she began to worry, she would just meet her mom. As she looked at the time, she realized that she should start getting dressed so she could meet Nick.

The address in question was exactly forty-five minutes away from Zola's house. As she pulled into the long side road, a yellow and white country cottage came into view. She eventually saw a sign that said, *"Adri's B&B,"* in front of the house. Zola pulled into one of the parking spots and got out. As she began walking towards the house, Nick's familiar face began to appear in the doorframe of the porch. Zola carefully watched him walk down the steps. She thought he was so attractive in his jeans and black button-up shirt with the sleeves pulled up to his elbow. "Hey gorgeous," Nick said as he approached her. Blushing, Zola embraced him. "Hi there. You're not looking too shabby yourself."

Nick second-guessed his decision to invite Zola to breakfast this morning. By meeting her at the B&B, Zola would be meeting his older sister today. He hoped he wasn't jumping the gun by having her meet another member of his family so soon. She hadn't even met his other daughters yet. Then he thought about his wardrobe. He was going for casual. When he walked downstairs this morning, Alex had approved. Hopefully, Zola will feel the same. As he watched her approach him, he examined her fully. There's always a peace about this woman that mesmerizes him. It made him desire to be around her all the time, or make excuses to keep her with him when it's time to part. Oddly though, he couldn't help but feel internally conflicted. He still felt as though he'd been cheating on Karmen. When Zola got closer, he tucked that latter thought away and drew her in for a hug. She smelled spectacular. Her intoxicating scent of lilac made him hug her tighter. They stood hugging for close to a minute with no words. Finally, she spoke, "How are you this morning?" Loosening his embrace, he stood back with a lopsided smile, "I am great. I am glad that you are here." She made him feel like a teenager. Zola simply smiled at him. "Welcome to Adri's," Nick said, gesturing for her to walk towards the house. "Nick, this place is beautiful," Zola mentioned, admiring her surroundings. As they walked towards the porch, she took in the beautiful scenery before her. Just off to the left of the house was a garden of vegetables. As the wind blew, she smelled rosemary lingering in the air. Looking straight ahead, behind the house was a lake. It was a crisp morning, but the water lapping at the shore looked rather inviting.

They were greeted at the door by a woman with jet-black hair and emerald eyes just like Nick's. Zola guessed the woman had some relation to Nick. "Zola, this is my sister Adrianna," Nick said. She wasn't sure, but she thought she heard a hint of uncertainty in Nick's voice. With a warm smile, the woman offered a hand to Zola. Zola shook it, and the woman said, "Hi, Zola. How are you?" Smiling, Zola replied, "I'm well. Thank you. Adrianna, this is a beautiful place you have here. It's like a little piece of heaven." With pure excitement on her face, Adrianna exclaimed, "That's the exact feel I was going for." "My sister has just opened her B&B, and we're among the first to try out her breakfast," Nick said to Zola. Zola nodded. She had no idea that she'd be meeting Nick's sister or any other member of his family any time soon. Sensing the apprehension on Zola's face, Adrianna spoke up. "I called my brother up this morning and I asked him to come up for breakfast, and I suggested that he bring you along. He mentioned that you two had been spending some time together." Adrianna didn't want this woman, who had begun to awaken something in her brother, to be scared off. She knew that their family, well, mostly her, could be a little pushy, and she didn't want Zola blaming her brother. Zola gave her a genuine smile and said, "Oh, no worries, Adrianna. I'm glad Nick invited me here." Nick's anxiety eased just a bit. "Well, come on in; let's get you guys seated," Adrianna said to the couple. She led them to the dining area through the parlor and down a hall. Zola loved the feel of this place. It was so quaint and intimate. Although she was a little thrown by Nick bringing her to his sister's B&B, she could understand the sentiment behind it. This place is so very private and romantic.

Looking up from her menu, Zola said, "So this is your sister's place." Nick sheepishly looked up at her and replied, "I apologize, Zola, for making this awkward for you. I know that we're not even close to meeting family members. You haven't even met my other daughters yet. Adrianna called me up this morning about visiting for breakfast today, and I immediately thought that this was a great place to take you. She was trying to cover for me before." With a curiosity in her glare, Zola asked, "Why is that?" "Well, judging from your home and our conversations, I thought you would appreciate this place. I figured you'd really like it." He added, "This place is virtually secluded, and being here with you gives us uninterrupted time." Zola's heart instantly melted. She reached across the table and lifted his chin with her index finger and replied, "Nick, this is not awkward for me. I was a bit surprised, but I'm glad you invited me here. I'm honored that you would want me to meet your sister." He took her hand in his and kissed it. "So, tell me more about your sister," Zola said. "Well, my sister, Adrianna, is older than me. She switched gears in her career about two years ago. For ten years, she was executive chef of *Token* restaurant," Nick explained. Zola's eyes widened. "I love *Token*. It is my favorite restaurant. I would travel a full hour from Rose Creek just to have her filet mignon. Wow, I didn't know your sister was the chef there." "My sister loved her job, but she and her husband rarely saw each other, and so she had to make a choice. She'd either have to slow down or lose her marriage. She chose the former. Long story short, she and Marco, her husband, both retired, bought this property, and they've spent the past two years turning it into a bed and breakfast." Nick told Zola.

"That's pretty cool. I admire your sister for making necessary changes in her life to make life better for her and her husband," Zola said. "She reminds me a lot of you," Nick said in a matter-of-fact tone. He told Zola that her strength, tenacity, and determination were very attractive to him. He went on to tell her that the more he knew about her, the more courageous he realized she was, and that if she would allow him to, he would love to stick around and know more about her. Zola looked across the table, speechless at Nick, and suddenly became very fearful of the emotion that was threatening to overtake her in that moment. She refused to admit that she might have been falling for this man, whom she didn't know very well. For years, Zola had closed her heart and mind off to the idea of romance and relationships because she didn't have the time for it with raising a child and building a life for both of them. Out of the blue, here comes this super sweet man who seemed to get her in ways she didn't think anyone ever would. He genuinely appreciated the qualities about her that turned many men off. However, as great as the connection was between them, she didn't want to get ahead of herself, so she wasn't bearing her feelings anytime soon. Zola had decided that she was just going to enjoy this man and the time spent with him. She was no longer that naïve young girl she was when she met Jonnie. She knew better than to create outcomes in her head that would ultimately lead to heartbreak. She would take this one day at a time and pace herself.

They talked about their daughters throughout breakfast. Nick leaned in with a serious look and announced, "I'm going to talk to my girls about us." Zola scrunched her face and said, "Wait, there's an us?" Looking utterly embarrassed, Nick said, "Well, I thought we were headed in that direction at least." Zola laughed aloud and said, "Nick, I'm teasing you. I was going to do the same with Sophie." Nick lowered his brows at her, stood up, grabbed her by the hand to stand her up, and kissed her with enough passion to make her knees weak. He broke the kiss off and whispered against her lips, "Now that's what you get for teasing me." Zola's thoughts were all scrambled up. When he was this close, she couldn't think straight. To gain control, she pulled away and laughed nervously, "Yeah, I guess that's what I get." Nick closed the space between them again. "Let's go for a walk. I want to show you something I think you'd like." He grabbed her by the hand and led her out of the back door. Zola was glad for the fresh air; Nick could be very intense. She looked out over the glassy lake and the white and blue boats out at the dock.

He led her down a rocky path and came to a threshold with wildflowers growing around it, with the word *"Sanctuary"* written across the top. "The ironwork is beautiful," Zola said. Nick smiled and guided her into a mini garden. She realized immediately why this place was a sanctuary. Purple, white, and pink asters took up one corner. She looked closer and saw yellow Biden and Echinacea in another corner of the small solarium-type area. In the center was a hot spring. "We came across this when we first started renovating the house. Marco and I were following this path, and then we came to this little oasis," said Nick. "This place is a dream," Zola said in awe. As she looked around the area in wonder, Nick watched her. He watched her reaction to this place. In that moment, she looked up at him and smiled; his heart stopped. Finally, he admitted the thing that he had refused to since they first spent time cooking at his house. The thing he simply couldn't admit was that he hadn't known this woman for very long. Heaven help him, but Nick had gone and fallen in love with this woman who stood before him, giving him the most beautiful smile he'd ever laid eyes upon. This realization hit him like a ton of bricks, and suddenly, in that moment, he couldn't get close enough to her. As if in a trance, Nick pulled Zola against his chest, and he crushed her mouth with a kiss that made her so weak, she clung to his shoulders as if she'd fall if she let go. That was fine by him because, as far as he was concerned, he wasn't letting her go anytime soon, maybe never.

On her way back home, Zola thought deeply about her time with Nick. She didn't know what to expect when he invited her, but she wasn't prepared for any of what happened this morning. She wasn't prepared to meet any member of his family. She wasn't expecting him to kiss her the way that he had. Well, she hoped. Most of all, she was not prepared to realize that she had begun to develop feelings for Nicolas Gallo. She was in uncharted waters here. She needed reinforcements. It was settled this weekend; there would be a meeting. Immediately, she thought of Veronica and thought perhaps the meeting wasn't such a great idea. She'll talk to Maranda and get her take.

Zola pulled into the parking lot of her mom's favorite bistro, Dehlia's. She always liked the ambiance in this place. From the linen tablecloths to the tea-light candles on each table, Zola could understand why her mom loved it here. As she looked around, she spotted her mother sitting at a table by the window. Her mom stared out of the window with a distant look in her eyes. Startled by her daughter's sudden appearance, Lila put her hand against her chest. "You scared me, sweetheart." Zola looked down at her mom and said, "I can see that. Are you alright, Mom?" Waving to dismiss her daughter's worry, "I'm fine, child; I was over here thinking, is all." Zola sat down across from her mother and studied her before talking further. From the moment she walked in and spotted her mother, she noticed that something was going on. Lila James has always had a tranquil presence. When people came around her, she had a way of immediately disarming and defusing any stress they had. So, to see her mom looking unsettled, Zola was just a bit worried. "Ma, can you tell me why we are having this clandestine meeting? Why can't we talk when Daddy is around anyway? Zola casually asked her mom. She tried her very best to look calm, but on the inside, she felt anything but. She wasn't used to seeing her mother looking this way, but she feared that if she panicked, her mother would change her mind about telling her.

Lila eyed her youngest daughter and felt confident that Zola would understand all that she was going through. She had made sure to keep open communication with both of her daughters and made sure to never pass judgment on them. She prided herself on being an understanding mom, and this is what made her daughters confide in her. Now the tables were turned. She wanted to talk to Zola and knew that she would listen and not judge, but more importantly, she knew that Zola would take her seriously. As she picked up her cup of tea to sip, she thought of how she could explain to her daughter about the plans she'd been making. Clearing her throat, Lila said, "Zola, I've decided to go back to school to finish my accounting degree." Zola looked at her mother with her manicured nails lightly tapping the table and giving her the most pensive stare. "Mama, really? You want to go back to school? That's all you wanted to tell me? I was silently panicking because I thought you were sick." Lila gave Zola an exasperated sigh. "Zola, nothing is wrong with me. I've been thinking that I want to go back to school." Zola's mother went on to explain to her that she'd been working on the books for a couple of her friends for years and that she'd really missed working with numbers.

Lila James gave up her goal of becoming an accountant when she met and married Zola's father. He was very traditional and didn't believe in his wife working. He thought her primary goal should be taking care of the house, raising his children, and nurturing the home environment just like his mother did. It was his responsibility to do the rest. Lila didn't have that kind of background. Lila didn't know her dad really. When she was six years old, her father left them and married another woman and had a whole other family two towns over. Her mother worked and fought tooth and nail to keep food on the table for her and her three younger brothers. Zola's grandmother was seemingly a very proud and strong woman. Everyone in the community knew that her husband had left her, but she would never take handouts. When someone would offer, she would politely turn them down. Lila once told Zola that she heard her mother crying in her room on countless occasions. Lila wished that her mom would show her vulnerability to someone, but she wouldn't.

When she was 21, Lila's mother became ill with cancer and refused to get treated. She continuously asked her mom to get treatment, but she refused. "Lilly, I don't have any money to give to those doctors. Besides, I have worked too hard to leave a pile of bills on you kids." she told her. Lila grew angry at her mom for giving up on her life. She had seen her mom fight for years to make ends meet, without accepting handout or anything. She fought for years for her children but would not fight now for herself. Lila couldn't understand her mother.

The last days of her mother's life were life-changing for Lila. She learned so much about her mother. Lila confessed that she had heard her mother crying at night and asked her why she never expressed how she felt to anyone else. Her mom looked at her and said, "Honey, if I had cried to anyone else, I probably would have never stopped crying, Lila." She went on to tell her, "I didn't have time to cry in those days. I had three young kids to raise all by myself in the 50s. I wasn't going to accept anyone's help because I didn't want pity, and I didn't want anyone to think that I was weak and needy. I know it might have been proper to have a husband, but I did, and he left. I wasn't going out to look for another one." Lila was grateful that her mom had finally opened up to her. She asked once about her father and why he left, and her mom didn't have much to say. "He stopped being happy, I suppose. At first, I thought he didn't want children, but then I found out that he had remarried and had other children." Lila asked her mom if she saw him again after that, and her mom said, "Yes, twice. Remember when your brother Billy had begged to go to that fair over in Burnside? Well, I saw your father there. He saw the four of us before I saw him. When I looked up, there he was staring." "Why didn't you say anything to him?" Lila asked. "He had this pleading look in his eyes, begging me not to say anything because, as I looked closer, I realized that his wife and his other children were there.

So, I ushered you children in the other direction." Lila's eyes immediately began to well up with tears. "So, he just let us walk away like that?" Her mom shook her head. "Wait, what about the other time? You said you saw him twice." This time, Lila's mother's eyes filled with tears. "The second time I saw him was on the day you graduated from high school." Lila sat quietly, so her mom continued. "This time the look on his face said something different than the last time. It was a mixture of regret, hurt, and pride. The first two belonged to him, but he didn't deserve the right to be proud of you because he left you a long time ago. Lila, when I saw him, I was filled with rage."

Lila sat back and stared at her mother. There were so many emotions she was feeling and thoughts floating around in her head. She wondered why her mom waited all this time to tell her these things. She wondered why her dad never came around except for those two times and why he never tried to contact them. "I was so angry. He had no right to feel pride as if he had a hand in raising you, Lila. You worked too hard and became valedictorian all on your own in school." Lila's dad told her mom that he had read in the newspaper that she was the valedictorian, and he wanted to see her. She told him that he could stay, but she dared him to come near any of her children. "They are my kids too," he said. "You want to bet? You stopped being their father when you left them and created another family outside of us." Lila's mom said angrily. As tears fell down her cheeks, she went on to say, "You threw my children away as if they were old shoes. You missed everything—all the important things. You missed them all because you chose to." In that moment, she grew stoic. "Now I could deal with you leaving and never coming back, but what broke my heart was that day at the fair, you saw your babies, and you pleaded with me not to say anything. That let me know right there you didn't care." Lila's father put his hands up. "I didn't stop loving them. I have always kept watch. I never walked away exactly. After a while, I was ashamed of what I had done. When I heard she was valedictorian, I just had to see her." Lila's mother did not soften. "I can't make you leave, but I forbid you to say anything to her today. This is her day, you hear? You won't ruin my baby girl's day because of your guilt," Lila's mother told her that her dad promised not to ruin their daughter's day. She said that was the last conversation they had. That was the first time Lila's mother cried in front of her, and she held her mother's fragile, ailing body. She never saw her mom the same after those days. Lila really believed that her mom forgave her dad.

When Zola's parents met, her mother practically gave up her dreams of becoming an accountant. Her baby brother, Jake, particularly had some things to say about it. "Lilly, how are you just going to give up everything for a man? You've worked too hard." On the day she was set to wed Richard James, her baby brother was trying to convince her not to. Lila promised her brother that she wanted this life, and it was her choice. Jake insisted that she was settling. She asked him to drop the subject and assured him that he didn't want to make her sad on the happiest day of her life. So, he did, and she never had that conversation with him again. The truth was, Lila James was afraid. She saw her mother struggle for years to make ends meet, and she was afraid that she would fail if she tried to go after her dreams. This wonderful gentleman was offering the world, and all she had to do was give up her dreams. Lila chose to be a stay-at-home mom and raise her children. Zola doesn't believe her mom regrets the choice she made, but she knows that she wishes she had decided to stand up for herself and have both. Lila James didn't want to end up struggling like her mom, and Richard attracted her because he was everything that her father was not. Now that her children are adults and have their own lives, there is no one to look after. Lila wanted to do something that she loved. For years, she's helped her friends out with taxes or looked over their books. The only thing left to do now is tell her husband.

Chapter 10

Zola thought about the events of the day as she kicked off her shoes and walked into the kitchen to grab the peanut butter. She thought about the conversation with her mother and how surprised she was at Lila's decision to go back to school. Zola realized that she was proud of her mother as a well of emotion began to overtake her. As long as she could remember, her mother was strait-laced, prim, and proper. Lila James rarely did anything out of the ordinary. In fact, she was rather predictable. She didn't believe her mom to be boring, but she did think she was certainly a creature of habit. The change in her mom was refreshing, and Zola felt as though there was another depth there that she never knew existed. "I think your mom is making a great move," Maranda mentioned. After her lunch with her mom, Zola visited Maranda, who was put on bed rest until she gave birth. "Zee, embrace your mother and her decision that she's making for her life. There is a reason why she came to you and not your brother, sister, or even a friend. She told you because I believe there will be a time when she is going to need you." Zola said, "You're right. I will be there in whatever capacity she needs me.

As she relaxed on the couch, recalling their chat at lunch, she began to dial her mother's number. "Hey, Ma. When are you going to talk to Daddy?" She listened to her mother explain that she'd talk to him after he came back from the Washington Bridge project. As they were talking, she received a text message from Sophie: *"Hey, Mom. With Alex, she invited me to her grandparents' house for dinner. I hope you don't mind. Don't worry, Mr. Nick or April will drop me off. Please don't be mad that I didn't ask first."* Zola sent her daughter a message back, *"Hi sweetie. Yes, you should have asked first, but we'll talk about that when you get home. Enjoy yourself. Be home by 8:30,"*

Sophie texted her back, promising her that she'd be home on time. Zola spent the rest of the evening completing paperwork for the stores and reflecting. She thought about Nick and the possibilities; she thought of her mom and dad and the transition that's about to take place in their lives. Most of all, she thought about how the pieces of her life began falling into place. For the first time in five years, she didn't feel as though she was holding her breath. Zola closed her eyes and silently thanked God for her life when her cell phone rang.

"Hey, Ronnie. How are you, sweetheart?" Zola said. "Hey sis. I'm good, and I'm back at work now and moving forward." Veronica replied. "Are you sure you're ok? I don't want you to fall back into the pattern of running away and avoidance," Zola asked. "Don't worry, Zee. These past few weeks have truly been the most emotional of my life. I've had to face the hard truths about my life, my self-image, my family, and my ideas." Zola listened intently as her friend began to explain her experience. "Hey, are you busy? If you're not, then I'm headed over because I don't want to talk over the phone." Veronica asked Zola. "No, come on over. I'm here. I'll order in," Zola answered. When she hung up with Veronica, Zola ordered from the Red Leaf Bistro. She ate there once and enjoyed their rainbow trout. Forty-five minutes later, Veronica was at Zola's door with wine in hand. With a tight hug, Zola invited her in." "Zee, this is a beautiful home," Veronica said, taking in the open floor plan of the kitchen and living room. She admired the exposed brick in the kitchen. "It has an old feel to it, but I love how you have updated the kitchen with stainless steel appliances. This house is all you, girl." Veronica remarked as Zola tugged on her to follow her down the hall to give her the rest of the tour. By the time they came back in from the outside studio, Veronica was ecstatic for her friend. With tears in her eyes, she said, "Zee, I'm so proud of you. I've watched you transform your life these past years. You rose out of a situation that was designed to defeat you. In the midst of everything, you discovered who you truly are. You are an inspiration." By the time Veronica finished, she was crying. Zola teared up at her friend's accolades and hugged her. Smiling, she said, "Girl, let's eat; enough of that mushy stuff."

The women sat to eat their dinner. Zola said, "Ok, now tell me what's going on, Veronica. Sounds like you've been doing some soul searching yourself." Looking up from across the table, Veronica said, "Yes, I have. After Eric walked away and the intervention with you guys, I had to really face myself. Zee, it was time that I was honest with myself and the decisions that I've been making. I went to my mom and dad about my birth parents. I guess I've always known that it all started with them. I want to know about them. In all these years, I've never asked about them, and Mom and Dad have never offered any information." "Wow. How did your parents respond when you asked?" Zola asked. "My mom said that she knew the question would come sooner or later. Dad didn't say much. He just said they would give me all the information that they had. They didn't have a whole lot, but I was able to find out that my adoption records were not sealed." Veronica said, pushing her food around on her plate. Veronica told of how her mother was in her teens when she gave her away. She discovered her last known address and explained that she was hesitant to reach out to her birth mother. There wasn't much information about her dad, except for his name.

"Well, what is your next step, Ronnie?" Zola asked, covering her hand. Veronica shrugged because she wasn't sure what she wanted to do. "Zee, what if she is a bad person? What if, when we meet, I find out that she has lived her life and never really wondered about me? Veronica kept throwing out "what ifs" until

Zola interrupted. "Don't do that to yourself. You are creating these worst-case scenarios in your head, and this is not the way to approach it. Keep an open mind and don't build any expectations, positive or otherwise. Your main goal is to discover your roots, and if you develop new relationships along the way, that will be wonderful. Veronica knew that Zola was right, and she also knew that contacting her birth mother was the start of the journey of understanding herself.

A little while after Veronica left, Sophie came walking into the house with Nick and Alex in tow. Zola looked up from the kitchen counter and smiled. Sophie hugged her mom and dragged Alex down the hall to her room. She was left alone with Nick. "How are you, gorgeous?" Nick said as he crossed the room to pull her into his arms. He gave her a tight hug and tipped her chin to look into her eyes. He kissed her, and her mind went blank. Zola couldn't think of anything else except for the wonderful man she had cared so much about. Nick broke the kiss and said, "Let's be careful; the girls don't know yet." Nodding in agreement, Zola wondered when they'd talk to their girls about their budding relationship. "Nick, how are we going to do this?" Gesturing her hands between them, Zola asked. Leading her to the couch, Nick said, "Well, we'll start by talking to the girls." Zola agreed. Taking her hand in his, Nick mentioned with a sly smile, "Besides, I want to take you out on a date. I want them to know that we're dating." She looked at him suddenly. "Wait, we're dating?" He blushed and shook his head yes. "Zola James, it would be an honor if you agreed to a dating relationship with me." She smiled at him and snuggled closer to him. "I'd love that." For the next twenty minutes, they learned more about each other. Zola looked at her watch. "It's getting late. I have to go to Crimson Art in the morning for another meeting with the curator." Nick, attempting to disguise the disappointment in his voice, said, "Sure, ok. Dinner tomorrow night? There is a restaurant that I'm sure you'll love." Zola smiled. "Yes, dinner tomorrow night is perfect." Nick really didn't want to leave, but he knew Zola had a lot going on. He would love to have more uninterrupted time with her, just like at the B&B.

Just as they were standing up, their daughters came bouncing into the room. "You ready, kid?" Nick asked his daughter, Alex. "Yes, I'm ready. Alex answered, pulling on her jacket. "Hey Dad, when I go to visit Adrienne at school, can I bring Sophie?" Alex asked. Nick looked at Zola's blank expression. "Maybe some other time, Alex. You guys just met. "Dad, that doesn't mean anything. Sophie met April and Adrienne through FaceTime." She mentioned it to her dad. With a shocked expression, Nick asked, "Really?" Alex went on to explain to her father that the girls had all be talking to each other, and Adrienne had no problem with Sophie coming up to school to visit with April and Alex. Still unsure about it, given the situation with him and Zola, Nick told his daughter he didn't think it would be a good idea just yet. Zola finally spoke up, "Besides, Alex, there will be plenty of time for you all to get together during Christmas break, right? "I guess so, Ms. James," Alex said with a long sigh. As the girls walked out of the house, Nick pulled Zola in for a tight hug. "I guess it's time to talk to the girls." Zola nodded her head in agreement against his chest but said nothing. When the house was quiet again, Zola's mind began to race. Was she ready to talk to Sophie about a man she's dating? Was Sophie ready for this change in her life? As she drifted off to sleep that night, Zola's thoughts were filled with Nick and their decision to put a label on their connection and tell their daughters. Zola certainly hoped that it would all go well.

4523 Trent St. NE was the address she'd plugged into her GPS two hours ago. Veronica sat in front of a Tudor-style house and observed a very neat and tidy yard with a swing. The house was brick with brown trimming, a heavy chimney, and a steeply pitched roof. So many scenarios ran through her mind as she traveled to her birth mother's house. Now that she was sitting out in front of it, Veronica began to doubt that coming was a good idea. That thought was shooed away by her internal pep talk that she'd given herself lately. "You came here for answers. You need to know who you truly are so that you can know where you're going. Don't chicken out now." After checking herself in the mirror, Veronica got out of the car and walked up the driveway to the door. She rang the doorbell and got no answer. She rang once more and heard a voice, "Who is it?" "I'm Veronica Calhoun. Is Peggy Wilson at home? Just then, the door unlocked and opened, and Veronica came face-to-face with a young lady who looked to be in her mid- to late twenties. Veronica looked into the girl's eyes and saw her own. This must be her sister. The woman said behind black and blue rimmed glasses, "That's my mother. She's not home right now." "Ok. Is there a better time that I can come back? Veronica asked the girl. The young lady eyed Veronica with a wary expression. "What do you want with my mom exactly?" Veronica was not prepared for the third degree. She really didn't know what to say. She didn't want to tell her the truth for fear of causing trouble in their family. For all she knew, Peggy Wilson never told anyone that she gave a baby up for adoption.

"There was a private matter I wanted to discuss with her. Since she's not available, I'll try to come back some other time." Just as she turned to leave, a blue SUV pulled into the driveway. In that moment, time stood still for Veronica. She stood there staring at the vehicle pulling into the drive and waited for the woman to get out. The woman she had thought about since she was fifteen years old. This was around the time her adoptive parents told her the truth. A caramel-colored woman stepped out of the vehicle. Her hair was pulled back into a neat bun. She also wore glasses but with red rims. She wore dark blue slacks and a white blouse. She was beautiful and elegant-looking, Veronica thought to herself. Looking at her was like looking into a mirror. This was, without a doubt, the woman who gave birth to her.

Veronica locked eyes with the woman, and she knew immediately that the woman had known who she was. Her birth mother walked up to her and said, "Veronica?" With a surprised expression, she replied, "Yes, I'm Veronica. How do you know my name?" Peggy's eyes began to fill with tears. "Because that's the name I gave you when you were born. I was not sure if they would keep your name or not, but if they hadn't, you would always be Veronica to me." Just then, all the emotions that Veronica had ever felt came gushing out of her. All the years of wondering who this woman was, wondering why she was left alone in this world, wondering if she was ever loved by her parents—all of it came out in that moment. Peggy walked closer to her and asked, "Can I hug you?" Unable to speak, she just shook her head yes. Veronica's mother hugged her like she had been waiting for the moment forever. In a soothing tone, Peggy said, "Shhh….it's going to be ok. I've waited and prayed for this moment for years." A voice behind them said, "Ma, is this her?" "This is her. This is your big sister, Veronica. Come here." Peggy loosened the hug and turned to her other daughter. "Veronica, this is your younger sister, Krista." Veronica looked back at the young lady who had her eyes and said, "Hi, Krista. Nice to meet you." Walking closer to the two women, Krista grabbed Veronica's hand. "Nice to finally meet you. We've heard so much about you over the years. I've always wondered when we would meet." Veronica grabbed her sister and hugged her tightly. Through her tears, Veronica chanted, "I have a sister, I have a sister." Peggy ushered them into the house. Veronica looked around the quaint home. Neat and clean, nothing out of place, but so full of personality. She could tell that living was taking place there. Suddenly, a pang of jealousy crept into her heart. As she looked around what looked like the family room, she began to imagine all of the memories that were made there with the family that she biologically belonged to. Just then, a flood of unexpected emotions came bubbling to the surface. "Why did you give me away?" When the words came out of her mouth, she recognized their harshness. Peggy and Krista, who sat opposite Veronica, looked at each other. "I was sixteen, and your father was seventeen. Our parents thought that you'd be better off with people who could properly take care of you. We were so young, Veronica; we didn't know anything about raising a child." Veronica looked at her quizzically. "Why didn't either of your parents keep me and raise me until you guys were old enough to take care of me?" Looking down at her hands in her lap, Peggy had a shameful look on her face. "I suppose after all these years, I should have been prepared for these questions, but it turns out that I am not. Look, sweetheart, I really don't know why our parents didn't decide to keep you themselves. I never even asked my mama. We just did what our parents thought was best at the time." Veronica sat quietly and mulled over what her biological mother was saying to her. "So why didn't you ever come for me?" she asked. Peggy looked up at Veronica with a sorrowful look. "Veronica darling, the adoption records were sealed. Your father and I weren't allowed to do that." With a confused look, "My adoption records were not sealed. It didn't take very long to get the information I needed to find you. Besides, my parents would have allowed you all to be a part of my life." Peggy didn't say anything. She sat with a blank expression on her face. Veronica could not decide whether this woman was caught in a lie or if she was realizing for the first time that she had been lied to. Krista spoke up, "Veronica, my entire life, I've heard about you, and I've wanted to meet you.

Mama and Daddy always believed that they could not contact you." Veronica's demeanor softened as she looked at her younger sister. She then realized something and looked at Peggy. "You married my birth father?" Peggy shook her head and explained that they had broken up for a little while, but after college, they had reconnected and had gotten married and had her sister and brother. "I had no idea that I had any other siblings." I've got three best friends, and they are the only sisters that I thought I'd ever have." Veronica realized that in the midst of the sadness, her sister and brother were the bright spots in this adoption story. Peggy straightened on the couch. "Veronica, would you be open to meeting Rick, your biological father, and your brother, Cameron?" She nodded and saw the faces of both women immediately brighten up.

The three women sat talking for about an hour and a half before Krista gave them a tour. The house had five bedrooms and three and a half baths. It was immaculate. As she examined each room, she realized that there were many Christmases and birthdays and other special occasions that she wasn't a part of. She realized that she had missed out on so much with her family, and this made her terribly sad. By the time she and Krista got to the kitchen, Peggy was making coffee. "Would you like a cup of coffee? I just made it fresh. Krista, your milk for hot chocolate is on." Before Veronica could answer, Krista interjected, "Mom, I drink coffee now." She looked a little embarrassed, not wanting to look like a child in her sister's eyes. It made Veronica smile that her sister cared about what she thought of her. "Thanks for the offer of coffee, but I'm a hot chocolate girl myself," Veronica spoke up, winking an eye at Krista. Krista smiled. "On second thought, I don't want my sister to feel left out, so I'll have hot chocolate as well." Peggy gave a knowing smile to Veronica for what she had done for her little sister. The three women sat at the kitchen table as Veronica told them all about her career, her parents, and her friends. "You've grown up to be a remarkable young woman. I am so sorry that we weren't around to see or even had a hand in it." She looked at the woman she'd been dreaming about since she was fifteen years old, and fat tears began to stream down her face. Peggy got up and threw her arms around her eldest child. She realized that this was something she longed to do: comfort her daughter. She also realized that she wanted to be the one to wipe her tears away and kiss all her boo-boos while she was growing up. They missed out on Veronica's entire life, and there was a sorrow deep in her heart that she wasn't sure she would recover from. For now, she would hug her and comfort her as a mother should. Just then, Rick walked through the door.

Veronica looked up into a familiar pair of eyes. "I have his eyes." She thought to herself as she stood up to greet her birth father. "Hi, I'm Veronica." She held out her hand, but just as Peggy had done before, he pulled her in for a hug. "I know who you are, my dear. We've been waiting for this moment for a long time." Veronica felt like a little girl again in his arms. He hugged her so tight. She never wanted to let go of this feeling. When he let go of their embrace, he looked to her brother, Cameron. "Cam, this is your big sister, Veronica." Cameron, standing at least six feet, looked down at her with a smile on his face. He resembled Peggy, from his caramel skin to his pointed nose. He pulled her in for an embrace. "Hey sis. It's great to finally meet you." She hugged him back. "It's a pleasure to meet you, Cameron." As they sat around the kitchen table, Veronica looked out at the family that she should have been a part of. She thought of all the time she missed and how much they missed out on in her life. She began to feel cheated, but she thought of the Calhouns and the life that they gave her. She had a wonderful life growing up. She never lacked anything, and they were always loving, patient, and kind to her. It's just that when she found out that she was adopted at fifteen, she'd always felt incomplete and a little out of place. Veronica felt that perhaps if she knew who her birth parents were, then she'd feel comfortable in her own skin, that she'd finally know who she was. In that moment, she didn't feel complete; she felt confused and realized that it would take a while to wade through the ocean of emotions from the past twenty-two years.

Zola had to meet the curator of the Crimson Art Museum at nine. She scampered around the house, making sure Sophie was up and ready to get to school. Kha'ren was tagging along to the museum today. Since she discovered her friend's love of art, she thought she'd expose her friend to different sides of the art world. After she dropped Sophie at school, she picked Kha'ren up. "I am so excited about your exhibit, Zo. I love that your work is being showcased. You really deserve all of this. I know how hard you've been working on this." Zola smiled. "Thanks, girl. It's been hard balancing moving, opening the new store, and finishing these pieces, but I'm finally here." She was so proud of the progress that she'd made. She was also happy to have Kha'ren with her because she had a surprise for her friend. Zola was told that Joshua Coven would be at the museum this morning, and she asked the curator if he'd be willing to meet one of his students in advance. She was pleased to hear that Joshua was willing to do it.

When they arrived, Kha'ren helped Zola pull the three extra pieces from her SUV. Zola had them wrapped so they would not be revealed until the showcase in a couple of weeks. Kha'ren walked with Zola and the curator throughout the area where Zola's work would be showcased. When they finished, Kha'ren looked at Zola. "All set?" Zola gave her a sly smile and replied, "Not quite. There is someone I'd like for you to meet." Kha'ren gave Zola a quizzical look. "You want me to meet another one of your artsy friends? I don't know, Zo; you know how it went the last time with that girl Ansley." Zola laughed loudly. "No, Cee-Cee, nothing like that. Just come with me, and you'll see." The two women walked down the hall and into a large room filled with familiar paintings. Kha'ren would know these paintings anywhere. They were Joshua Coven's paintings. She walked through the gallery, eyeing each painting carefully until she looked up and saw a tall chocolate man. He had his back turned to her, but she'd know him anywhere. She'd googled him enough to know who he was on the spot. She tugged on Zola's arm excitedly, "Is that the Joshua Coven?" Zola replied with a satisfied smile, "Yes, ma'am, that is the Joshua Coven. Do you want to meet him?" Kha'ren gave a quick inventory of her attire. She was dressed in a fitted black tailored pantsuit with white lapels. Her black stilettos were pointy and high. "You look gorgeous. When have you ever been self-conscious?" Kha'ren gave Zola a cynical look. "Hush, he is a celebrity, Zola." "I know who he is, Cee-Cee, but you are a powerhouse, a force to be reckoned with." Before she could respond, Zola walked ahead of her, calling Joshua's name. He turned around, and Kha'ren froze.

His pictures on the internet did him no justice. He was the most beautiful man Kha'ren had ever seen. With his chocolate skin, high cheekbones, and big piercing eyes. He smiled at Zola, and she immediately noticed that famous dimple on his right cheek. Zola began waving her over. "Joshua, this is one of my very best friends and possibly one of your biggest fans, Kha'ren Sage." Joshua turned and unleashed one of the sexiest grins on her. Her mind went blank as he extended a hand to her. "Hi, Ms. Sage, I'm." Before he could finish his introduction, Kha'ren said, "Mr. Coven. It's a pleasure to meet you. I am a huge fan of your work." "Well, I am flattered. I heard you will be one of my students next week. Perhaps you want to tour the gallery with me briefly and talk about the pieces?" Joshua asked with a look Kha'ren could not quite describe. "Sure, I'd love that. I mean, if

Zola has the time." Zola waved her off. "Of course, I have to go finalize everything for my showcase anyway." Before Zola walked out of the gallery, she met her friend's gaze. "Thank you." Kha'ren mouthed, and Zola gave her a thumbs up.

"Oh my God, Zola, I can't believe you did that!" Kha'ren exclaimed, blushing. Zola looked over at her friend. "I thought it would be a great opportunity. You love his work, and when I found out that he'd be there this morning, I knew I had to get you to meet him." "Thank you so much; that was a once-in-a-lifetime experience," Kha'ren said as she opened the car door. Looking over at her, Zola said, "What I didn't realize was that you had a crush on this guy." Unable to contain her embarrassment, a blush crept up Kha'ren's olive-colored cheeks." Kha'ren was all smiles as she thought of her encounter with the man she had several daydreams about. "Do you think there was a connection?" Zola asked. "I don't know about that, Zola; this man is very famous and could have any woman he wants and probably has one now. I don't think he's checking for me." Kha'ren replied. "Cee-Cee, don't sell yourself short. I saw the way he looked at you. He had the same dumb grin that you had looking at him. There's something there, believe me."

The next few months went by in a blur. Zola and Nick got together as much as they could with their busy schedules. They both finally got around to telling their daughters about the relationship. Zola was extremely nervous about talking to Sophie. "Mom, I kind of figured that something was going on between you and Mr. Nick." Zola worried, as this was the only response from her daughter. "So, what do you think about it? I mean, I have not dated anyone since your dad and I divorced, and your opinion means a lot to me, Sophie," Zola said. She knew her daughter was not used to her dating. To her chagrin, Sophie hadn't said much after her initial comment. Zola knew that Alex was excited, but she wasn't sure about April and Adrienne. He did mention that his girls recently said to him, "We've always said that if you did tell us about a woman, she would be pretty special because you haven't dated since Mom died. Zola knew that the idea of someone else in their father's life was different from the reality of someone being in their father's life. He held his breath waiting for his daughters' responses. April told him that she wanted him to be happy, but had her reservations because she did not want anyone coming into their lives to replace their mom. Nick assured her that no one could ever replace Karmen, and those aren't Zola's intentions. Adrienne's response took him by surprise because he didn't imagine that his oldest would oppose him dating someone, especially so long after their mom passed away. "Dad, this seems kind of sudden. One day you're single, not even thinking about dating, and the next here's this woman that you want us to meet. You never said anything about her before." Adrienne lamented. She told her dad that she wanted him to be happy, but like April, she had her reservations, and she didn't want someone coming into their lives trying to take their mom's place. Just as he had with April, Nick explained to Adrienne that their mom could never be replaced. Nick and Zola planned an evening where everyone would come together for dinner. They both crossed their fingers that all would go well.

The morning of the dinner, Nick decided to talk to his daughters while all of them were finally home together. "I think you all should give Ms. Zola a chance. She really is a nice person, and she's talented," Alex told her sisters. "I'm not saying I don't like her, nor would I give her a chance; I just don't want Mom to be replaced," replied April. Nick expected some type of apprehension from his daughters, but meeting and getting to know Zola has been like a breath of fresh air for him. He's fallen in love with this woman, and he wasn't ready to let her go. He knew that once April and Adrienne got to know Zola, they would love her. At least Alex likes her, and she and Sophie get along very well.

Zola and Sophie showed up at Nick's house at six thirty sharp. He introduced his daughters to them, and immediately Zola could sense tension. This made her a little nervous because Nick told her that his daughters were warming up to the idea of him being in a relationship. Alex asked her father if she and Sophie could be excused to go upstairs until dinner was ready. Nick walked everyone into the family room, took drink orders, and went into the kitchen. Adrienne and April were cordial but made very little effort at small talk. She attempted to break the ice by asking each girl questions about themselves. April spoke liberally about her studies in school, hobbies, the college she'd like to attend, and her dream job. When it was Adrienne's turn to speak, she gave only minimal details about herself. Zola could feel the icy attitude that Nick's eldest daughter was giving her, so she felt an amicable approach would be best. Unfortunately, the more she tried talking to Adrienne, the less friendly she became with Zola. April eventually elbowed her sister. She was thankful Nick had brought the drinks because by this time, she was feeling so nervous that she needed something to do with her hands.

At the dinner table, Nick asked if everyone had gotten to know each other earlier. April responded that she talked a little about herself, while Alex and Sophie said in unison, giggling, "We already know each other." Adrienne kept silent, but after a moment, looked at Zola and asked, "How is it that you know so much about us, but we know virtually nothing about you?" A little caught off guard, Zola began to answer her, but Nick put his hand over Zola's and began to answer his daughter's question. "Adrienne, I believe that's a question for me." He explained to her that he made the decision to keep quiet about his relationship with Zola because he hadn't dated anyone since their mom, and before he brought a woman into his kids' lives, he needed to be absolutely certain. He went on to explain to his daughter that he also wanted to be sure of his feelings for Zola, and he didn't want to be hasty in bringing a woman around his daughters before he knew for certain that he loved her. He expressed how being in a relationship again was just as new for him as it was for them and that Zola meant so much to him. Adrienne's resolve softened a bit, but she retorted, "Alex seems to know her very well. Why was it ok for Alex to be around her, and you practically said nothing to April and me?" "Alex knows Zola because she is a student of Zola and Sophie. Sophie and Alex have become fast friends, but neither one of them knew about our relationship." Zola interjected, "Girls, listen. We know that we kept our relationship from you, but we did it out of caution for all of you. We wanted to make sure it was right. You all have faced a lot in the past few years, and we didn't want to add any unnecessary stress to your lives by bringing someone in for you to get attached to, and then they go away because things didn't work out. "Alex, April, and Adrienne, I truly care for your father, and I'm grateful to have him in my life, but I also want to get to know all of you as well. I hope you give me a chance to do that." Nick turned to Sophie and expressed the same sentiment. Everyone ate in silence for a few moments until April spoke up. "Dad, I want you to be happy, and if Zola makes you happy, then I'm fine with your relationship. I just don't want you to forget about Mom." Her eyes began to fill with water, and Zola's eyes welled up too. She realized at that moment just how vulnerable Nick and his three daughters were. She didn't want to do anything to jeopardize her connection with him or her possible connection with his daughters. "That could never and will never happen, April, Adrienne, and Alex. Your mom will always occupy an important yet special place in your hearts, and no one could ever replace her. Nick looked at Zola in such awe. He wondered how he could have fallen in love with two wonderful women in his lifetime. He felt so blessed in that moment. When dinner was over, and the girls went to their rooms, Zola and Nick were left alone to unpack the evening. "Well, that was a little intense," Nick said as he pulled Zola into his arms on the couch. "It was, but our daughters are just apprehensive and scared of the unknown. I think, though, that if we are patient with them and keep showing them that we love them, they'll eventually settle down," Zola replied. Kissing her forehead, Nick said, "Man, how did you become so wise? I was completely at a loss as to how I was going to get my daughters on board with our relationship. You seem to always know what to say, Zola." She smiled. "I don't actually, but I'm trying to trust my gut here. Neither one of us has faced the situation our girls are currently facing, and I just believe that right now they need our love, attention, and patience." Holding her tighter, Nick knew he had made the right decision to love this incredible woman.

Chapter 11

Maranda sat holding her new baby in her arms, thanking God for the blessing that He'd given her and Mike. As she looked down into the angelic face of her baby boy, Samuel, she began to reflect on her journey. Her unwavering faith in God is what has always kept her through the hardships in her life. At this moment, though, she began to thank Him for the hard times. Tears rolled down her cheeks as she began to see how God was the artist who created the tapestry of her life. When she was younger, she had her life all mapped out. Each decade of her life was filled with plans, wishes, hopes, and dreams. She chuckled to herself as she thought of a conversation with her grandmother. They were talking about Maranda's plans for the future, and she said to her in her thick southern accent, "Darling, you can plan all you want to; if your plans aren't God's plans, then you have no plans." Oh, how many times has that statement proven to be true in Maranda's life? In all the plans she made, she never planned to be a pastor's wife, a teacher, a group counselor, or any of the other things she does in her community and for her family. Having cancer wasn't in her plans either, but she had it, endured it, and is now in remission. She looked down at little Sam in awe. Because of ovarian cancer, her doctors told her that it was a growing possibility that she wouldn't have been able to conceive. She found herself grateful for it all. She gave God thanks for her husband, who taught her that just because life can throw curveballs and you find yourself floating along in the storms of life, it doesn't mean that God hand isn't in it all. She marveled at how her challenges caused her to grow spiritually. They increased her faith, patience, love for her family and community, and love for herself, but most importantly, love for God. Because of all that He's done for her, she was determined to serve Him for the rest of her days.

Shortly after she came home from the hospital, her three best friends came over to spend the day with her and little Sam. She appreciated the time that each woman took from their busy life to lavish her family with love. She knew she would do no less for them, but it's always wonderful to know that you're loved. Their church congregation had been wonderful to her and their little family by cooking dinners, sending cards, and sending gifts. Maranda truly felt blessed. In all her gratefulness, she couldn't help but feel the tug on her heart for more. More of what, she wasn't quite certain, but she felt it. She knew that God had more for her and that her heart was being prepared for the tasks ahead. She felt it so deeply. She and Mike talked about this feeling that she had a little while ago, and he told her to be patient, and God will reveal everything in time. Maranda took a deep breath and snuggled her son closer, contented for the first time in a long while.

Her phone buzzed next to her just as she finished feeding her baby. The caller ID said New Hope General Hospital. "Hi Maranda, this is Dr. Lewis from New Hope. How are you today?" She greeted the woman on the line with a cheery tone. "Congratulations to you and Mike on your new addition, and I apologize that I have to call you with this, but it is imperative that you come into the office this week." Maranda's heart sank. Dr. Lewis is her oncologist, and she just went in for her routine imaging scans. The concern in Dr. Lewis's voice alerted Maranda. "How's this Friday?" Maranda asked the woman. She agreed to the date and explained to Maranda that she was just a little concerned about one of the scans, and she needed to come back in for further tests. Eyes filling with unshed tears, she could no longer speak. She kept nodding her head to the doctor's explanation. "Maranda? Are you there?" said Dr. Lewis. She was pulled out of her reverie and said in a teary tone, "I'm here." "Maranda, I'm so sorry to call you with this, with everything that is going on in your life, but this isn't something that I could wait on. In these situations, we must be proactive." Maranda replied in an understanding tone to her doctor. After they hung up, with shaky hands, Maranda dialed Mike's number. "Babe, please come home. I need you."

Staring down at her phone, Kha'ren could not take her eyes off the message that flashed before her eyes. "Will you have dinner with me?" He asked her out. Joshua Coven, an incredibly talented artist, asked her out to dinner. That day in the art gallery when Zola introduced them, they had a great conversation, so great in fact that he asked for her phone number. She didn't tell her friends because it all felt too good to be true. She could come up with several reasons why she should keep this to herself, but truthfully, she didn't tell anyone because she didn't want to get her hopes up again. Every time she met a man, things fell apart. She learned a long time ago to stop wishing and hoping that Prince Charming was coming her way. The problem is that it's been such a long time since she felt any kind of connection with a man. Since he asked for her number a few weeks ago, they've texted daily and, between their busy schedules, found time to chat on the phone a few times. Now he's asked her out. Admittedly, as much as they hit it off, she didn't expect much more than what they were doing. He was a renowned artist with great influence in the art world and beyond. She was simply Kha'ren. She could not imagine how she could keep the interest of a guy like him when he could have, or maybe even had, any woman he wanted. She could not believe she was contemplating turning him down, but she really was in no mood to experience another failed relationship. On the other hand, she has had a crush on this guy since she saw his picture in *Artworld Magazine*. When Zola introduced her to the art scene, she was instantly in love with the vibe and creativity of the artists she encountered. Her firm even represented some of them. Joshua was no exception; his art spoke to her. She would never admit this to him, but when she looked at his paintings, whether in a magazine, gallery, or even on her own wall at home, she felt such peace. She firmly believed that artists express so much about themselves through their work. Art tends to evoke emotions out of her, and she has never quite understood why. It's as if each piece sang a lyric from the song of her life. Joshua's work just made her feel peaceful. Getting to talk with him has been a great experience, but now he wants to have dinner, and this made her nervous.

Familiar feelings of contempt and self-loathing crept back up. These have been her constant companions throughout the years. They've come along and sabotaged all that has been great in her life. She had no reason to believe that things would be different with Joshua. She would just end up messing things up with him. She felt like such a hypocrite preaching to Veronica when she had done the same thing throughout her adult life. Not knowing how to respond to his text message, she put her phone down and plowed through the rest of her day. Luckily, she was busy with meetings all day, but that didn't stop him from crossing her mind. She contemplated talking to the girls about it, but thought better of it. She just wasn't ready to hash this out with anyone. If she were really honest with herself, she wasn't ready to face the root cause of her inability to keep a healthy relationship. So, for now, she'll just play another game of avoidance. Later that night, Joshua called her, but she didn't answer his phone call. She crafted some excuse about a case she was working on and assured him that they'd talk the next morning. As she sank her spoon into a quart of cookie-dough ice cream, she thought to herself, "Who does that?" She closed her eyes and let her head fall back on the couch and answered herself, "Only me." They didn't end up talking for the next two days. She didn't text or call him. A little anxious, she noticed that he didn't actually respond to her text message from the other night. How could she have missed that? However, when she returned to her office from a lunch meeting on the third day of no contact, she found him waiting for her. He looked so handsome. She just adored his caramel eyes. He was looking down at his phone when she walked in, but their eyes met, and a shy smile spread across his face. He stood up and began to speak. "Listen, I know I showed up here without an invitation, but this is day three without talking to you. I asked you out for dinner, and then you went radio silent. One could read that as a no, but I figured that if you were going to turn me down after some of the best conversations I've had in a long time, I wanted to hear it from you in person." Kha'ren stared, flabbergasted that he was in her office and their connection was mutual. An unexpected blush crept up her cheeks. When he saw her blush, his eyes lit up. "Hi Joshua. I know we haven't spoken, and I never gave you a response to your question. The truth is, I really wasn't sure if I should accept your invitation to dinner. Our lives are totally different, and our schedules are crazy." This was not the complete truth, but she didn't want to scare him off with her baggage. She wanted more than anything to go to dinner with him, but she was just so unsure and scared. At six feet three inches, Joshua moved closer to her five-foot-four-inch frame and slid his hand into hers. He said, "Well, that's why I'm here now. I know we're busy, but I'm willing to make time in my schedule. Are you willing?" She looked up into his irresistible eyes and realized that there was no refusing him. "Yes, I can make time." With a smile that reached his eyes, he said, "Good, then it's a date. How about this Friday night? I know a nice, quiet bistro that has great food." Kha'ren gave him an incredulous look. "Quiet on a Friday night? What kind of place is this?" He chuckled in response, "You just be ready when I pick you up and let me handle everything else." Blushing again, she agreed to let him handle all of the details.

Upon leaving, he kissed her on the cheek and told her that he'd call her later that night. Kha'ren sat back in her desk chair, feeling more hopeful than she had in years.

A month later, while working in her office, Zola's phone rang. She looked down and saw that it was her father. "Hey, Daddy. Everything alright?" asked Zola. "I'm doing alright, baby girl. I'd be doing better if your mom wasn't so mad at me." Zola's dad replied. "Dad, Mom told you that she wanted to go to school to get her degree, and you told her no. Honestly, how did you think Lila James was going to take you saying no to one of her dreams?" Her dad fell silent for a moment and said, "Zo, why would your mom want to go to school at her age? This is a time when we should be settling down and traveling. I'm retiring next year, and I thought that we'd get to spend more time together, and I'd get to take her places that my schedule wouldn't allow us to go." Incredulously, Zola said, "Ok, so I get it. She is interrupting your plans?" Her dad sighed heavily and responded, "I know how this sounds, Zola, but I have sacrificed and spent so much time away from my family because I wanted to support all of you. Now I just want to make plans with your mother." "Daddy, it sounds like you've already made plans and you expected Mommy to go along with them. What about what she wants?" Her dad asked her with an edge in his voice, "Did you have any influence on your mother wanting to go back to school? This sudden decision sounds an awful lot like your handiwork and encouragement." Zola looked from her computer screen and down at her phone when she heard her father's tone and accusation come through the speaker. Rolling her eyes, she replied, "No, Daddy. I am not influencing Mama. This is something that she wants to do. I support her, by the way. You really should as well." There was a hush over the line, and finally her father spoke up, explaining that this just wasn't something he envisioned. He said he felt like he missed so much quality time with Zola's mother because of his career, and now that part of his life was coming to a close, it felt like they were starting all over again. While she listened with sympathy for her father, she knew that his view of things was completely self-centered. "Dad, it's as if you planned this entire life for Mom without allowing her to give consent to it. Yes, it was a great life that you both created for us, but you weren't the only one who made sacrifices. Mom did as well. I get that you want more time with her, but does that have to be at the expense of her dreams?" Zola told her dad before they finished their conversation.

Richard James was a proud man. His father instilled in him that the role of the female should be in the house and the house only. Not that he thought Lila incapable. If he was honest, he knew what his bride was giving up when she agreed to marry him. Guilt spread through him. He knew how he was raised, and it seemed to have served his parents well, but did his mother sacrifice because his father wanted her to stay at home and raise him and his siblings? He never considered this before Zola pointed it out to him. Yes, he adored his wife, and they had built what he thought was an incredible life for their three children, but at what cost to Lila? He knew she had plans before she met him, and he introduced his plan to take care of them, but she never hesitated to go along with it. He didn't know why she didn't protest his plans for her, but he intended to find out. "My baby girl just continues to teach me." Zola's father chuckled to himself.

That evening at dinner, he watched his wife as she ignored him while she ate. He hadn't imagined that she wanted to go to school. He figured that doing her friends' books was just a hobby, something she simply enjoyed doing. "Are you unhappy or something, Lilly? Why would you want to do something like that at your age?" He said those words to her when she first mentioned the idea of her going to school for accounting. He couldn't imagine how that must have hurt her feelings. His words were insensitive and insulting. She gave him a disbelieving look, and then he could see anger clouding her eyes. "No, Richard, I am not unhappy and definitely not too old to get a degree." She walked away with her head and shoulders held high. For weeks, he couldn't understand why she was upset with him. Every time she tried to talk to him about it, he would shut her down. She finally said stiffly, "Richard, with or without your support, I'm going to get my accounting degree. While I would prefer that you be by my side, I won't allow your antiquated ideas about the role of women to hold me back." Since then, she hadn't said much else to him. He sat across the table observing her, wondering how he could begin to make her understand how sorry he was for minimizing her feelings. "Lilly, I'm sorry," Richard said to his wife and lowered his head." Lila looked up doubtfully. "That's all, Richard? That's all you have to say?" He met her eyes. "Lilly, you know that I'm not good at these kinds of things." She replied, "Good at what? Apologizing? Admitting when you're wrong? Yes, you're right, Richard. You have a real issue with these things." He noticed the tears in her eyes. He had really done it this time. "Lila, I know I've been an inconsiderate and selfish fool. I had this plan for us for when I retired. I thought that we'd get to spend more time together, travel, and do the things we couldn't do because of my career." Richard lamented. "You made plans, but you didn't bother to include me in the planning. They involved me, but that's it. Not once did you consider me. I supported you throughout your entire career, and when I asked for your support, you wouldn't give it because it did not fit in your plans." Lila responded. He tried to speak up, but she held her hand up. "I'm not finished talking, Richard. For years, my life had been devoted to you and the kids. I don't regret it because it's a choice that I made, but our children are all well into adulthood, and they don't need me anymore. Your work continues to take you all over, and I have been left home alone more times than I can count. I figured that this would be a great time to focus on the things that I want to do. I know that you've always had these archaic notions that women and men have specific roles in life. I also know that you were taught this by your father, but I was hoping that perhaps you would break that cycle one day after raising such strong-willed, successful daughters." Richard was suddenly filled with shame. He had raised strong-willed daughters, but he realized that it had nothing to do with him. It was all Lila. She instilled the free spirit and thinker in Zola and the driven mindset in Tori. It was as if he was seeing his wife for the first time. Richard sighed, "Lila, you are right. I allowed my old-fashioned ideals to disqualify you from doing and being anything other than a mother to our children and a wife to me. I'm sorry I didn't see or wouldn't see how this made you feel." He got up and sat in the chair next to her, and covered her hand with his. She looked at him with tears in her eyes. "You have allowed your father's ideals to shape your relationship with your children and me. This is why you have always conflicted with Zola. She doesn't fit the mold that you created. You've had this prescribed life for all of us. When our son switched careers, you nearly disowned him. When Zola decided that she wanted to pursue her art career, you counted her out as well. Tori seems to be the only child who hasn't disappointed you, but that is because she is so starved for your approval, she'd nearly do anything to keep it." Lila explained to her husband. She told him that she went to Zola about school because she knew that she was going to have her full support. Zola would give her the confidence she needed to talk to him about her next step. When she was finished talking, he sighed and held his head down. "Lilly baby, I can't apologize enough for what I've done to our family. I didn't realize I made any of you feel inadequate because of my expectations. I'll admit my thought process is archaic and that I was wrong. You have my full support; I'll never hold you back again." She grinned at him, and he felt as though he could breathe again. He loved this woman with everything in him, and he hated it when they were not speaking to each other.

Chapter 12

Zola agreed to hold the girls' night at her house so she could give her friends a tour of her new little town. She and Sophie had lived in Ridge Haven for almost a year, and she'd fallen in love with its charm. She settled in nicely and loved how connected everyone seemed to be to the town. She was excited to see the girls again. They make it a point to get together once a month for a girls' night, but the past three months have been frenzied for all of the women. They'd talked on the phone, but there was nothing like coming together. Instead of ordering in, she thought she'd cook and had Nick make the dessert. She thought about him and smiled. She wasn't looking to meet or date anyone, let alone fall in love, at this point in her life. She reflected on her life over the past years and felt grateful for it all. When her husband filed for divorce and then moved on with someone else, she was devastated. She wasn't sure how to move on with her life. There were all of these realities that she had never had to contend with before. For instance, being a single parent. In all of her dreaming and imagining how her life would be, raising a daughter on her own never made the list. Financially supporting herself and a child on her own didn't make the list either. Yet there she was, faced with the reality of bills and responsibilities all on her shoulders. Then there was her career. At that time, she had sold a few pieces, but she was building her collection. She remembered a particular conversation she had with Jonathan before he left: "Among other things, Jonnie, you promised to support me while I built my career as I supported you! How could you just walk away like this?" As he was walking towards the door, he glared at her and, with an icy tone, said, "Well, I guess you'd better get a job, princess."

Tears filled her eyes as she thought about how heartbroken she was. There were so many days that she didn't want to get out of bed, but she would think of her little girl. Her family and friends rallied around her and loved her. They gave so many encouraging words, but it wasn't until she had a conversation with her mom that she began to stand tall on the inside. Her mom sensed that she had fallen into depression and was determined to lift her spirits. She showed up unexpectedly early one Saturday morning, let herself in the house, and began making breakfast. She woke Sophie, fed her, and got her going for the day. Then she went into Zola's room and opened the curtains and the blinds. "Get up, get up, get up," she exclaimed. "Ma, what are you doing?" Zola asked, sighing heavily. "I came to see about my child. Now, Zee, it's been four months since Jonathan left this house, and it's time to get back to living life." Lila said. Zola rolled over and covered her face with the pillow and responded. "I am living life; I'm just tired of it right now." Lila grabbed Zola's arms and told her to get up in a stern, motherly tone. Reluctantly, she got out of bed and stood. Her mom pulled her into the bathroom in front of the mirror. "Zola, look." She looked in the mirror as her mom requested and said, "What am I looking at, Ma?" "Who is this woman staring in this mirror? What does she want? What does she want to do? I know that your heart is broken, but you are not in despair. While this is not a situation you thought you'd be in at this point in your life, it's still your reality. What are you going to do with it? Who are you going to be, Zola? Who is Sophie going to see when she looks at her mama?" At these questions, the tears came pouring down Zola's cheeks. She answered, "I don't know who I am, Mommy. I have no idea who I am." Hugging her daughter, Lila said, "Sweetheart, you have spent so much time helping Jonathan build his identity and making his mark in the world that you never got around to doing that for yourself. Your identity is not wrapped up in your marriage or even being a mother. These are parts of you, but they don't make you complete. The story of your life has not ended. A new chapter has just begun. Rejoice in this because just like the paintbrushes you use to create art on your canvases, the canvas of your life is waiting for you to create your greatest masterpiece yet. You, my dear, get to decide from this day forward how you want your life to be. You get to decide who you want to be." Lila's words pulled Zola right out of her low place. Eventually, she realized that Jonathan had truly given her a new start. She didn't want to waste another moment of it lamenting over what was and what could have been. During that time, she remembered what her mom told her when she was in high school after her first breakup. She smiled, remembering how hurt she was that Trevor Smith dumped her right there in front of her locker. She was so mortified that she pretended to be sick and called her mom to pick her up. She wept in her mother's arms. Lila said, "Baby, when someone wants to walk out of your life, let them walk right out. Never beg for love or affection from anybody. People are always going to show you your place in their lives. If it's not the place you deserve to be in, given the nature of your relationship, then they aren't honoring your value and worth. You are certainly valuable and worthy, Zola James." Patting her daughter's shoulder, she urged, "Let him go, baby girl." Those words rang loud and clear in Zola's head in the months and even years after her divorce. She decided that she wanted Sophie to see her as a strong woman who can stand in the face of adversity. She wanted her daughter to see her as triumphant.

Zola also reflected on her life as a single parent, a single woman, and eventually her marriage and life partnership with Jonathan. She could see that from the beginning of their relationship; she never spoke up for what she wanted. Of course, he knew her goals, dreams, and aspirations, but somehow hers never shone as bright as his. She recalled them talking one night after they got engaged. He was in law school, and she worked on her art at night while working as an assistant during the day. "Zo, it's best for me to just finish up before you go back to school. It's my career that's really going to bring the income in anyway." He said this to her while she was explaining that she herself wanted to go back to school to further her art education. Zola realized that she had allowed him to dim her lights. She never went back to school, and after he became a lawyer and began making good money, they settled into a routine. She was a stay-at-home mom who worked on her art part-time while he worked to advance his career and ultimately made partner. All her mom's words rang in her head as she built a new life for herself and Sophie. She realized that in addition to creating art, she loved to teach it and celebrate others who created it. Therefore, the idea of her first store, *A Messa Stuff,* was born. Thanks to her parents' connection in their city's Chamber of Commerce, she secured a business loan and toiled to get her business off the ground. Now she's opened her second location. Looking down at the clock, she realized that she'd been walking down memory lane far too long. Her friends were due to show up within the hour.

The four women laughed, ate, and caught each other up with the happenings of their lives. Everyone noticed that Maranda didn't seem to be herself, although she tried to cover it up with her usual sunny disposition. No one bought it, though. Veronica leaned back on the sofa next to Maranda and sighed, "Ok. Spill." With a shocked expression, Maranda looked at her. "What do you mean, spill? What am I supposed to say?" Kha'ren spoke up, "How about telling us what's wrong instead of pretending everything is fine all night long? Randi, we clearly see that something is off with you tonight." Maranda looked into the eyes of her three sisters and began to sob inconsolably. The women rushed to her side. "Randi, will you please tell us what's wrong?"

Zola asked as tears filled her eyes. She hated seeing any of her friends hurt. Wiping her cheeks with the back of her hands, Maranda explained her possible health crisis to the women. Each woman listened intently, cried with her, and held on to her. "How could I have cancer again? God just blessed us with our baby boy. What if I don't get to see him grow up? It's not fair." "Randi, they don't know if what they found is cancerous yet. Don't go assuming the worst-case scenario." Kha'ren said in a soothing tone. Swiping a tear from her cheek, Veronica asked, "How's Mike holding up?" "He is holding up. He's very encouraging and trying to be strong for me, but the other night I heard him crying and praying in his study." This response brought on a whole new set of tears for Maranda. She explained that she and Mike hadn't told any of their family members, anyone in the ministry. She explained that they didn't want to get anyone worried, and it could turn out to be nothing. "So, you guys have just been carrying this for a couple of months with no outlet? Oh, Randi, I wish you had told us when you first found out. We could have all been there for you guys. We are family." Nodding, Maranda said, "I know, guys, we just didn't want this to overshadow any joy anyone felt about our baby boy. Our moms are so excited. He is the first grandson on both sides. How could we tell our parents this now when everyone is so happy?" Giving her a peck on the forehead, Kha'ren told Miranda, "Well, you guys aren't alone in this any longer." "Ok, ok. Enough about my situation, you three have a lot going on, and I'm not the only one who needs to spill tonight." Maranda smiled at her best friends. "Ok, I'll spill." Veronica spoke up. "As you all know, I met my biological family a little while ago. At first, it was surreal. I could not believe that I finally met them. I had no idea that my biological parents stayed together. Zola asked, "How do you feel now that you have met them, and you got the whole story?" Veronica hesitated, thinking about how best to answer the question posed to her. She had felt so many different emotions since meeting her birth family. "I have had so many feelings about the entire situation. At first, I felt relieved to finally know the truth and finally be able to lay eyes on my birth mother and father. I dreamed of what that day would be like from the moment Mama and Daddy told me that I was adopted. After that, I felt a whole gang of emotions. Some included anger, envy, and joy, but these days all I've been feeling is left out." Wrapping her arms around Veronica, Miranda said, "Aww, Ronnie, I'm sorry." Kha'ren leaned in. "Why do you feel left out? I thought you'd be happy that you've met your birth parents." "I feel like this because they have built this life together and raised two other children, my younger siblings, without me. While I understand what happened, I still feel that I missed out. My brother and sister seemed to have turned out perfectly fine; why couldn't either of their families keep me?" Veronica said with tears falling down her face. Zola put her hand over Veronica's and said softly, "Veronica, who's to say that if your parents' parents had kept you, your life would have turned out alright? Your siblings were born to your parents, who were adults. They were virtually kids when your mom got pregnant with you. You're measuring what you missed out on based on their lives now, not what their lives were back then before your brother and sister were born." Shaking her head, Veronica said, "I know that everything you're saying is right, Zee, but my heart keeps going back into this place." The room fell silent as each friend thought about the best way to respond to the way Veronica was feeling. Then Kha'ren exclaimed, "I think you should sit down and talk to a therapist. At some point, I think your parents need to join you." Veronica gave her an incredulous look but said nothing. "Hear me out, please. Ronnie, you have spent most of your life not knowing a huge chunk of who you were. You've expressed to us so many times over the years that you've had dreams of what kind of woman your birth mother would be. You assumed that your parents weren't together, so you figured you'd eventually have another parental reunion after you finally met your mom. No amount of imagination could have prepared you for realizing that your mom and dad married, created a life, had two other children, and didn't come looking for you. I completely understand why you feel that you missed out. They created a life without you, and they knew that you were somewhere out there. I just think that you need to work through your emotions, and you need to share your feelings with the two of them." Maranda and Zola nodded in agreement. She looked around at her friends and sighed. Veronica was not ready to pour out her feelings to some stranger. She didn't do well with this kind of thing. She was, however, aware that not dealing with her feelings affected just about all her relationships. "I can see you've got your internal dialogue going. You've got the look. "Kha'ren said. The women burst into laughter. "Girl, what are you talking about?" Veronica asked. Zola said, "Ronnie, girl, please! You get this real pensive look when you are thinking to yourself." She smiled sheepishly. "Maybe there's something to this therapist thing. Honestly, though, I'd like to sit down and talk to my birth parents alone before I do that.

The rest of the night, the four women enjoyed each other's company and talked endlessly about their lives. Zola even told them about her meeting with Nick's daughters. "Boy, that must have been uncomfortable," Veronica told her. "To say the least. The tension was extremely thick at that dinner table," Zola said. "How have things been between you all since then?" Maranda asked Zola. "We're coming along. I figured that taking it one day at a time was the best. We've decided it's best to give the girls some time, even Sophie. What we've realized is that neither of our girls has ever had to experience this before," Zola said. She went on to explain, "Nick's girls have only seen him with their mom, and Sophie's only seen me with Jonnie. The last thing we want to do is force our relationship on them because it's a huge change from what they're used to." "Who would have thought that you'd be in a new relationship with a man and happy after all that you've gone through since your divorce?" Maranda retorted. A giggling Zola said, "I know, right?" Veronica leaned forward on the couch with a mischievous grin and said, "You know what I've noticed? Kha'ren hasn't given much of an update on her life. Anyone else notice that?" Kha'ren narrowed her eyes at her friend. "Come to think of it, she sure hadn't." Maranda said, smiling. "You might as well spill, girl," Zola said. Rolling her eyes in her head, Kha'ren responded, "There isn't much to tell. You all know my life; I work and come home." The women gave her an incredulous look. "Are you kidding me, Kha'ren?" Veronica exclaimed. "What about Joshua? Are you guys dating?" Maranda asked. "I wouldn't say that we're dating. We've gone out a few times." Kha'ren responded. Her friends saw the blush that crept up on her face. "You really like him!" Zola exclaimed. "Of course, she does, Zee. Look at her face!" Veronica teased. With an exasperated sigh, Kha'ren said, "Ok, I like him. I really like him." "So, what's wrong then?" Maranda asked her. "What do you mean? Nothing is wrong?" Kha'ren responded, raising her eyebrows and feigning curiosity. Maranda gave a slight frown. "Kha'ren, please don't insult my intelligence. There is something going on that you're not telling us." "Wait, is he a jerk or something? Veronica asked. Kha'ren looked over at Veronica. "Ronnie, calm down. No, he did nothing to hurt me, and he most certainly is not a jerk. It just all seems too good to be true. He is truly a great guy, but I don't want to get my hopes up. You guys know that my relationships don't work out. I just can't get my hopes up this time, only to turn around and end up heartbroken again. I just can't risk that." With sympathetic eyes, Maranda turned to her friend and hugged her. "Kha'ren, loving is a risk. You cannot approach every new encounter with a man as if it's doomed to fail, or else it will. It's perfectly fine to be apprehensive when moving into something new like this, but it's not alright to walk in fear. You begin to respond to fear, and you will psych yourself out of what could be one of the greatest experiences in your life. This man could be the one for you. Give it a chance to work." Tears pooled up in Kha'ren's eyes. She knew her friend spoke the truth, but she couldn't see how this situation would be any different from other relationships that didn't work out. She never felt this way about a man like this before. He is a totally different guy than what she is used to, which is why the thought of a relationship frightens her so much. Being with him increased her chance of heartbreak, and she wasn't sure she would be able to recover from that. She didn't share these thoughts with her friends. "Kha'ren, Joshua really is a good guy, and I think he is the one who is feeling blessed to know you right now. We see the value in you, and so does he." Zola mentioned to her friend. Smiling, Kha'ren admitted, "There is something there between us. He asked me out, and I never answered his question. It was great chatting through texts and even a phone call or two but getting together was something different. Out of fear, I ignored his invitation to dinner. It seemed to have worked until he showed up in my office." The women gasped. "I was coming back from a lunch meeting and walked into my office. There he was sitting in my chair on his phone, looking so confident." Kha'ren told the women. "That's because he was coming to get his woman," Veronica spoke up. "I don't know how he does it, but Joshua has a way of disarming me, and that causes all kinds of internal alarms to go off." Kha'ren said. Maranda covered Kha'ren's hand. "Kha'ren, I encourage you not to build walls around your heart to protect yourself. You miss so much that life has to offer. You miss out on building rich and loving relationships with people who really are worthy of it. You have so much more to give than you give yourself credit for. You, my friend, are worthy. You are worth the love that a good man wants to give you, but you will not see that until you see that you are worthy of the love that God wants to give you. You have to receive God's love. Allow him to mend all that is broken on the inside of you. It's at this time that you will be able to receive love from others." The three women sat in silence as they digested the words Maranda had spoken. Kha'ren shared so many things about her life with her friends, but there's one thing that she's never shared with anyone, outside of her family. She had thoughts of sharing, but she could never get the words out.

Chapter 13

Three weeks later, Zola was putting the finishing touches on the final piece of her showcase at the Crimson Art when her cell phone rang. On the other end was her sister Tori. "Hey sis. How's it going? Is everything ok? You don't usually call this early in the day." Zola answered, glancing at the clock on her table. There was silence on the other end. "Tori, are you there?" asked Zola. Sighing, Tori replied, "Hey, Zola." Zola noted a hint of sadness in her sister's voice. "Is everything alright, Tori? "No, my marriage is over. I just can't do this anymore." Tori responded to her sister, sobbing. "Wait. What do you mean when you say your marriage is over? Why? What happened, Tori?" Zola asked with concern. "We just want different things, Zola," Tori said. "Different things? You two have always been so in sync with each other. I can't imagine that you all would want different things now." Zola listened to her older sister sob over the phone. Torie had always had everything under control, even when she was young. She's always been so reticent. Sure, she showed emotions, but vulnerability is something very few people have seen from her, and even those moments are few and far between. "Zola, I want to have a baby." Tori blurted out between sniffles. "As you already know, Tim doesn't want children. I know having no children is what we agreed upon before we got married, but things have changed for me in the past two years." Tori explained. "All I know is that one day I began to think about my life as a mom. I began to wonder what kind of mom I would be and how wonderful it would be for Mom and Dad to have more grandchildren. I began to imagine Tim and me having a baby and how different our lives would be if we were parents. I kept it to myself for a solid year. Chalking it up to me getting older and perhaps being bored with life." Tori explained on the other line. Zola never met anyone more driven and career-focused than her sister. She had been declaring that she wasn't going to be a mom since they were younger. "They are just going to alter the plans I have." Tori often told her family. Their mom would often say, "Tori, you will not always feel like that, sweetie." Tori would respond with some quick quip about not sacrificing her dreams. After years of listening to Tori's rants about not having kids, her family accepted it. Their parents accepted that their grandchildren would not come from their firstborn. Now, here she is, singing a different tune. "What are you going to do now, sis?" a concerned Zola asked. "Well, I've hired a divorce attorney. Tim is going to move out of the house, and we're just going to come to an agreed settlement." She went on to say, "Zola, I'm exhausted. Things have been strained between us for over a year. About a month ago, he asked me where his wife had gone. I told him that I never left. He told me that we had an agreement and that we had made all these plans, and none of them included children. I agreed that we didn't have plans to be parents, but told him that the desire to be a mom grows stronger. He didn't want to hear that, and he got really angry. He was going on about how unfair I was being and how I'm destroying everything, all of our plans and goals. He was upset that we're no longer on the same page. Zola, he went on and on. Afterwards, we barely spoke. He had already started using a condom since I told him that I wanted children, except when we went to a dinner party at our friends Mark and Sariyah's house. We had such a great time. There was a lot of wine and good conversation. It felt like we were us again. That night when we got home, he made love to me for the first time in a long time without any protection. The next day, things went back to the same strained silence." "Wow, Tori! Why didn't you tell me before? I could have been there for you." Zola said. Tori sighed before responding. "Honestly, Zola, I was ashamed. I was so vocal about not having children, and I judged every woman who had them. I had some pretty stupid ideas about having children. I couldn't come to you after behaving the way that I have." Zola exhaled, and her heart filled with sympathy for her sister.

Never had she thought her sister would be saying any of this. She's always been too resolved and in control. This woman speaking to her now seems shaken and uncertain. "Tori, I am here for you. I'm so sorry that things have happened this way. Is there anything that you need?" Zola responded, trying to console her sister. She honestly didn't know what to say to make Torie's situation better. There are no magical words that could make things better. It seems her sister's marriage is over, and her ideals are shifting. "Zola, I'm pregnant," Tori said. Gasping, Zola said, "What? Pregnant? Are you sure, Tee?" "I'm sure; I've been to the doctor to confirm. We conceived the night of the dinner party. Zola, he is going to think that I've planned this, but I swear I did not. I was never on birth control, and we were just careful over the years. That night was different." Tori thought back to how they reconnected that night. Neither one of them was thinking about contraceptives nor conception windows. "Tori, what are you going to do? Have you told Mom and Dad? Are you going to talk to him? You'll have to tell him; he's going to be a father." Zola sputtered out a barrage of questions. "Even if he doesn't want to be one." She kept that thought to herself. Tori thought about the conversation that was ahead with dread. "Zola, I don't even know how to tell him this, and yes, Mom and Dad know. We're getting a divorce anyway. Can't I just not tell him, and we go our separate ways?" "Tori, that's nonsense and wrong. You know this. He deserves to know that he has fathered a child. Don't take his choices away from him," Zola replied. Once Tori told her parents the situation, they offered to get on the first plane to Chicago, but she told them that she'd come home at the end of the month. "Wouldn't this be helping him? I mean, he doesn't want to be a dad anyway. If he doesn't know, it won't be complicated for him." "Tori, you know that isn't right. You're trying to avoid the inevitable. I'm glad you told Mom and Dad. You know Daddy was going to come up there to try to convince you to come home, right?" Zola said to her sister. Tori sighed, "I know. How did my life blow up like this? I want my life back, and I want my marriage. Ever since the doctor confirmed my pregnancy, I've been feeling like I've been walking in a fog. I've picked up my phone to call Tim a number of times, but I chicken out. My mind keeps racing. On one hand, I'm ecstatic that Tim and I are going to be parents, but then I'm devastated about our situation. I really didn't imagine having a baby, even when I decided that I wanted to be a mom, but I never thought of things turning out this way. He's going to be so upset with me, and he's going to think I've tried to manipulate him." Tori said to her sister, crying. "Hold up. You could not foresee this situation happening. You made love with your husband, and the two of you conceived a child. This happens to couples every day. Things are complicated right now, but they won't always be that way." Zola said. She went on to tell Tori, "Tell Tim that you're pregnant, and whatever his response is, you, my sister, will be just fine. You're not alone in this." Wiping her cheeks, Tori thanked her sister for her support and told her she'd call her back because she was going into a meeting.

Zola picked up the phone to find Nick's name flashing across the screen when it started ringing. "Hello, handsome. How are you today?" a smiling Zola said to Nick. "Better now that I've heard your voice." Zola and Nick have had multiple dinners with their daughters since they first told them about their relationship. Nick's oldest daughter, Adrienne, has come around to accepting their relationship; Zola still believes that giving all of the girls time is the best way. "Listen, our children hadn't seen us with anyone other than their other parents. They need time to adjust, and we need to be patient with them. Zola cajoled Nick as he told of his fears that Adrienne would never accept their relationship in one of their late-night conversations. "You're making me blush, Nick." Zola giggled. "Well, that's exactly what I intended to do. I do love hearing your voice, though. I called to see if you were free on Friday night. I'm ready to have some alone time. I was thinking that I could take you out," Nick said. "I'd love to go out on Friday. You ran across my mind this morning. I was lamenting how it seems like forever since we were together without the girls. I mean, I know the times we've all spent together have been great, but I miss you." Zola replied. "I've been missing you, too, beautiful. What do you think about us staying together at my sister's inn overnight? Just one night? Nick asked. Zola hesitated before answering him. It would be lovely to spend that kind of time with Nick, but she wondered how she could pull it off with her schedule, and she had Sophie to consider. "Well, let's see how things go." Zola replied to Nick. "Nick, I would love for us to spend that kind of uninterrupted time together, but are you sure that you're ready? Nick sighed for a moment. He didn't expect that he would ever care for another woman in this way. He knew there was a possibility, but that largely depended on him. He chose not to date in the past years. "I have the girls to think about." He'd always tell his family members, friends, or pretty much anyone who asked him about that part of his life. Many have speculated why he wasn't dating, but truthfully, he chose to put his focus on his daughters. He promised Karmen that he'd take care of them and make sure they were healthy in every area of their lives. Zola's entrance into his life was unexpected. When he saw her in his bakery, she took his breath away. She's spectacular inside and out, and he knew he was falling in love with her. "Zola, I'm sure that I love being with you, and I really would love to have alone time with you." Nick responded to her question. "Ok, so what about the girls?" Zola questioned him again. "What do you think about telling them together? We gather them and tell them our plans," Nick answered. Zola pondered the idea for a beat. The girls now know about their relationship, and they've all been spending significant time together for the past few months. "I agree. I think we should do it together." Zola's nerves began to swell. She wasn't sure how either of their daughters would respond. She was particularly concerned about Sophie. "Mom, I like Mr. Nick. I can tell he really likes you and you like him." Sophie said to her mom right after the first dinner with Nick's daughters. With teary eyes, Sophie lamented, "I just always hoped that you and Daddy would work things out and get back together so that we can be a family again." "Oh, baby, don't cry. I know that this is something that you've wanted for a long time, but your dad and I are better off as co-parents. You're our baby girl, and we'll always be a family, Sophie. Know that no matter who your father and I date, you'll always be our first priority." Zola consoled her daughter. Zola thought back to that night and remembered that she wanted to make sure that Sophie knew that her feelings were valid and that it was all right to feel the way she felt. Because her mother had done it for her and Tori, she wanted Sophie to have a voice in their little family. "Nick, I'm excited about us being together this weekend, but I'll admit, I'm nervous about how my daughter is going to feel. Although Jonathan and I divorced years ago, she has always wanted us to reconcile and be a family again. I've not dated since the divorce, so she had no reason to believe that this would not happen. Our dating is somewhat of an eye-opener for her. I want to help her process and accept that her dad and I will not be reconciling." Sighing, Nick responded, "Zola, I absolutely understand. I've had a similar conversation with my girls. They imagined that one day I'd date again, but they assumed they'd all be adults by the time it happened. They told me that they weren't ready for my time to be divided. Like you, I feel my girls' concerns and feelings are valid. I've been thinking about that conversation. What should I do? I break up with you because my girls don't want to share me, only to have them go off into adulthood. Yes, I would have honored what they wanted, denying my desires. I'd also be lonely and kicking myself. Since Karmen died, Zola, I've devoted myself to being there for my daughters. I never thought about or even desired a relationship. Our family was broken, and my girls and I were heartbroken. We'd become closer through our common suffrage. We built a cocoon around ourselves with our grief. That wasn't healthy for them, nor was it healthy for me. We began seeing a grief counselor, and he helped me to realize that we weren't grieving; we were stuck in the moment of Karmen's death. We've been working it out since." As Zola listened to Nick open up like this, it made her cry. "My God, Nick. Thank you for sharing this with me," she replied. She didn't know what else to say. "Zola, you have been an unexpected blessing in my life. When I saw you in the bakery, I thought, "Wow, now that's a beautiful woman," but I didn't expect to see you again, but I hoped. When Alex brought your flyer to me and asked me if she could attend your class, it was a definite yes. That meant that I'd get to see you again. I'm so glad I said yes." Zola blushed in response. Nick had a way of doing that.

Chapter 14

Since meeting her birth family months ago, she's had multiple Sunday dinners and several impromptu evening barbecues in the backyard with them. Veronica enjoyed this time with her new family. "Are they really my new family since they've always been family?" She pondered how to refer to them. She loved the laughter and the closeness that they all seemed to share. She had that too with the family she grew up with, but she couldn't help but be grateful that they went out of their way to include her. "Veronica, you are welcome here any time. You are our child, and I want you to feel like you belong here as well. Her birth father said to her while they sat on the back patio. Ronnie didn't know what to say. He misread her hesitation and amended, "Of course, we could never replace the family you already have. We just want you to know that we carry you in our hearts, and we want you to feel like you belong." She listened to her dad talk with uncertainty. "Thank you all for going out of your way to make me feel comfortable and loved." Veronica replied, trying to ease the tension of his remarks. He smiled suddenly and said, "Each month, we take a kid out to dinner or whatever they have time to do and spend time with them. Do you think we could add you to the rotation?" her father said. She wrinkled her nose and asked, "You take intentional time to spend each month?" He nodded yes to her and told her, "We decided to do that when they were both in high school. They were getting older and were soon going to live their own lives. We just wanted to spend as much time with them as we could. Years later, they've come to expect it and throw a fit if we have to miss one of their months." Veronica asked, "Well, wouldn't I take off their months? I wouldn't want to stir up any trouble." Her dad chuckled, "It was your sister's idea, and your brother agreed. They have known about you ever since they were little. We didn't keep you a secret from them, Veronica. They always believed they'd meet you one day, and your mother and I did too." A few weeks later, Veronica found herself sitting at the dinner table with her parents. She opted to cook dinner with them. "It's simple, I know, but it's the little things that I've thought about over the years," she explained to her friends on a group chat. The evening was light and fun, but Veronica felt like a weight was on her chest. Although she loved being around them, it was a reminder of what she missed out on. She felt guilty about feeling this way because she grew up in a wonderful family. "Ronnie, you do know you are entitled to your feelings and questions, right?" Kha'ren asked her. "There are no blueprints for this situation. Your feelings and emotions are valid in this situation. You should be able to ask these people any question you want, even if it makes them uncomfortable." Kha'ren attempted to encourage her friend. Veronica was on needles and pins, trying to figure out how to navigate through both families. She took two bites of her dessert and put the fork down. "Why didn't you look for me? Why didn't you come get me?" Veronica asked her birth parents. Her mother's eyes softened and began to well with tears. "Oh, baby, I'm so sorry. We should have pushed the issue when they told us that your adoption records were sealed. We got married after college, and I went to my mom and told her that we wanted to find you. She shut me down and convinced me that you were happy and our presence in your life would just complicate things." Her father reached to grab her hand from across the table. "Veronica, we know that there is no amount of explaining that could make up for the years that we weren't around. I'm so sorry, baby. If you would give us a chance, we aren't trying to replace the family you grew up in. As a matter of fact, we owe so much thanks to your adoptive parents. They are the reason you are the woman you have grown to be." Veronica replied, with tears in her eyes, "That's just it. It seems that from the moment I found out that I was adopted, I didn't feel whole. I've always felt like something was missing. I had trouble staying in long-term relationships. Actually, outside of my three closest girlfriends and family, I haven't created quality relationships. I never wanted anyone to get close enough because I was afraid that they'd leave me." She went on to explain to her parents that she prayed every day when she was a kid that they'd show up and come get her and take her home. "I used to wonder about you two all the time. I never imagined that you were together all these years. I always wondered if I had siblings and if I'd ever get a chance to meet them." After she finished talking, the tears began to flow. Her mother got up and wrapped her arms around Veronica, and her father wrapped his arms around both of them. "Veronica, our hearts ached for you. We should have fought harder to search for you. We're so very sorry for it all, sweetheart. The three of them sat like this for a while. Veronica said, "I am in therapy. I can communicate this to you because of that. I was a real mess. I have some real abandonment issues, but I'm working on them." Her mom said, kissing her forehead, "It breaks my heart to know that we are the source of your pain. We are so sorry. Please forgive us." She breathed in deeply and realized that this was really what she wanted. She needed answers from her birth parents. She needed to know her history, to know the other side of her that was a mystery. "Ronnie, you have to find out everything. This is a part of your journey to healing and wholeness." Maranda said to her at one of their dinners. She knew that Maranda was right, which is why she was open to building a relationship with her birth parents.

"Mrs. Collier?" A nurse called out to an anxious Maranda in the waiting room. Her husband, Mike, joined her for this appointment. He was so supportive during the time of waiting. The day she told him about the oncology report, he wrapped her in his arms, whispering, "My love, don't worry. We've already declared your healing. God is faithful to us." She wept, burying her face in his shoulder. She was so grateful to the community of people around her who showed her little family so much love. Maranda thought back to the calls from her best friends. Most of all, she was thankful for the man who sat beside her, holding her hand. He was with her when she went in for more tests, and she could not imagine being without him for the results. Maranda's mind drifted as she walked hand in hand with her husband. "Thank you both for coming in today. I know that this has been a stressful time for you. With that, let me talk to you about the results of your scans," Dr. Lewis said. Mike squeezed Maranda's hand tighter. Dr. Lewis explained to them both that she was fine. Because her scans came back abnormal, additional testing was needed to clarify what they had seen through the image. Mike and Maranda both sighed in relief. Mike hugged his wife and whispered in her ear, "I told you God was a healer." This time, when Miranda shed tears, they were tears of joy. Maranda was filled with so much joy and thanksgiving. She said to her husband, around sobs, "He's so faithful to our little family." That evening, they called all the important people in their lives and told them the good news. The weeks that followed were simply bliss for Maranda. She felt a sense of normalcy. She went back to teaching when her maternity leave was over. The hospital called her to lead more groups for patients dealing with cancer. She worked in the church alongside her husband. For the first time, Maranda felt like her life was exactly how God intended for it to be.

Zola's mother had finally begun taking classes for her accounting degree. Achieving this goal at her age was challenging, but this is something she's been thinking about since her children were little. Lila felt that, finally, this was her time to achieve this goal. She wasn't sure what she was going to do with it besides helping the few clients that she has, but this was something she was doing for herself. She was extremely disappointed when her husband wouldn't support her going to school. Lila thought back to all those years that she supported Richard. She gave up her goals to be his wife and the mother of his children. What angered her for a long time after they were married was that Richard did not stop her. He let her walk away from her aspiration so that he could fulfill his. It took her a while to get past that. She made up her mind years ago that there would be a time one day when she would get her college degree. She knew that her husband had adopted outdated ideas about the role of women and men in society, but she expected him to be supportive just as she had been supportive of him all of these years. It was devastating for her when he told her that she could not pursue her dream. Lila realized that when she gave up on her dream to be his wife and mother to their children, she consented to his self-centered mentality. There wasn't a lot that she would have changed about their lives together, but following her dreams would be one of them. She was willing to stand her ground, and Richard was just going to have to come around eventually. She didn't like any conflict between them, but she couldn't budge. Lila wasn't sure what made Richard's heart change towards the situation, but with his apology and acknowledgment that his mindset had not promoted mutual love and respect in their marriage, she loved him even more than she thought she ever could. "All these years of marriage, and I'm still learning about you, my love." Richard said as he took her in his arms. She wrapped her arms around his waist contentedly. "Don't they say it takes a lifetime to get to know someone?" she asked. "Well, I'm here for it," Richard replied, kissing her forehead. Her phone began to ring. She dug in her pocket, wondering who could be calling her at this time when she only had a few minutes between her classes. "Mama, can I come home early? "A sobbing Tori," said on the other end. Lila listened to her eldest daughter sobbing on the phone about how her life was falling apart. After years of declaring that she didn't want any children, Tori is pregnant with her fourth grandchild. "You won't always feel this way, my love." Lila said to twenty-year-old Tori, who was home on break from college. Her daughter had always been an overachiever, and she had made all of these plans to have what she called "the perfect life." She graduated from high school and undergrad early. After getting her bachelor's degree, she went on to obtain her MBA. Lila always wondered why Tori ran towards the future at full speed. She'd always encouraged both of her daughters to stop and enjoy life. She didn't have to twist Zola's arm to live her life, but she felt as if she was still working on Tori. She knew that her daughter's plans would change one day. She just hoped that her marriage would survive Tori's shift. "I can't stay in this city another day. I called Tim and told him that I wanted him to meet me at the house so that we could talk. When he got there, I told him that I was pregnant. Mama, just as I suspected, he accused me of manipulating him into being a father." Lila gasped. Tori went on to explain to her mom that she reminded her husband that they both had a lot to drink that night. "I told him that I knew he didn't want to be a father, and he doesn't have to be a part of the baby's life. Zola told me that he deserved to know, no matter how he felt about being a father, and she was right," Tori said to her mother. "Baby, are you ok? You know you can come home anytime. If you want to get on a plane and fly home tonight, you can," Lila said, soothing her daughter. "I know, Mama. I'll be home in a couple of days. I just took a leave from the firm." She went on to tell her mom that she needed some time and spoke with the senior partner about working remotely and flying in a few times a month. He reluctantly agreed, but Tori didn't care what his response was. For the first time, she was realizing that she came before her career. "Ma, Tim asked me how I could put him in this situation. When he said that, I got so angry. He was acting as I set him up." Tori explained to Lila. He said, "What kind of man would I be if I had a child that I knew was out there but didn't want anything to do with? I feel like you're forcing me into a situation that I don't want to be in." With tears falling down her cheek, Tori told him to leave. He stormed out of the house. "That was four days ago. I have been feeling so numb. I feel so happy to become a mom, but I'm so depressed that my marriage is over. I can't believe this is my life." Tori said to her mother, starting to cry again. Lila said to her daughter, "Baby, you know that God doesn't make any mistakes. If this wasn't God's plan for you, your heart would have never changed towards being a mother. God is going to bring you and Tim through this. I don't think that this is going to destroy your marriage. I am believing for total restoration in your marriage." Lila said. "Ma, we've both been talking to divorce attorneys. I don't see how this can be fixed between us. He doesn't want the child that I'm carrying. He feels like I tricked him. He hates me." Tori replied to her mother. She explained that Tim texted her the day before, saying to her, "You got what you wanted. You wanted the baby, and now you don't want me. You didn't talk about working things out. You got a lawyer instead." She told Lila that for six months, he had been cold to her. They barely spoke to each other. When she tried to talk to him, he'd shut her down. She said that it was as if they had become strangers to each other. They agreed to go to the dinner party because Mark and Sariyah were their closest friends, and they weren't ready to share what's been happening in their marriage. "Tori, God has fixed more broken circumstances. Trust me. We'll all be waiting on you to get here." Tori's mother encouraged.

Kha'ren sat in her office thinking about the time she and Joshua had spent together. She had fallen for him, and this both scared and elated her. She had never met a man like him before.

Joshua's the first man with whom she could be herself. Not a version of herself he might like, but Kha'ren. "Kha'ren, I want you to know that I'm in love with you. I see you, all of you. I love everything about you. I love your highs and your lows. I'm here for every mood swing, every smile, and every tear. I want it all." When Joshua had told her these things a couple of weeks ago, she was speechless. She never had anyone love her this way. Caught up in her thoughts, she missed the look that he gave her when he assumed she wasn't going to respond or at least acknowledge that there was some sort of reciprocity between them. He began to turn away; she touched his face with her hand to turn him to face her. "Joshua, I'm in love with you. I've wanted to tell you, but I was so afraid that you didn't feel the same way. I know I was in my head after you told me, but." He didn't let her finish her statement; he gathered her up in his arms and kissed her. "How did I become so blessed?" he said as she lay her head on his chest in their embrace. She thought to herself, "Blessed? How could he feel blessed? Doesn't he know that I'm damaged goods?"

Kha'ren began to tear up at the thought of the moment they shared. She did not feel like she deserved this man. Her thoughts were filled with doubt. Kha'ren truly believed that if Joshua knew everything about her, then he would be repulsed. Her cellphone rang, filling her office with Corrine Bailey Rae's Put Your Records On, startling her a little. "Hey girl! What's going on? How's your day?" Veronica tripped off rapid questions. Kha'ren rolled her eyes up in her head. "Why do you do that? A chuckling Veronica said, "Do what?" Kha'ren sighed, "You know what I'm talking about. You always have all these questions right after you say hi. You never give me a chance to even say hi." "Does that bother you?" Veronica asked her. "Veronica, you know that bothers me." Kha'ren said with an elevated voice. Veronica laughed aloud. "That's why I do it."

"What do you want?" Kha'ren asked Veronica. "I'm just calling to check on you. You've been on my mind this week." Veronica answered in a concerned tone. I've been ok these days. I've been busy with work, and there's been a lot on my mind. "So, what's on your mind?" Veronica asked. "I don't feel like talking about it." Kha'ren responded. "Are we really going to do this again? You know you're going to end up telling me eventually. Just save both of us the breath and tell me what's going on." "Whatever. Ok. I've just been thinking about Joshua this week. We've confessed our feelings for each other." Veronica screamed over the phone. "Oh my God, Kha'ren! I'm so happy for you." "I mean, I'm happy with Joshua, but I don't know how long this is going to last with him." Kha'ren said, sounding melancholy. "What do you mean? Didn't you guys confess your feelings for each other? That doesn't sound like you guys will be splitting any time soon." Kha'ren reminded Veronica about her past. She attempted to convince her friend that it would never work out between him and her. "Listen, I'm going to say this because you are one of my best friends and I love you. I need you to deal with your past and get some help because you are right. You and Joshua will split up if you keep going on like this. You are going to push him away," Veronica said. "Help? What do you mean, "get help"? I don't need any help, Veronica, and you know it." Kha'ren said in an angered tone. "Girl, please. You have been walking around with your trauma for nearly two decades. Aren't you tired? Listen, you know I know about walking with demons that you don't want to deal with. It was your words that helped me deal with my messed-up behavior. Now I just want to do the same for you," Veronica replied. Sighing, Kha'ren said, "I'm fine, Ronnie." "How could you say that, Kha'ren?" her friend replied in an incredulous tone. "You don't get close to anyone. Just how many people have you spoken to about what happened to you besides me?" Veronica said. "You know I haven't told anyone, but you and I trust that you'll keep this to yourself." Kha'ren replied. "Do you know how difficult it has been over the years watching you struggle with creating lasting relationships with people outside of us? You walk around like you are fine, but you are not. Until you face this and get healing from what happened to you, your relationship with Joshua will eventually fail." Raising her voice, Kha'ren said, "Veronica, how could you say that?" "I can say this because I've watched you push a few good men away over the years. You have done what I've done throughout the years. You wear this trauma of your past like it's a badge, and you use it as a license to not be happy. You deserve better for yourself, Kha'ren." Veronica said with resolve. "Kha'ren could not say anything to her friend's response. Veronica was right about everything. Tears began rolling down her cheeks as her resolve not to deal with her past came to an end. She had wanted to say what happened, to get it out, but she had felt so much shame, and she was afraid that others would feel the same way. "Kha'ren?" she prodded, "Kha'ren?" "I'm so tired, Ronnie," a sobbing Kha'ren replied. "I know, love. Would you consider telling Randi and Zee tonight at dinner? You need the support of all who love you right now. That includes Joshua." Kha'ren agreed to tell Maranda and Zola about her past.

That night, the girls came together at Maranda's house for their monthly dinner. They loved going to Maranda's house; she always made home-cooked meals when it was her turn to host. She'd try new recipes out on them so that she could tweak them for the cookbook that she was writing. "Girls, I have missed you all," Zola said as they sat in Maranda's living room with cocktails in hand. "Yes, I know what you mean. So much has been going on since we last got together. It's been a difficult couple of months." Maranda replied. Veronica spoke up, "Yes, Lord. It's been an emotional rollercoaster for me, y'all. I am long overdue for one of these nights." They usually come together once a month, but last month their schedules would not allow it. Maranda had her cancer scare, Veronica was working things out with her birth parents, Kha'ren had a budding romance, and Zola had her art show at Crimson Art Gallery. The women led busy lives, but they didn't let too much time go by before getting together. "I missed you ladies, too," Kha'ren said. Zola turned to Kha'ren with a sneaky smile. "Oh, we know why you were busy, Ren. Did you see Kha'ren and Joshua at my exhibition? They were inseparable." All the girls laughed. "Please," Kha'ren said, rolling her eyes. "We saw you and your guy. You guys look great together. I'm so happy for you two." Maranda chimed in. Kha'ren smiled, thinking about that night. She had a great time with Joshua. After the exhibition, he had the executive chef from *The Sauvage* make them a private dinner. It turned out that they were friends. Joshua made the night so special for her. Her birthday was the following day. She was never big on birthdays, and in the beginning of their conversations, they mentioned their birthdays. She purposefully didn't mention it again. Her mother passed away on her thirteenth birthday. She didn't tell him, of course. He remembered the date and made plans to make her feel special. He accomplished just that. No man has ever gone out of his way to make her feel so loved and cared for. "Um, what's up with that dreamy look in your eye?" Zola asked her. "I was just thinking about the night of your exhibition. You all know I don't celebrate my birthday, and I told him only once what day my birthday fell on. He remembered and had the executive chef from *The Sauvage* cook a magnificent meal for us. Joshua pampered me the entire weekend." Kha'ren said. "We know," Maranda said. "He came to us and asked us what would make you feel special on your birthday. He kind of guessed that you didn't celebrate your birthday because you never mentioned it as the time drew closer to the date." Veronica said. "We did not tell him why you didn't celebrate, of course, but we didn't confirm his suspicions about you not celebrating your birthday. We left the "why" up to you to explain," Zola also said. With her eyebrows reaching the top of her forehead, Kha'ren said, "So you guys were behind this?" Her friends said sheepishly and with uncertainty about her response, "Yes." Kha'ren looked down at her fidgety hands with tears falling and said, "Thank you." They engulfed her with a hug. "You deserve it, sweetheart," Zola said. Sighing, Kha'ren said, "I don't know what I'd do without you girls. I love you so much. You're not only my best friends but also my sisters." Maranda said to her, "Look at how God does things. You grew up an only child, and he gave you the sisters that you never knew you wanted." "No, Maranda. You all are the sisters that I didn't know that I needed." Kha'ren said through her tears. She felt so safe in her friends' embrace.

The night was filled with laughter. The ladies had truly missed each other. They took the time to update each other on their lives. "Nick and I are going away next weekend. I'm so nervous that I don't know what to do," Zola mentioned. "Ok now, Zee!" Veronica exclaimed. "Why are you nervous?" Maranda asked. "Are you kidding me? I've not been in a relationship in five years. I'm so out of the game that I don't know what to do. I've loved only one man for most of my adult life. Now Nick has gone and captured my heart." Zola replied. "And just what is wrong with that?" Veronica said to Zola, giving her a pensive look. "Nothing, I guess. I do love him; I have to admit. I'm just scared of things not working out." She went on to tell them that Nick made her want to be better in every area of her life. From the business side of life to parenting. He had influenced her. He'd help her love herself in areas that she didn't know she needed loving. She told them that she had a conversation with Nick about abstaining from sex. She explained that she loved him, but if things were going to work out between them, she didn't want it complicated by getting physical. She made that mistake with Jonathan when she was younger, and she wanted things to be different with Nicolas. Maranda spoke up, "Zee, I think that is an amazing decision that you've made. I can't tell you how many couples Mike and I have counseled about this very subject. Abstaining gives you an opportunity to really build a friendship. Your judgment isn't clouded by emotions from the physical attachment." "So, what was Nick's response?" Veronica asked. "Well, he admitted that he hadn't been with a woman since his late wife, so he was fine with it. After talking extensively about it, we agreed that we were both extremely attracted to each other, but we were more excited about our relationship being built on the right things. We've both made mistakes in the past and we don't want to make them with each other." Zola explained. The women nodded in agreement. She went on the say, "I was nervous about telling Sophie about me going away with him for the weekend. I feared her reaction, but she surprised me. "Ma, I know that it probably isn't in the cards for you and Daddy to get back together. I let that go a long time ago. I like Nick, and I like that he's so into you." Sophie said the night of their discussion. "Do y'all know Nick went to his daughters and to mine to talk to them about the weekend before he brought it up to me?" Zola exclaimed. Maranda said, "Zola, why are you shocked that he would do that? He is in love with you, Zola. From what you told us, he's not dated since his wife died. Which means you're the first and only woman that he has brought around his daughters." "Yeah, Zee. He's got it bad." Kha'ren said from across the table. "I'm just so happy," Zola told them. "Well, make sure you stay that way, Zee. You deserve it." Veronica said, covering Zola's hand with hers. "Ok, enough about me. Ronnie, have you been dating? You haven't mentioned anyone recently," Zola said. "That is because I have been balancing two families, healing from my past through therapy, and working." Veronica replied.

Veronica explained that she didn't want her adoptive parents to feel like they no longer matter now that her birth family is in her life. She told them that she saw fear in her birth mother's eyes when she told her parents that she was going to meet them for the first time. Since then, her mom hadn't asked anything about them. "I think she's fearful that I'll walk away from them." Veronica said. She explained to them how she had gone out of her way to spend time with her mother. "Ronnie, though she is happy for you, she's probably feared these days. I'm sure both your parents knew that one day you would ask about your birth parents. As a parent, I cannot imagine sharing my little one with anyone else." Maranda said to her. "My dad explained that they were trying to give me space to process meeting my birth family. He said that when I was ready to talk to them about my birth parents, they would be there. "See, look at that. Your parents are in your corner." Maranda said to Veronica. Veronica knew that her adoptive parents were there, but she didn't want them to believe she was replacing them. "I feel incredibly blessed to have been adopted by two of the most wonderful people that God has placed on this earth, but I'm equally as pleased with my birth parents." Veronica said, feeling torn. "Maybe, Veronica, you should stop feeling like you must choose between the two families. You are a part of both groups. How blessed are you?" said Zola. "Also, Veronica, how many people find their birth parents? How many people find them married?" added Kha'ren. "I know I'm blessed, guys; I just don't want my adoptive family to get hurt behind my desire to know my birth parents." Veronica said with a sigh. Zola explained to Veronica that she has every right to want to get to know her birth parents. Learning who they are is a part of her journey of healing. Veronica had always felt that a piece of herself was missing. Her habits, triggers, and responses—she wondered if they were similar to either of her birth parents. She wondered who she looked like or even if she had siblings. Now that she had those answers, she, along with the help of her therapist, began to heal the wounds. Veronica had been on the road to self-discovery, and there are things she absolutely loved, but then there are things she abhorred. She knew now that she had the power to change. She was no longer stuck in a mindset and a disposition. "You know, I could not fully enjoy life and all that it had to give me because I didn't see myself as whole, because I didn't know where I came from. It's as if I had a mark on me that everyone could see. In reality, it was how I viewed myself," Veronica said. The women sat in silence for a few minutes, eating their dinner. Kha'ren broke the silence, "I was gang raped in college." The heads of her three friends snapped in that direction. Veronica got up from her seat and walked around the table to sit by Kha'ren. "Take a breath and tell them." Veronica said in a soothing tone. Zola and Maranda both looked at Veronica. "You knew about this and didn't tell us, Ronnie?" Zola said. Veronica replied, "Zee, I only found out by accident, and this was not my story to tell, sweetie." Zola looked at Kha'ren and reassured her that if she wanted to tell her story, they would be there to listen. With a deep breath and Veronica's hand covering hers, Kha'ren told her story to her three closest friends. "I was a sophomore in college. My roommate and I had become pretty close. I was studying for my finals when she invited me to come out to this party. I initially told her no and that I had to study, but she kept on insisting that we would have a great time. She suggested that I needed a break from all the studying. I was tired of studying, so I said I'd go for a little while, but I'd have to get back to the dorm. When we got to the house, there were quite a few girls there. The fraternity was having a more intimate party. My roommate left to go upstairs with one of the guys at the party. I sat in the corner nursing my rum and Coke. A guy came up to me, Bradley Corson. We had a little small talk. He seemed to be a nice guy. I remember him making me laugh that night. We talked for what seemed like hours, and then two of his friends joined us on the porch. They mainly spoke to Bradley, but two more guys entered the porch. There were too many guys on the porch for my liking, so I excused myself to the restroom. When I got out of the restroom, Bradley met me in the hallway with my drink and suggested that we go somewhere quieter. I agreed, thinking we were just going to finish our conversation. We continued talking until I got really sleepy. I remember thinking that I should go home because I was feeling so tired. I was so drowsy that I couldn't move. I fell asleep. When I awoke, a guy, not Bradley, was pulling my panties down. I fought to stop him, but I was so drowsy. I don't know how many were in the room; I lost consciousness. I woke up naked in bed, obviously having passed out the night before. I could not remember how I got there. I must have been sleeping for a long time because it was the middle of the afternoon. I found my clothes and quickly put them on. I went to my dorm room and found my roommate there. She questioned where I was all night and all morning. I told her that I woke up naked in a room in a house. I couldn't remember anything. I'll never forget the pale look on her face. I asked her if she knew what happened, and she told me that she didn't. She told me that the guy she was with told her that I had been escorted home. She said she called my cell phone multiple times. I told her that I think that I had been raped. She was frantically crying by this time and asked me to go to the hospital with her and to call the police. I told her that I wanted to take a shower first, but she advised me that showering wasn't a good idea. She borrowed a car from a friend and drove me to the emergency room. I told them that I believe I had been drugged and raped at a party the night before. They took me back and did a rape kit. I was there for five hours. They took pictures of me and took swabs of everything. I felt so embarrassed and exposed. The nurse asked me if I wanted to call the police, and I told her no. My roommate tried for hours to get me to go to the police, but I didn't want to. That night I had the most terrible dream about the events, though I don't know if what I dreamed about were actual events. I woke up screaming and crying. My roommate did not ask me again if I wanted to go to the police because she called 911. I was so hysterical. She crawled into the bed with me to calm me down. The police finally arrived, and she told them what had happened. I could not speak, so she did the talking for me. She told the police that there was a rape kit at the hospital. She told the police which fraternity house we were at the night before. She gave them the names of all the people she knew at the party in hopes that someone had seen something. The police told me that I would eventually have to come to the station to make a statement. I told them that I couldn't remember anything. I told them that I know that I was sexually assaulted because I was a virgin. The nurse who examined me explained to the detectives that I had a lot of bruising down there. There was more than one DNA specimen that they found. Soon, what happened to me got all around campus. Random people were walking up to me asking me about that night. Some were calling me a liar and a whore. There were some girls in my hallway who said that I was asking for it. There were a lot of people who supported me. One night, I was lying in bed, and I heard a knock at my door. When I opened the door, Bradley was standing on the other side. I tried to close the door, but he blocked it with his foot. He said all he wanted to do was talk to me. I told him that if he didn't leave, I was going to scream. He let the door close and said that he had nothing to do with what happened to me. I told him that he was the one I was talking to when I fell unconscious. I told him that if he didn't leave, I was going to call the campus police. He eventually left, but three days later, I received a message in my inbox from Bradley. In the email, he explained his side of the story that night. He said that I had suddenly fallen asleep that night, lying by him on the bed. He said we were watching a movie and that one minute I was laughing and the next I was sound asleep. He said he will regret leaving me there for the rest of his life. He explained that he tried to wake me up, but I was out cold. He said he told Stephon, the guy whose room it was, that I was asleep and that he was going home. They apparently told my roommate that Bradley had escorted me home, so she left without me. He told me that he didn't know specifically who assaulted me, but he told the police the names of everyone in the house that night. His and my roommate's stories coincided with each other. The police investigated Bradley, but his roommate was up and in the room when he got back to his dorm. We exchanged numbers that night, and the records from his phone showed that he called me three times that night. He was cleared. This nightmare went on for months. I began receiving threatening phone calls to my cell phone and room phone. I didn't go anywhere alone at night. Eventually, three guys, Matthew Ryson, Arthur Wise, and Sean Wilson, were arrested and convicted of rape. This was all over the news and a counselor at school encouraged me to leave and transfer to another university, but I didn't want to leave. I had been dreaming about attending this college my entire life. My mom graduated from this school. I tried to establish some sort of normalcy in my life until I discovered that I was pregnant. I could not believe that I was pregnant and carrying the child of one man who raped me. What was I to do? I know I could not tell my dad and risk disappointing him. Turns out that Bradley really was a decent guy. He stood by my side despite the backlash that he received. He took me to the abortion clinic. I was so ashamed, but how could I bring a child into the world who had been conceived in such a violent way? After that, I could not stay in that school. I withdrew and went home for the remainder of the year. The following school year, in the second semester, I enrolled in the school that we all graduated from."

By the time Kha'ren had finished telling her truth, her three friends were sobbing. They enveloped her in a protected embrace. "We got you, sweetheart," Zola said, sniffing. Kha'ren felt lighter after telling her story. She hadn't uttered a word of this story to anyone outside her father since that year. Maranda asked, "Veronica, how did you know?" "She left her journal open, and when I went over there, I only read where she said she was raped. I have tried for the longest time to get her to tell you guys. She refused," Veronica replied. "I didn't want to say anything to anyone because I wanted to put it behind me. I also didn't want to get judged for anything." Kha'ren said. "Honey, why would we judge you? We love you." Maranda said. "Maranda, you don't believe in abortions. I didn't want you guys to look at me differently." Kha'ren responded, looking down. "Kha'ren, we would never look down on you, nor would any of us judge you. You are our sister," Zola said. "This thing has been my constant companion for almost twenty years. It has crippled me emotionally. I can't live like this anymore. I love Joshua, but I was going to call it off because he was getting too close." Kha'ren said. "Please don't do that. He is good for you. Why do you think you are in this place now? He makes you want to be healthy enough to give your relationship a real chance to work. There is nothing like the love of a good man, Kha'ren." Veronica said, placing a hand on Kha'ren's back. "We'll get you some help. Your healing started the moment you told us your story." Maranda told her. A few days later, Kha'ren called Joshua over to tell him what had happened to her. He spent the night holding her and ensuring that she was safe with him. She was grateful that he didn't judge her. "Kha'ren, why would I ever judge you? What happened to you was not your fault, baby. You were the victim. I'm here for you every step of the way." Joshua said to her. For the first time since the incident, she felt like she could breathe.

Zola's alarm went off at 6:30 am. She had a long day ahead of her. She and Nick were going out of town this weekend. He made sure the timing was right because the girls are on their winter break. When they told the girls one night at dinner, they confirmed they were fine with the idea of them going away. "Isn't this what couples do?" Alex asked with curiosity. "Yes, it is, baby, but we still wanted to run it by you girls," Nick replied to his youngest daughter. Suddenly, Alex's face lit up. "What if Sophie stayed the weekend here with me and April?" Nick's face frowned. "Alex, why do you assume you're staying here while I'm away?" Crestfallen, Alex said, "Come on, Daddy. We are in high school, and April is practically out of school now." Sophie chimed in with a pleading look at her mom. "Mom, please, can I stay over here that weekend? We promise we won't get in trouble." Nick replied to both girls, "It really depends on your sister April. You don't know what kind of plans she has." Both girls turned to April, pleading with her to stay with them that weekend. April rolled her eyes and reluctantly agreed. "You two better not get into anything that weekend. You'd better stay chilled." They both promised.

Zola was so excited about the fact that their families coming together for dinners or other activities became the norm. When either one of the girls has an extracurricular activity, Sophie or either of Nick's daughters expects Nick or Zola to show up. They all have truly come a long way. Though Nick and Zola didn't share a residence, they, along with their children, had created a rhythm. It's been almost a year since she and Nick became a couple, and for the most part, they have taken things very slowly because of their children. For that, each milestone for them is special. She recalled when they met each other's parents for the first time. Zola met Nick's parents a month after they made it official. Not that Nick was ready, but Alex had told her Nonna all about her dad's new girlfriend. His mom insisted that they meet Zola immediately. "You don't want me to meet your parents? Zola asked him. "Darling, of course I want you to meet my parents, but I didn't expect to introduce you guys so soon. My mom is insistent because Alex has been telling her about us. Nick's parents invited her to their biweekly Sunday. At this dinner, Nick, his siblings, and the grandchildren were required to attend. She noticed right off that his family, from his parents to his siblings, were all protective of Nick. His mother and his sisters fussed over him. When they arrived at his parents' home, everyone was already there. "Here we go," Nick said with an exasperated sigh. "What? What's wrong?" Zola asked, looking over to Nick. "Everyone's already here. This never happens on Sundays. My mom is always fussing because my sisters and their families are never on time." Nick got out of the car and opened Zola's side. They walked hand in hand up the step, and he opened the door. As she walked through the door, a delicious scent hit her senses. "Oh my." Zola said as he took her coat. "My mom is a fantastic cook," Nick told her. Before they could get to the foyer, a familiar face smiled at Zola. "Zola, nice to see you again." Adrianna, Nick's sister, said. She grabbed Zola into a warm embrace. As she was expelled from Adrianna's embrace, the rest of Nick's family came around the corner speaking all at once. "Mom and Dad, this is Zola James. Zola, these are my parents, Elena and Nicholai Gallo," Nick said. Despite her nerves, Zola smiled warmly and extended her hand. Elena looked at Zola and hugged her. "No handshakes for the woman who brought life back to my son." She whispered this in Zola's ear as they embraced. Nick's father hugged Zola as well, kissing her on both cheeks. She was embraced by his other sisters and their spouses as well. At dinner, Nick's family hit her with a barrage of questions about her life, her business, and Sophie. Alex inquired about Sophie's whereabouts, and Zola reminded her that she was with her father. "That's right. I forgot. I wish she were here. "Nonna, you would love Sophie; she is my best friend," Alex said to her grandmother. "Aww, I'm sure I will, my love. I cannot wait to meet her." "So, Zola, Nick tells us that you are a professional artist as well." Nicholai asked her. "Yes, sir, I have an exhibition coming up in a few months. My pieces will be on display at Crimson Art Gallery. "Impressive. Do you sell many pieces?" Adrianna asked her. "I've sold quite a few over the years," Zola responded. "So, could I see your portfolio? Marco and I were just talking about purchasing more art for the B&B," she said. "Absolutely, let's exchange information, and I'll get in touch this week." Zola said to Adrianna. Zola could see Nick smiling in her periphery. He squeezed her hand under the table. She thought the rest of the evening went lovely. She adored Nick's family. They were such a close-knit family. There was so much love and care among them. While assisting the women in cleaning the dishes, Elena began to talk to her about Nick. "Zola, I want to thank you for loving my son. Since Karmen died, my son shut down. He didn't do anything pleasurable. He only looked after the girls and ran the bakery. I told him that I wanted him to live his life, and he wasn't interested in that. My response to him was that when the right woman comes along, she will pull him right out of his low place. Now, here you are, my dear." Nick's youngest sister, Caterina, spoke up in agreement. "My brother became a shell of who he used to be. He put all of his energy into the girls. I told him that there is more to life than raising the girls and his career. He told me that he simply wasn't ready. I've been worried about him these years. My brother is different now. He smiles a lot. Nick's sisters and mother were all in agreement that Zola and Nick's connection was great for Nick. They asked Zola about the family she grew up in and about her life growing up. For the next hour and a half, the women talked about their lives. At some point, Nick's mom pulled out his baby pictures. She thought he was an adorable little boy. On the drive back to Zola's house, Nick grabbed her hand and thanked her. "Thank you so much for meeting my family. I know that they can be a bit much at times, but they are full of love. I hope they didn't overwhelm you tonight." "Of course, they did, but I enjoyed every minute of the evening." Zola replied, smiling at Nick. They spent the rest of the drive talking about the dinner and the time Zola spent with his mother and sisters. When they arrived at her house, he walked her to the door. He put his arm around her waist as she slid her arms around his neck. "You are an amazing woman, and I am so blessed to have you in my life, Zola James." She blushed. "I'm blessed to have you in my life as well, Nicolas Gallo." He kissed her sweetly. "Would you like to come in and stay a while?" she asked him. He nodded, and she led the way into her house. That night, while they watched a movie, he discussed what the future could hold for them. Zola thought back on how the months had flown by for them. She was excited about what the future held with Nick.

They arrived at his sister's B&B later that afternoon. They were led to their rooms to freshen up. Marco had prepared a late lunch for the two of them. After they ate, they walked the grounds. Marco and Adrianna had done so much since they were last up there. "Hey, I scheduled us a canoe ride this afternoon. Marco and Adrianna will go with us. There is so much beauty in this place." Nick said to Zola. "Ok, well, let me change," Zola replied. "No, what you have on is perfect, sweetheart," Nick told her, kissing her neck. Even after almost a year together, he still made her weak in the knees. She loved everything about this man. She loved how his eyes sparkle when he is talking about his daughters, she loved the way he touched her with such love and care, and she loved the intimacy between them. Zola loved her friendship with Nick. This is something that she knows that she didn't have with Jonathan. In the end, they didn't have a foundation to fall on when things got tough. With Nick, though, things are so different. He is a communicator, and she loved that about him. She never had to guess what was on his mind. What she also loved about him was his ability to get her. It's no secret that Zola's life hadn't gone exactly as her parents would have liked it to. This fact still bothers her from time to time. "My love, you are exactly who you should be. Celebrate who you are and what you have accomplished in your life. Celebrate your strength in following your dreams when your parents wanted you to go down the path they laid out for you. Look closely at your life now, darling. Because of your tenacity and individuality, you are a successful business owner, and you're a professional artist. You are doing exactly what you've wanted to do." Nick encouraged her one night when she admitted to her insecurities about how her parents viewed her life. "The truth is, Zola, how many people are living their exact dream right now? So many have compromised along the way, but you haven't. You've been living in the fruit of your labor, not just since your divorce, but even before you were married. Of course, Sophie looks up to you. My girls are blessed to have you in their lives as well." Nick went on to tell her. That's when she knew she the right choice to love Nicolas Gallo.

On the canoe ride, Adrianna and Marco took Nick and Zola to an island that came with the land they purchased. "We didn't know this was back here," Adrianna said with excitement. Marco and Adrianna were planning on building a cottage on the island as an extension of the B&B. "Oh my goodness! This is breathtaking, guys. I love it back here," Zola said. They explored the island for a while. On the way back to the B&B, Adrianna asked Zola, "So what do you think?" Smiling widely, Zola told her that she was sitting on a gold mine. "I know that your father is an architect and he's designed buildings, but would he design our cottage?" Adrianna asked. "Well, he designed and built the home we grew up in, so I'll ask him. If he doesn't do it personally, I know he can connect you guys. He knows everyone," Zola replied. Later that night, Nick took Zola to a very nice dinner in the neighboring town. They both thought the food was delicious and the ambiance lovely. She felt so special on her date with Nick. The next day, they travelled to the town once more to attend their festival. Zola and Nick laughed all day. They shopped in the local shops. "You know, there's always something in these small downtown stores that you cannot get anywhere else," Nick said to Zola. She nodded in agreement as she spotted something she wanted to purchase for Sophie. Nick could hardly believe how this woman had changed his world. When Karmen died, he was resolved to taking care of the girls and build the business that he and Karmen started together. Throughout the years, friends and family suggested dating again, and he would simply refuse. He felt like he'd be cheating on Karmen, but he knew in his heart he wasn't ready. He felt like that up until the day he laid eyes on Zola. It was such a chance encounter. She has such warmth and life. She was a spontaneous and fearless woman. She managed to pull him out of the place he was in. She came in and shook his world up, and he knew he was the better for it. He worried about his daughters after they first met her, but once they got to know her heart, they accepted Zola and Sophie into their little family. He didn't see a reason to put off asking Zola to marry him. Nick never thought that he'd be in love again, much less contemplate asking another woman for her hand in marriage. All he knew was that he wanted to be her partner for life. He watched her interact with the other patrons in the store. He loved her smile. It seemed to brighten up any room she was in. He watched as she walked towards him.

She connected her arm with his. "Ready?" He nodded at her. He was indeed ready.

Chapter 15

Nick arranged to have their dinner in the Sanctuary, the place where he realized he was falling for Zola. "Everything about this place is romantic," Zola said. Marco got the staff to set a table just for the two of them. They sat out in the Sanctuary for a couple of hours talking, laughing, and dancing. Nick and Zola had such a lovely time. There were a couple of times when Nick almost proposed to Zola right there in the Sanctuary, but he didn't because he wanted to do it right. Zola deserved that and so much more. They slept in the next morning and met downstairs for brunch. The perk of being related to the owners is that they could stay as long as they wanted today. Nick really wanted to keep Zola to himself for as long as he could. At the table, Nick mentioned, "My sister messaged me last night and told me that we can stay as long as we want. I hope you weren't in a rush to get back," Nick said. "Rush? Why would I be in a rush to get back to responsibility? The girls are all in one place. We've spoken to them throughout the weekend, so we know they are fine. We can stay as long as you desire." Zola replied to Nick. "Hey, would you mind accompanying me to my friend's wedding in a few weeks? You remember Billy? I introduced you guys when you and I were getting to know each other. He has popped the question to his girlfriend, Krista," Nick said to her. "A wedding, really? I haven't gone to a wedding since Maranda got married. I'd love to," Zola replied. "Good. How do you feel about going to dinner with them sometime soon? Nick asked her. "I think that's a lovely idea. I'd love to meet her," she answered him. After brunch, they did not come back down until it was time for them to leave that evening. They spent the rest of the day in Nick's room talking, watching movies, and spending quality time. On the ride back home, there was a comfortable silence between the two of them. Nick had the jazz station playing. He absently stroked the back of her hand with his thumb. He loved jazz music and listened to it all the time. Etta James's Sunday Kind of Love blared on through the speakers. As Zola listened to the words, she looked out the window. Tears began to form in her eyes. She found herself full of joy. There is a completion that Nick and his daughters brought to her and Sophie's life. "Mama said it would be like this," she thought to herself. When they arrived at Nick's, Zola gathered Sophie, and they headed home. On the way, Sophie told her mom all about her weekend with Nick's girls. "I had the best time ever, Mom. Adrienne came home, and the four of us hung out all weekend. "April and Adrienne took us to the mall, and Alex and I watched a movie," Sophie said. "Wait, the two of you went by yourself?" Zola asked. "Well, the movie theater is in the mall, so Adrienne and April shopped while we watched a movie," Sophie replied. Zola knew what that was about. They were getting Alex and Sophie out of their hair for a while. She smiled at the thought. Zola and Sophie spent the next hour talking about their weekends.

Tori rolled over and looked at the clock. It was five thirty in the morning, and she had been wide awake. She had not been able to sleep through the night since she came back home to her parents. Almost since the moment she stepped off the plane, her parents had been by her side. Though she was grateful, she did not expect that at forty-four, she would be with child. She wanted to be a mother, but she wanted to raise this child with her husband. "What a mess this is," she thought to herself. She's been here for a week now, and she's had no contact with him. He's called her several times in the past few days, but she sent them to voicemail. "Tori, we're all here for you. Zola told her at lunch one afternoon. She was happy to see her baby sister thriving in her life, and she wanted that for herself. She didn't want to face the fact that Tim was still walking away from her knowing they were going to have a baby. "Good morning, baby girl." Richard James said to his eldest daughter. He came into the room and sat on the edge of the bed. "How are you feeling this morning?" he asked. "I'm feeling alright. Daddy, why are you up so early? You're retired now." Tori asked. "Well, you know how the body works. I may not get up to go to work these days, but I always get up early. Besides, there is always something to do. Speaking of that, I wanted to see if you wanted to grab some breakfast with me. Your mom has class this morning, so it would be the two of us if you'd like to go," Richard answered. Just then, she felt a hunger pang. She thought it would be nice to have her dad all to herself for a change. "Tim called your mom and me last night. He has been trying to get in touch with you. Have you not been answering the phone?" said Richard. "Daddy, I know he's been calling, but I'm not ready to talk to him. I'll talk to him soon," she responded. "Baby, make sure it's sooner rather than later. "Dad, I can't believe this is my life. I never imagined that I'd even want to be a mom, let alone carry a child," Tori said. "Well, baby, you know that the good Lord doesn't make mistakes. You might not have thought you'd ever be a mother but pay attention to how he softened your heart to the point of desiring a child to prepare you for this moment. If God changed your heart, then he can change Tim's heart. Have faith in Him." Richard encouraged her. She sighed. She didn't look at this situation the way that her father described. She had been so angry with him for how he'd been acting towards her since she told him that she wanted a baby. He had become cold and distant to her and eventually moved out of the house. When she showed up at his office one day, he told her to leave. Now he's calling her. She didn't know why he was reaching out, but she returned the favor and sent his calls to voicemail. He's left several messages and texts, but she hadn't checked any. She wanted to avoid any confrontation with him. Besides, Tori had to clear her mind and plan.. She resolved to listen to his voicemail and check texts from him in private when they returned home.

"Tori, are you kidding me? Where are you? I have been calling you for a few days now. Call me back. My lawyer wants to talk to your lawyer about setting up a meeting." Tim left the first message. "Tori, why aren't you answering the phone? You cannot put off the inevitable. Call me back." Tim left the second message. "I've gone to your office, Tori, and your assistant said you weren't there. Your managing partner said that you're working remotely. What are you doing, Tori? Why are you avoiding this situation?" Tim left the third message. He sent her a long message about arbitration. "Tori, my lawyer has set a meeting date for January 27th. Get with your lawyers, and if that is not a good date, please let my lawyer know. He's Lee Joseph of Joseph, Hurd, and Wilson. Please stop avoiding me. Where are you?" He sent another text before he called her parents. "Tori, did you go home? I'm calling your folks. I hate that it had to come to this because I don't want your parents in our situation, but you leave me no choice." Her father explained that Tim had called their home, and her mother answered the phone. "Hello, Mrs. James. This is Tim. How are you?" her husband said to her mom. "Hey, Tim. We're doing quite well. How are you? Are you well?" Lila James said to her son-in-law. "Yes, ma'am, I'm maintaining. I have been trying to get in touch with Tori. I've been calling and leaving messages, but she's not answering. Is she there by any chance?" Tim said. "Yes, Tori did come home. She is not here at the moment, however. I will have her call you." Lila responded. "Yes, ma'am. Thank you. Take care." Tim said before he hung up. Immediately upon hanging up the phone, he sent Tori another text message. "So, you went home? You cannot run away from this. Come back to Chicago and handle this. Call me back and talk to me." Tim sent his last message to Tori.

Tori sighed after reading and listening to his messages. She dialed his number, and he answered on the first ring. "Hey Tori. Why have you been avoiding me?" Tim asked her. "I have not been avoiding you. I needed to get away and think, Tim. I'm pregnant and you accused me of manipulating you. We conceived this child the night of the dinner party. I know you position on being a parent, and I want you to know that I am not trying to trap in you a marriage that you don't want. I did not expect to get pregnant, given that things were so strained between us. Tim was silent. She nervously waited for his response. "Tori, I don't know what to say. We were drunk, and we weren't careful. Are you keeping the baby?" Tim said. "What do you think, Tim? This baby is as much a surprise to me as it is to you. I'm keeping it. I want this baby that you and I created. We don't feel the same way about wanting kids, but that does not negate the fact that this baby was conceived in love. Should you decide that you don't want any part of parenting this child with me, I will move accordingly. I will have my lawyer contact Lee Joseph." Tori replied to him. She felt a resolve take hold of her. "Ok," was all Tim said to her before they disconnected the call. Tears streamed down Tori's face. What was she going to do now? Part of her wished that he'd change his mind. Tori accepted that this was how her life was going to be. She lamented losing her husband. They had not missed a holiday together since they became a couple almost two decades ago. She spent Thanksgiving with her family without him. She loved seeing her nieces and nephews and her siblings. Richie and Zola made her laugh constantly. She had missed them terribly. Why didn't she come home more often? She'd always loved Richie's wife, Dominique, as well. She was so proud of her brother for letting love guide his heart. She has changed him in ways that she, Tori, never imagined. Her brother had always been high-strung and singularly focused. Now, he's relaxed and easygoing. He is on his second novel. When their brother shifted his life, he and their father were constantly at odds, but just as he accepted Zola's differences, he accepted Richie's. Both of her younger siblings had carved their own way in life, defying their father had expectations. Zola was supposed to be an architect like him, Richard was supposed to continue in his career as a headhunter, and she was to excel in advertising. She was the last to veer off their father's prescribed plans. It amazed her how completely understanding he was compared to her siblings' situations. When she called her parents, she half expected them to tell her to stick it out. She was so glad they welcomed her with open arms. She needed her mom and dad now more than ever.

"I want to ask Zola for her hand in marriage," Nick announced to his best friend, Billy, one night at the sports bar. They made plans to meet after work. "What? Are you serious? You want to marry Zola?" Billy exclaimed, smiling and high-fiving Nick. "I'm happy for you, man. She is good for you. You are a different man. It's as if she came in and brightened up your entire world. Keep holding on to her, Nick; she is the one." Billy went on to say. "Thanks, man. We went away a few weeks ago, and I was just observing her. I've been observing her—how she interacts with strangers, how she interacts with my girls, and even my parents and sisters. The love that she has attracts others to her. I mentioned this to her before, and she said, "It's the love of the Father, Nick." That is what she told me. She is exactly right. She makes me want to be a better man, a better father, and a better son. She brings an upgrade to my life. How could I not want to spend the rest of my life with her?" Nick gushed. Billy slapped Nick on the back. They discussed how and when he was going to ask Zola. "First things first, though, I need to have a conversation with her parents. Her dad is as traditional as they come," Nick said. He thought back to the first time he met Zola's parents. She had invited him and his daughters to a barbecue.

Upon entering the James home, Nick noticed the photos of the moments captured throughout the years of Zola's family's lives. He saw preschool, high school, and college graduation photos. He saw vacation photos and photos of the grandchildren. The home that Zola grew up in was so warm and inviting. Her mother greeted him with a hug. "Nicolas, it's nice to meet you. My baby talks about you all the time." Lila James said to him. Her dad gave him a very firm handshake. "Nick, nice to meet you," was all that Richard James said. Zola's father was understandably protective. Zola had gone through a lot in her previous marriage. Zola's father, brother, and Nick were sitting on the grilling porch watching the football game. Her father and brother asked him a barrage of questions, sizing him up. Almost immediately, he and Richie, as he preferred to be called, hit it off. They had a lot in common. Nick grew up playing soccer, and while Richie played American football, his preferred sport to play was soccer. Richie was a fan of Chelsea F.C., and Nick loved Inter Milan. They both followed the clubs faithfully. Richie told him that his wife, Dominique, who's Colombian, purchased tickets to a Chelsea F.C. match. Dominique was a die-hard Atletico Nacional club fan. His favorite NFL team was the Baltimore Ravens. Her father had been a San Francisco Forty Niner fan since Zola was in diapers, he told Nick. During a commercial, Richard James Sr. asked Nick what his intentions were with his daughter. "What is your end game, son? See, I'm proud of my baby girl. She's so strong and self-assured now. It took her a while to get into that place. I can't have anyone coming in to take that away." Nick's heart began to pound. "I love your daughter, Mr. James. She is the best thing that has happened to me. She is just who my girls and I need in this season of our lives. I'm happy that she allowed me to prove myself to her and Sophie. The two of them have become a part of our family," Nick responded. "My girls are special to me. Jonathan has put Zola through a lot. It took her a while to recover. I'm warning you now. Don't put my daughter through that," Richard said. "Sir, I would never purposefully hurt your daughter. She carries a light that the world needs, that I need." Nick said. He could see her brother nodding his head out of his periphery. Nick's daughters loved Zola's mother. April said on the way home, "Ms. Lila is so classy, Dad. I like the way she dresses. Ms. Zola reminds me a lot of her mother." "I like Sophie's aunt Dominique. She's so nice. Her hair is so beautiful. She let me brush her curls," Alex said. Nick asked Adrienne what she thought of Zola's family. Shrugging her shoulders, she said, "I see where she gets her mannerisms from. April is right; she is a lot like her mother. I like them all. I kind of want to get to know them more." Nick didn't push any further. "This was a good day," Nick thought to himself.

"Well, whatever you plan, let me know how I can help," Billy said. "Well, I have to talk to Mr. James next." When he told his mother and father that he was planning to propose to Zola, his parents told him that he needed to talk to her father. "Son, you know how I did this. I went to your grandfather for your mother's hand in marriage. You will go to Zola's father." Nicholai said to him. "I know, Papa. I would never asked her without getting her father's blessings." Nick said to his father. "I'll be headed over to her parents' house in a few days," Nick said to Billy. "Good luck, man," Billy said.

"Josh, can I talk to you about something?" said Kha'ren, who was snuggled up next to Joshua on the couch. They made plans to spend the weekend together at his house. They had both had some busy days, which didn't leave very much quality time. They were talking on the phone one evening about how much they missed each other, and he suggested that they spend a weekend at his house. "Are you getting ready to show in LA?" she asked him. "Yes, I am, but you are definitely a priority. I want to be with you, so I'm going to make it happen, even if I have to rearrange my schedule," Joshua answered. This made her blush. This man was one of a kind in her eyes. "Of course, you can talk to me. What's up?" Joshua said. Kha'ren took a deep breath and thanked him for standing by her as she went through the healing process. Tears were pouring down her cheeks. "I love you so much. I'll always be here," he said, taking her into his arms. They sat there holding each other for a while. She cried, and he cried with her. His weeping felt like an intercession for her. "I'm here for you, for whatever you need. I want you to know how strong you are. You carried this trauma for a very long time and kept surviving. Please see someone professionally so that you can continue to heal." Joshua said to her. "I've already made an appointment. You know, it wasn't until recently that I realized how much that affected my life. I thought I was damaged goods, so I pushed men away. I didn't think I deserved happiness in a relationship, especially since I got an abortion. I walked around with guilt and shame all the time." Kha'ren explained to him. "I'm here for you, my love. Whatever it is you need. I'm here," he told her. The night she told Joshua about what happened, she felt a release in her soul. Twice she's told this story to people she loved, and both times they comforted her. The fears she had of being rejected never came to pass. No one thought less of her, no one blamed her, and no one thought she deserved it. They simply supported and loved her. This has given her the strength to talk to a professional. "I want to learn how to live without this incident in my life. Everything in my life, in every encounter, in every relationship, and in every experience, the rape has accompanied me. I want to be in a place where it simply happened, and it's not my identity," she told Joshua. "You do know that what happened to you doesn't define you, right?" he asked her. "I know, but sometimes I have a hard time believing it." He kissed her cheeks and reassured her. From then on, Joshua made sure to speak words to Kha'ren that brought life to her. He'd send her messages that encouraged her. Joshua went out of his way to show her that he loved her. For this, Kha'ren counted herself blessed.

Nick knocked on the Jameses' front door. The door swung open, and a tall, caramel-toned woman answered the door. "Yes, can I help you?" the woman said. "Hi, I'm Nick. Is Mr. James available?" Nick asked her. "Nick? Zola's Nick?" the woman said with a smile. "Yes, ma'am," he responded. Nick held out his hand, but she pulled him in for a hug. When she pulled back, she introduced herself. "I'm Tori, Zola's sister." "Really? It's so nice to meet you. I was hoping that we'd get to meet one day," Nick said to her. Tori led Nick to her father's study. "Dad, Nick is here to see you," she said after opening the door. "Have him come in," her dad said. Nick walked into the office. Her dad stood, and the two men shook hands. "What can I do for you, Nick?" Richard asked. Nick was so nervous that his hands were sweaty. He took a deep, shaky breath. "Mr. James, I would really like to ask you for your daughter's hand in marriage. I love her with everything I have," said Nick. Zola's father leaned back in his desk chair as he squared a look at Nick. "Son, my wife and my daughters are the sun and the moon to me. Zola has had to overcome too much in her life. She's faced a lot, and I have been there for every bump, bruise, and hurt. I've been there for the divorce, for the single parenthood, for the highs and lows, and for the struggle to find her voice in business as a Black woman. I, her father, have been there for it all. I've protected and held her through it all. Now you want to take the reins? Nicolas, I need you to understand that Zola is one of the most important people in my life. I was her first love. When she divorced, I continued showing her how she should be loved. Her mother and I took care of her heart these past few years. "Sir, I promise that I see her. I know her value and her worth. You and Mrs. James have influenced her. I love her so much. I want to spend the rest of my life showing her just how loved and valuable she is to me." Nick responded. Richard smiled at Nick and saw him take a notable exhale. "Nicolas, I believe you love my baby girl. I'd like to think she is a good judge of character. Welcome to the family, son." Nick stood up and shook Richard's hand. "Sir, thank you so much," Nick said. "Call me Richard," Zola's father said. Richard called Tori and Lila in to tell them of Nick's plans. "How are you going to ask her?" Tori asked him. "Well, I have a yearly catered Christmas party at the bakery, and I was thinking of asking her during the party. I would love for all of you to be there." Nick responded. "Of course, we'll be there!" an excited Tori said. Zola's father smiled and slapped Nick on the back. "Zola's mother and I wouldn't miss it for the world."

Nick set out planning the Christmas/engagement party for Zola. He realized that he didn't know a thing about planning an engagement, so he orchestrated a meeting between his mother and sisters and Zola's mother and sister. The women were introduced and exchanged pleasantries. Nick came out of the kitchen with an assortment of desserts, teas, and coffee. The women were ecstatic at the news, and all offered him assistance. They asked him what he had planned, and he explained to them that he was just going to throw the party and then propose. Shaking her head, his mother, Elena, said, "Oh, thank goodness we are here, my boy." The rest of the women seconded. The women determined that it would be best for them to take over the planning. The only responsibility he had was to buy the ring. After an hour and a half of planning, laughing, and fellowshipping, all the planning was complete. "I can't tell you all how thankful I am that you all came here to help me. Elena grabbed him in a hug. "Baby boy, it is my pleasure to help you. Zola makes you happy, and she's brought a brightness in you and the girls." Lila explained to Nick that they had never seen their daughter this happy, not even in her first marriage. "Of course, we'd be here, my dear," Lila exclaimed, pulling on her coat. The women set aside some dates on which they would get together to meet again. Lila mentioned that she was going to bring in Zola's three best friends to also help with the planning. "The more hands we have, the better," Elena told Lila as she embraced her.

Though they overwhelmed him, Nick was glad that the women came to help. His phone buzzed as he cleared the tables. "Well, hello there, beautiful. How was the rest of your day?" Nick said to Zola. "Hey! My entire day was tiresome. Inventory is always so much work. I was there a lot longer than I intended to be. Are you home with the girls?" Zola replied to him. He hated lying to her, but he had to come up with a quick excuse as to why he was still at the bakery. "Oh, no, I'm at the bakery working on a new cake. Will you be coming over this evening?" he asked. "Sweetheart, if it's ok with you, I'd like to go home, take a long bubble bath, and crash." "You should get some rest, as you have to do inventory in the store here in town tomorrow. Sophie is already scheduled to stay with Alex tonight, so she's squared away this evening. They chatted a little while longer until Nick heard a knock at the bakery door. "Hold on a second. Someone is at the front door," he said. When he came through the double doors, he saw her standing at the door smiling. Enveloping her in a hug, he asked her, "Why didn't you tell me you were coming by?" He pulled away a bit so that he could kiss her. She leaned in and stood on her tiptoes and kissed him back. "Now it wouldn't be a surprise if I told you I was coming. Thank you for understanding about tonight," she said to him. "Zola, you need to rest, and I know what inventory is like. You have to do it in both stores this week," Nick said. "Well, now that I'm here, I don't want to leave," she said as she slipped her arms around his waist to snuggle in closer. Zola truly loved this man. Over the past year, their lives had become intertwined. Both of their families had accepted them as part of their family. Nick and Zola showed up for each other's children in major ways. They ate dinner together and went away a few times for long weekends. Nick and his daughters had become a normal part of their lives. "You might feel that way now, but you must rest, my love. Besides, I've ordered you hibachi from your favorite Japanese restaurant. You've got to beat the delivery guy." Nick responded. She looked up curiously at him and asked, "When did you order dinner for me?" He explained that when she said she couldn't come over on account of her exhaustion, he ordered her dinner. Zola kissed him and hugged him tightly. Nick made her feel so loved. "You know I love taking care of you, Zee," Nick said to her. He loved taking care of her and Sophie. They were an integral part of his life. He had long thought of Sophie as one of his daughters. In fact, when he had Billy drop some fishing gear off at his house, he told him, "You can go on over; my girls are home." Later, Billy was talking to him about his encounter with the girls and realized that he was referring to Sophie as one of his girls. "So, things are serious between you and Zola?" Billy asked him. "Yes, man. They are about as serious as it gets. I love that woman." He knew that Zola could take care of herself and didn't need a man to do it, but it was a pleasure for him to take care of and support such a woman. "See, this is one of the reasons why I love you, Nicolas Gallo," she said, dropping a kiss on his cheek. "I love you too, Zola James. It's the little things that count, my love. I always want you to feel secure in the fact that I will always be here for you." Nick said. For the first few months of their relationship, Zola had been waiting on the proverbial shoe to drop with Nick. She had expected something to go wrong. Her mother made her realize that she was approaching her relationship with the expectations that she had of Jonathan. "Baby, not all men take good women for granted. That was a choice your ex-husband made. Don't make this guy pay for the poor decisions of another man. You're going to push him away for sure." Lila said to her. Her mother's words rang in her head. It took her a while, but she finally understood the truth of what her mother was saying. She had to give Nick a chance to be who she suspected he was. She was so glad she took her mother's advice. Her life with Nick was so satisfying. She had become attached to him rather quickly, and that scared her. It did help, too, that they were big on communication. She eventually talked to him about her fears, and he made sure he made her feel secure. He went out of his way to show her that he cared. He gave her his time, attention, affection, truth, and consistency. In return, she gave the same things back to him. She loved him deeply and made sure she told him every day.

Zola had no idea Nick was planning to propose to her. She was gushing about how beautiful Billy and Krista's wedding was and what she'd do if she ever got married again. She went on about decorations and flowers, and venues. He smiled and listened. Nick was more than ready to marry Zola. He'd love Karmen with all of his heart and soul. Which is why he couldn't conceive of loving another woman. He mourned her for years, and he held his daughters in mourning as well. It had been long past the time to start living again. Nick thanked God daily for his mother. Had it not been for her honest conversation about the state of his life, he would have never pursued Zola.

Not too long after Nick asked Richard for permission to ask Zola to marry him, Richard took his wife and daughters to dinner. He had been so thankful to have his children together again. Tori lived away in Chicago, and it was difficult to get her home because of her busy career. Zola moved two towns away, and although she was closer than Tori, her schedule wouldn't allow her to come home as much either. This holiday season, Richard will have all three of his children at the dinner table. "Girls, your mom and I are so happy that we'll all spend the holidays together. It's been so long since we've gotten together," Richard said. "Yes, my heart is so glad to have all three of my babies in close proximity." Richard and Lila both listened to their daughters catch them up on the events of their lives. They gave advice when it was asked of them, but mostly they listened. "I'm so proud of both of you. Zola, you've overcome much, and you've allowed God to heal you. You're expanding your business, and your art career is thriving. Sophie is following right in your footsteps. Don't be like me, though. Allow her to forge her own path; don't try to create one for her like I tried to do with you all," Richard said. "Aww, Daddy. I love you too!" He went on to talk to Tori. "Tori, baby girl, you've had an amazing career, which has afforded you the experiences that most people won't ever get. What amazes me the most is your courage to stand up for yourself. You're giving us another grandchild. I know it was God who moved on your heart about children. I know you love Tim and your heart is broken, but darling, it doesn't matter how long you've been married to him; if he doesn't show up for you and his child, then he doesn't deserve either of you. We've got you, and you are not alone." Tori had tears streaming down her cheeks. "Thank you, Daddy." Richard covered Lila's hand with his. My love, I want to thank you for loving me all of these years and raising our children. You have loved and accepted me. You have lifted me up and encouraged me through every venture. You were patient with me when I wasn't patient with you. I'm such a blessed man." He leaned over and kissed his wife. The rest of the evening was filled with laughter.

The holiday season was always busy for Maranda. From Christmas shopping to dinners to volunteering to counseling, there was always something to do. Usually, she and her husband, Mike, gladly work tirelessly during the holiday season to make sure everyone has a great Christmas, but this year, they are parents. They both spoke about having time for their little family. She explained to her husband, "Darling, I know that we're always on the go this time of year, but I really want us to have time for our family. This is Sam's first Christmas." He agreed, and they delegated some of the work this season to their ministry leaders. She continued Christian and grief counseling because it was simply important to continue this work. Maranda could not wait for Nick to propose to Zola. She was extremely happy for her friend. Zola had come so far, and she was grateful to watch God do a great work in her life. She deserved to be happy and with a man who loves her unconditionally. She remembered how broken Zola was when Jonathan walked away and how she was stricken with grief from the loss of her marriage. God, however, pulled her up out of the low place and ministered to her heart. He sent believers such as herself and mutual acquaintances to minister and encourage her and Sophie. He sent wisdom to her through her mom. She loved how God went out of His way to love and care for her friend. Now, she's healthy, whole, and healed. Her phone rang. "Hi, Veronica. How are you?" Maranda answered. "Randi, Eric called me and left a voicemail message," Veronica said. "What did he say, Veronica? Maranda asked. "He wants to meet me for dinner, though I don't know why. He broke up with me." "Reconciliation, perhaps?" said Maranda. "I don't know about that. He was very clear that I had all of the problems that broke us. I can't imagine why he'd come back to these issues." Veronica replied. "First of all, you didn't have all of the issues in that relationship. Secondly, you are not the same woman you were at the beginning of the year. You've done a lot of work, and more importantly, you've allowed God to take you on the journey of healing." Maranda rebutted. "That may be true, but Eric made me seem like I was not worthy of giving and receiving love. said Veronica. "I know that unkind words were said between the two of you, and you may still be angry at him, but under all that vitriol is love. So, I'd suggest you meet him and talk to him," said Maranda. "I want to meet him, but I am afraid of being rejected by him again. I just want to escape that horrible feeling," Veronica replied. "You don't know what this man is going to say, Veronica. Why not show up to hear what he says? At the very least, you can get closure." Maranda tried to encourage Veronica. Veronica tended to run away from tough situations. Maranda knew that she really needed to hear the truth. Veronica loved Eric, and Maranda knew he felt the same. "Face the music, my sister, and no matter what the outcome is, you're going to be fine," she went on to encourage Veronica. They spoke a little while longer that day. She truly prayed for her friend's happiness.

Days after speaking with Maranda about Eric, she texted him. *"Hi Eric. Give me a call when you're available to talk about dinner."* He called her almost immediately. "Hi, Veronica. How have you been?" Eric greeted her. "Hello, Eric. I'm doing well. How are you?" He told her how busy he'd been. Then there was a silence between them. She cleared her throat, and he spoke up. "So, I, uh, wanted to know when you'd be available to have dinner with me," Erica said. "Eric, why do you want to have dinner? I can't imagine what we'd have to discuss, as you've said everything when we broke up." Veronica replied to his invitation. He sighed and fell silent. "Veronica, listen, I know there was a lot spoken between us months ago, but I'd really like to speak with you once again. Will you hear me out?" he said. Now it was her turn to fall silent. "You there?" he asked. "Yes, I'm here. When would you like to meet Eric?" she asked him. "Can we meet this Friday night at Walton's? It's that new restaurant around the corner from your office." Eric said. "I know the place. Seven o'clock fine with you?" she replied. "Yes. Seven is perfect," he said. Eric hesitated once more. She knew he was having some kind of internal dialogue. "Eric? You there?" Veronica asked to pull him out of his thoughts. He cleared his throat. "Ah, yeah, I'm here. Ok, so seven it is. I look forward to seeing you on Friday, Veronica," answered Eric. "Looking forward to it too, Eric. I'll speak with you then; I have a meeting in a few," she said to him. "Um, ok then. I'll, uh, see you then, Veronica. Enjoy the rest of your day."

Tori sat at the desk in her childhood bedroom. She had been on conference calls all day for a major account. She realized that she was going to go to Chicago next week to finish her work on the account. She sat back in the chair and sighed after booking her plane ticket. She also knew her meetings with the lawyers were coming up next week as well. She was not ready to deal with this. She could not believe that Tim, after knowing that he was going to be a father, didn't budge on his decision. They hadn't spoken much since she told him that she was pregnant. She jumped when her phone buzzed on the desk. She answered the phone with her headphones. "Hello, Tori Collins speaking." "Hello, Tori." "Tim," said on the other end of the phone. Upon hearing his voice, she sat up. "Hello, Timothy. If you're calling to tell me about the meeting, your lawyer has already contacted me." Tori said. "No, I'm calling to check on you. Is everything alright?" Tim said to her. Deflated by the indignation she felt, Tori replied, "Oh, I'm fine. We're fine." "Ok, great. Umm," Tim said to her, but fell silent. "Tim, I'm busy right now. Is there anything else you wanted to say?" she said. "I miss you, Tori," Tim told her. Her heart sped up. She had missed him terribly, but she was determined not to fall to pieces because of it. It was easier to be angry and keep her indignation so she wouldn't have to feel the heartbreak over her broken marriage. She had resigned to feeling the worst things about it and called him cold and heartless for not rushing to her side when she told him she was pregnant with their child. She sighed. How should she respond? "Will you have dinner with me when you come to Chicago next week?" "Ahh, why?" she asked him. "I'd like to talk to you, but more than that, I'd like to see you. I know you're getting in a day early. I got it out of Shaun." "Shaun, one of the partners, Shaun?" she asked. "Yes. I saw him on the golf course, and we began talking about you," Tim replied. "Why do you want to have dinner, Tim? "There are things that I want to say to you, but I'd like to say them in person," he replied. "Ok," was all she said to him. She thought about that phone call from him for the next few days. She noticed that he had begun texting her throughout the day. At first, she was hesitant, but she began to respond. Before long, she had come to expect to hear from him. He did not disappoint her. He called and texted her very often, but he didn't often ask about the baby. That disappointed Tori, but she didn't dwell on it. She heard her parents' doorbell ring. "Coming," she yelled out. She's been so tired lately. Her mom and sister explained that she would be exhausted during her first trimester. Tori felt tired and sleepy very often. She slowly schlepped down the stairs to the door and gasped. "What are you doing here, Tim?" she asked him as a smile spread across her face. He smiled back and captured her in a hug. "I decided that I didn't want to wait until you came back to Chicago." Tim responded tightening the embrace. She returned the embrace, burying her face in the crook of his neck. He eventually released her from his grasp. "Come in, Tim." She led him into the living room. They sat down, and she waited expectantly for what he had to say. Tim looked at her and lowered his head. "Tori, I'm sorry for how things have played out between us. I feel like we were on this journey together and in agreement on the direction we were going in, and you decided to go in another direction. We were on the same page about not having children, but you changed things," he said. Tori rolled her eyes. "I'm pregnant now because we have slept together." Sighing, he told her, "I know that, Tori. I'm talking about before you got pregnant. Our marriage was strained because all we did was argue about having children. I was so angry with you, and then when you told me that you were pregnant after the night of the dinner party, I got even angrier. I thought you were forcing me into this situation. I had begun to question whether or not you planned it." Tori's eyebrows rose. "Are you kidding me? You think I planned this, Tim? Did you come all the way here to accuse me of trapping you into being a parent?" With each question, Tori's voice rose an octave higher. He stood up and paced in her parents' living room. "This is not going how I planned it. " He turned back to her and walked back towards the couch to sit down next to her. "Tori, please listen to me. I'm trying to explain my thoughts to you. I'm not proud of how I treated you or what I was thinking about you. I know you didn't plan on getting pregnant. You and I had too many glasses of wine that night. This baby was conceived out of love. We both wanted to be missed and wanted to be together that night." She visibly relaxed after hearing him out. "When I realized that you had taken a leave of absence from the firm and gone home, I was devastated, but it came out as anger. I know I had no right as I made you feel unwanted. I was so angry at you. I felt like you blew our lives up. Then the only way you would communicate with me would be through your parents, text, or your lawyer. I was not used to not having access to you, let alone not being able to talk to you. I sat in anger and thought that if I could get the divorce quickly, then it would hurt you. I wanted you to feel the pain and devastation and loneliness that I felt about losing you. I have done a fine job of pushing you away, and I blamed you for it. I stopped communicating with all our friends because I knew someone was going to ask about you. One night, my mom showed up at the house. You obviously told my sister because she told my parents what was happening between us." Tim said. She nodded in confirmation that she had told his sister about their marriage. "I expected my mom to come hear me out and take my side, but I should have known better. She never takes sides. That's probably why I didn't tell her, because I wanted someone to feel sorry for me, too. My mom said, "Are you telling me that Tori is having my grandchild and you are mad at her for it? I don't care what kind of agreement you came to when you first got married. Timothy, you both were so young. You had to know that one or both of you would have changed your mind. Son, I don't know what you expected me to say. I came over here because your sister told us about it, and I wanted to see if you lost your mind. Do you realize how precious a baby is? Tori is not being selfish; you are. You're a grown man having a tantrum because things have changed in your life. You're going to be a father, Tim, and you're afraid. You've always been afraid, which is why you are in this headspace. Ok, so you two did not plan this, but that doesn't mean it's not meant to be. You may not want anything to do with his baby, but your father and I do. This is our grandchild, and he or she will not grow up thinking that their father's side of the family didn't want anything to do with it," Tim explained. "She told me to grow up. Can you believe that? he said. Tori nodded her head yes. Tim's mother was known to speak her mind. She meant well, but she did not spare feelings when she was telling it like it was. She never tried to hurt anyone's feelings, but she was very matter-of-fact. "I thought about what my mom said to me, and after a while, I felt like such a fool. I began to reach out to you, hoping that we could communicate again. I was so glad when you began to respond. After a while, I felt like I was getting my best friend back. I wanted to ask you about the baby so many times. I would text you asking how he or she was doing, but I would delete the message. I felt like I didn't have the right to ask. I wanted to talk about the baby, but I didn't know how to broach the subject. I thought you would shut me out." He said. When he finished, tears were meeting under her chin. "Tim." "Was all," she said, and he moved closer to her and wrapped his arms around her. She wept in his arms, and he hugged her tighter, whispering apologies and comfort in her ear. "Please forgive me, baby. I'm so sorry that I pushed you and our baby away. I know that I have a lot to make up for. I broke something between us, and I intend to fix it," he said. When the sobbing subsided, she cleared her throat and said, "I was so angry and scared. I didn't know how I was going to raise this baby and hold a career by myself. That's why I came home. I needed to be with my family. I prayed for this day. I prayed for you to want the baby and me," Tori said. "You should never have to pray for that, Tori. I'm sorry." Tim replied to her. She looked up at him. "Why not? When we got married, we gave our marriage to God. We promised to give all our problems and concerns about our marriage to Him. Well, we definitely had problems. I'll always pray for you, Tim." He looked her in the eyes and felt silly. "How can I make this up to you, Tori? How can I make things better between us?" he asked her. "You being here is a start," she said, kissing him. He hugged her tighter and touched her stomach and removed his hand. He realized that she might not have been ready to let him in yet. "I'm sorry, Tori. Can I touch your stomach?" She grabbed his hand and placed it on her slightly swollen belly. His eyes glistened with tears. "My God, I'm going to be a father," he said, trembling. "Tim, where did the fear of being a parent come from? You mentioned that your mom told you this." Tori said. He looked at her embarrassed. "My uncle Charlie. When I was fourteen, he and my aunt Catherine were arguing about my older cousin, Tristan. I don't even know what they were arguing about exactly. I was sitting in their garage when he stormed out. He looked at me and said, "Look here, kid. Don't have children. All they do is come between you and your wife." Then he walked off and got in the car and drove off. My aunt filed for divorce later that year. My young mind had no reason not to believe my uncle Charlie. I guess I carried that into adulthood. When you told me that you wanted children, my uncle's words came back to me. Then, when you told me you were pregnant, I thought that it was over." "Do you know why your aunt and uncle divorced?" she asked him. He admitted that he didn't really know the reason they got a divorce. "Maybe you should talk to them and find out why. They may not have divorced for the reason you believe." As he held his wife, he thought about what she said. He had allowed an incident from his childhood to shape a very important part of his life. He fervently believed that if he and Tori had children, it would tear them apart. He could not believe how foolish he had been. "How's the baby?" he said, looking down at her. Tori gasped.

Zola sat at her desk, looking over her schedule for the next few weeks. She had multiple buyers from her art show. She created pieces for Nick's sister, and that paid off for her. His sister and her husband told almost everyone they knew about Zola's artwork in their bed and breakfast. Since then, she's had a few meetings. She never thought of marketing her art in this manner. She created art and hoped that people would buy it. "It's a little different to have my work commercialized." Zola mentioned it to Nick one night at dinner. "Think about it, Zee. Your artwork can be reproduced and put up in more bed and breakfasts or even hotels. Think of this as the blessing that it is." Nick encouraged. She had ruminated on the possibilities in her mind. When her mobile phone rang, it startled her. "Hello, this is Zola James." She answered in a cheery tone. "Good afternoon, Ms. James. This is Dr. Francis Carter from General East Hospital. You are listed as the next of kin for Jonathan Pendleton," said a man with a gruff voice. Zola sat up in her chair. "What's wrong with Johnathan?" "He has been in a car accident and has a collapsed lung, broken ribs, and a shattered leg. He's in stable condition, but I wanted to inform you." Dr. Carter said. Tears welled in

Zola's eyes as she thought of Jonathan lying in the hospital, hurt. "I'm on my way," she told him before hanging up. With shaky hands, she called Maranda. "Maranda, Jonnie's been in an accident. I'm headed to the hospital now. Can you all come when you can? With a panicky voice, Maranda assured her that she would contact Veronica and Kha'ren. She then asked her about Sophie, and Zola explained that she would contact Nick so that he could bring Sophie to the hospital. On the way to the hospital, she called her parents to tell them about Jonathan. Zola arrived at the nurses' station and grabbed the attention of a young brunette. "May I help?" said the nurse whose tag said her name was Amanda. "Yes. My name is Zola James. I received a call about Jonathan Pendleton. He is my ex-husband, and I'm his next of kin. How is he doing?" Zola replied to the nurse's question. The nurse looked up Jonathan's file and gave Zola a wary look. "Can you hold on for a few minutes? I'm going to get the nurse who helped the doctors work on him when he first came in. Zola nodded her agreement, and the woman quickly walked away. There were so many thoughts flowing through Zola's mind as she stood there. Finally, after almost ten minutes, another nurse, a little bit older, came walking up to her. "Good afternoon. I'm Nurse Charlotte. I was with Jonathan when he first came in. He was suffering from a collapsed lung, and we were putting a chest tube in for his lung when he went into cardiac arrest. We were able to revive him, but he's in surgery now. We won't know anything for a while." Charlotte said, placing a hand on Zola's shoulder. The doctor will come to see you when the surgery is complete. With tears streaming down her face, Zola shook her head. Suddenly, arms wrapped around Zola. "My love, how is Jonathan?" Nick asked her. She swung around and wrapped her arms around him. Sophie approached them both. "Mom, is Dad alright?" Zola opened her arms so that she could capture her in a hug as well. "He's in surgery now, baby. He was in a car accident and has broken ribs and a leg, but his lung had also collapsed. When they were working on his lung, he went into cardiac arrest." Zola explained to Sophie. Sophie cried in Nick and Zola's embrace. "We're all praying for your dad to pull through." Nick consoled Sophie, wiping her tears. They sat in the waiting room in silence. Sophie sat between Zola and Nick. He wrapped an arm around Sophie, and she leaned into his embrace. Zola was moved by this, and at that moment, there was no doubt in her mind that Nick was the one. He rubbed the back of her neck to get her attention. "Hey, are you ok?" She shook my head at him. "I'm just really concerned. Thank you for this." She replied, pointing to Sophie, who had snuggled in the crook of his arm. "Sweetheart, I'm always going to be here," Nick said. Zola silently prayed that God would bring Jonathan through this. Half an hour later, her parents came rushing into the waiting room. Sophie and Zola jumped up and rushed into her parents' arms. "How is Jonathan? Richard asked Zola. "Well, when the doctor called me, he told me that Jonathan had sustained injuries from the accident but was in stable condition. They were prepping him for surgery. By the time I got here, he had already gone into cardiac arrest. He's been in surgery for the past hour now." Zola told her parents. "Is there anything that we can do, baby?" Lila asked her. "Not right now. You're being here for us is more than enough." Zola replied to her mother. Richard shook Nick's hand, and Lila gave him a hug. "Thank you for being here for our girls," Lila told him. "Think nothing of it. Zola and Sophie are family to the girls and me." Nick said, wrapping an arm around Zola and kissing her temple. Richard nodded and slapped Nick on the shoulder, assuring him that he was glad that he was with his girls. Twenty minutes later, Nurse Charlotte came to the waiting room to get Zola. "Hi, I just wanted to give you an update. He has undergone a coronary angioplasty. He had blockages in his arteries. The doctor will come out soon and speak to you in a little while." Zola thanked the nurse and wrapped her arms around Sophie. Her three best friends came walking through the door just then. They rushed to her side and hugged both her and Sophie. "How are you doing, love?" Veronica asked her. She explained what the doctor and nurse told her. "We've got you, sweetheart." Maranda assured Zola. The group held hands and prayed.

For the next hour, they all had small talk. Someone asked Zola if they could get them food. Sophie clung to her arm tightly, and Nick kept staring at her. An older gentleman came walking through the door and looked around at the small crowd of people that had assembled in the waiting room. "Ms. James?" Zola stood up. "Mr. Pendleton is in recovery now. You can see him in an hour when he awakes. We were able to repair his arteries by widening them so that the blood could flow freely. His leg is in a cast, and of course, his ribs will need to heal on their own." "Thank you, Dr. Carter. How long is his recovery?" she asked. "Recovery will take a few months, but please urge him to be patient with himself as he recovers. Many patients want to get back to the life they had before their cardiac emergency before they've fully recovered," Dr. Carter explained. "Will he need to stay in a facility, or can he live alone?" Richard asked the doctor. "I would suggest that someone stay with him for two to three weeks after he is released." Dr. Carter replied to Richard's question.

Zola told the group, "Now that he is out of the woods, you all can go. He's going to be out of it for a while longer, and they will only allow family in the back right now. I don't know when he'll move to a room, but I'll ensure that you all have his room number. They all simply looked at her. Her father said, "Zola, we aren't leaving you." They all shook their heads in agreement. "Zee, we're here for you," Veronica said. Just then, Nick's daughters, Alex and April, came walking in. Sophie stood and embraced Alex while April hugged Zola. "See, we're not going anywhere," Nick said to her. Zola was truly grateful to the friends and family who rallied around her. No one left their side until after she and Sophie were both able to see him. When Sophie entered the hospital room, she grabbed her father's hand. He opened his eyes and looked at her. "Oh, my baby girl has come to see me." Sophie lay her head on her dad's shoulder. "I'm so glad you are alright, Dad. I was so scared, but Mom was praying for you." He looked over at Zola. "Thank you." She shook her head. He explained to them that someone swerved into his lane and hit him. His car began to spin, and then it flipped. He told them how grateful he was to be alive. Sophie told him about all the people who were in the waiting room. "I'm so glad that you two weren't out there alone," Jonathan told them. They sat with him a while longer. "Ok, I'm going out there to tell them all to go home." When she and Sophie reached the waiting room, they flooded her with questions. She explained what happened to cause his accident and how he said he was feeling. She told them that they were giving him a room within an hour and encouraged them to go home. They obliged this time. "Baby, you make sure you give us updates on his progress," Lila said as she hugged both Sophie and Zola. "Yes, Mom, I'll let you guys know. Tell Tori and Richie that he is fine. They've both been texting me. I told them not to come." Zola told her parents. Her friends approached her, and each gave her a hug, promising to call and check on them. Nick's girls gave their hugs and told Sophie that they hoped her dad would get better soon. Sophie walked out of the waiting room with them. Nick looked at her. "You know I can stay here with you. April has driven her own car. I'll stay right here by your side," he said, kissing her. "No, we're actually not going to be here much longer. They are moving him to a room. Sophie and I are going to go to his house and pack a bag for him and drop it off for him." Zola explained to him. He nodded at her. "Ok, well, the girls and I will make sure you guys have dinner waiting when you get home tonight." She smiled at him. "That would be lovely, babe. Thank you so much for being here for us."

An hour and a half later, Zola and Sophie were entering Jonnie's home and going to his bedroom to pack a bag. "Ok, so you know your way around her better than I do. Help me pack your dad's bag." Zola said to Sophie. They packed three days of clothes and gathered his toiletries. Sophie stacked dirty dishes in the dishwasher while Zola tidied up his bedroom and master bath. "We cleaned your house, Dad," Sophie said as she sat in the chair next to his hospital bed. "You cleaned my house? You girls didn't have to do that," he said. "Well, clean isn't exactly the word. You're a neat freak, Jonnie. We tidied up." Zola said with a chuckle. He smiled at her. The three of them talked a little while longer until visiting hours were over. Sophie and Zola promised to visit him the next day. Left alone, finally, Jonathan began to think about the day's events. He was so grateful for his life. His mobile phone rang. He looked at the caller ID, and his aunt Rebecca's name flashed on the screen. "Hey!" he said. "Hello, my boy. How are you feeling?" she asked. He explained all that had happened to him. "Oh, my sweetheart. I'll be catching a flight out as soon as I can." She assured him. His aunt was in her late seventies, and he did not want her flying across the country alone. "No, Aunt Rebecca. I do not want you to travel across the country by yourself. I'm ok, and I'll recover, but I don't want to have to worry about you." He said to her. His aunt Rebecca raised him after his mother died of cancer. It has always been just he and her. As far as he knew, Rebecca was the only family he had. He didn't know anything about his father, and his aunt said that his mother refused to talk about him. "Jonathan, you are like my own child; why would I not come to make sure you're alright?" she rebutted. "Listen, I'm fine, Auntie. It's going to take some time to recover, but I'm fine. Sophie and Zola will be here for me. "Oh, Zola! I'm so glad. You know, she called me to tell me what happened. She's always been a good girl. She's always been good for you. It's a shame you divorced," Aunt Rebecca exclaimed. Jonathan closed his eyes and lay his head back on the pillow. In almost every conversation, his aunt mentions Zola. "They left a little while ago. I'll probably be in here a few days longer, and then I'll be released." He told her. "You are going to need help, son. You've got a broken leg and ribs, and you're recovering from a procedure. If you don't want me to come over there, then you need to hire a nurse temporarily." His aunt said. Jonathan sighed, "I'm not sure it'll come to that, but I have Sophie and Zola. They've been here all evening and will be here in the morning. It's going to be alright. Don't worry so much, Aunt Becca." His aunt sat quietly as if to ponder what he had said. "Alright, Jonnie. Make sure you keep me posted on what the doctors say. I want to come, but I'll listen to you for now." Rebecca said to him. He noted her 'for now' at the end of her response to him. After he hung up with her, the gravity of the day came crashing down on him, and tears began to spill down his cheeks. He felt so grateful to be alive and have family and friends around to care for him. He was most grateful to have Zola and Sophie there. He began to lament, which is something he's been doing for months over his divorce. He knew that it was his fault that they divorced, but if he could go back, he would have fought for his family. He did not love her right, but he was certain that he could love her the way she deserved this time around.

"Do you have everything squared away for the party?" Zola asked Nick as they were curled up on the couch, looking at a movie. They had come to the realization that they needed to be intentional about spending time together because their busy

194

schedules would not allow it. They decided that they'd spend quality time two nights a week, and the rest of the week would be filled with their businesses, kids, and everything else going on in their lives. Though they didn't plan it, their families ended up eating dinner together at least three times a week. "Yes, everything is covered," Nick replied to her. "I don't know why you wouldn't let me help you plan it," she sighed. "Babe, you are already very busy. You know I didn't want to put anything extra on you." Nick consoled her, kissing her temple. "It wouldn't have been extra. You know I love doing stuff like this," Zola said. "I know, babe, I just didn't want to worry you about this," he said, hoping that she would drop it. The fact is, this was their engagement party, and he didn't want anyone to let it slip that he was planning to ask her to marry him. Her mother told him to keep her as far away from the planning as possible because she was certain that Zola would find out. He hated to keep her out of it, but he wanted to keep it a surprise. "Ok, but next year my hands are all over the planning," Zola said in a pouty tone. He chuckled at her declaration and agreed. The women had really done the planning. Their mothers came together very often without him to go shopping and to discuss food options. He was grateful that they seemed to really get along quite well. As a matter of fact, his mother told him that she felt as if she'd known Lila a lot longer than just a few months. Things were going as planned until her ex-husband got into an accident a few weeks ago. She and Sophie had been by his side ever since. He knew this was Sophie's father, but he was still bothered by the fact that Zola spent so much time helping him recover. "Don't they have nurses for that?" he said as he was talking to his friend Billy. He lamented to his friend about Zola and Sophie helping him. "Sounds like someone is jealous?" Billy said. "Jealous? No. I just know men. If he is truly sorry for how he treated Zola, then he will want her to give him another chance." Nick said in a knowing tone. "Also, I know that Sophie is not my daughter, but I feel like she is, and she and Zola have become a very important part of our family. I feel like he is going to try and take my family away," Nick admitted. "So, you're jealous." Billy looked at him quizzically. "You're not hearing me, Billy," Nick said, sighing with annoyance. Chuckling, Billy said, "Oh, I hear you loud and clear. You've become possessive of this woman and her daughter. You've let them into your life with your daughters, not to mention your heart. Now, you are afraid that Zola will choose to go back to her ex-husband, take Sophie, and effectively leave you and the girls. Am I right?" Sitting back in his chair, Nick said, "Well, when you put it like that." The fact is, Nick was terrified of losing Zola and Sophie. He loved the family that he and Zola were creating with their girls. He and their girls missed Zola and Sophie. "Have you spoken to Zola?" Billy asked. He looked incredulously at his friend. "To have her thinking I'm insecure and jealous? No." "You are insecure and jealous, sir. I think you should talk to her. You're getting ready to ask for this woman's hand in marriage. Don't you think communication is important?" his friend said. Nick sat quietly for a moment, contemplating his friend's words. He knew he needed to talk to Zola, but pride was getting in the way.

Chapter 16

Veronica showed up a few minutes late for her dinner date with Eric. She had been working on an account with her staff, and she lost track of time. She had intended to go home and change, but after glancing at the clock, she realized that there was simply no time. "Oh well. I'll have to go as is." She said to herself as a man opened the door to the restaurant for her. She exchanged pleasantries with him and gave him Eric's last name. The host escorted her to their table. She saw Eric sitting and looking down at the menu. He looked up and stood when he heard the host bidding them a good dinner. He smiled down at her and pulled her in for a hug. "Hi, Veronica. You're looking beautiful as usual." She hugged him back. "Hey, Eric. Thank you for the compliment." He pulled a chair for her to sit. "I ordered a bottle of wine for us. I hope that is alright," Eric said, smiling. "Oh, that's perfect. It's been that kind of day," Veronica replied. "So, tell me about your day," Eric insisted. "It was long. I have been working on a new account with my team. There's been a lot of back and forth between my client and my team. At first glance, you'd think they are picky, but not really. He has a vision, and he wants to see it manifest just as he envisioned it. As a result, that means a fair bit of going back to the drawing board. It's ok though because I love what I do," Veronica explained. Nodding, Eric said, "I can tell. You've always been passionate about your career." Just then, the waiter came to take her drink order. Once he was gone, they sat in silence for a moment. Because she didn't like awkward moments, she spoke up. "So, Eric. What did you want to talk about tonight?" He sighed, "Well, I wanted to talk about the way things went down with us. First, I want to say that I'm sorry for the way that I walked away. I know that I hurt you, and for that I apologize." He put his head down after that statement. Veronica sat quietly, looking at him for a moment.

She said, "You walking away hurt me, but it pushed me on a trajectory of healing in my life. I had to face myself, and that was one of the hardest things I had to do. Eric, I know you walked away, but I did my share of pushing you away. In those days, I had no idea who I was because of my past." He gave her a questioning look. "I didn't share this with you, but I'm adopted. My adoptive parents took me home from the hospital. I was still young when they told me, and I appreciate them for not waiting until I was an adult. Unfortunately, it sent me on a spiral. I didn't feel complete. I was hurt, and I took that pain out on everyone I dated. I was angry at my birth parents for giving me up. I was so grateful to my adopted parents. They have been so amazing to me, but I felt like pieces of me were missing. I mean, who did I look like? My proclivities? Where did they come from? Who has my eye color and shape? The more I ruminated on these things, the more terrible I felt. I functioned in my life feeling rejected. You got that part of me that was so unsettled in my mind and spirit. For that, I'm sorry. I was bleeding my past all over you." He looked at her with compassion in his eyes and covered her hand with his. "Veronica, my God. You were dealing with a mountain of things. I'm sorry." She smiled. "Listen, I'm healed now. My best friends had sort of an intervention with me after we broke up. I'm grateful to God for them. They loved me right through everything. I began seeing a therapist. I still see her. The best part of it all is that I met my birth parents, and we are building a relationship." Veronica went on to tell him everything about her journey to healing and wellness. They talked through dinner and dessert. She talked, and he listened and asked questions along the way. He looked at her with amazement. "You are a strong woman. I'm proud of you, Veronica. I'm so sorry I walked away instead of trying to get down to the root of the situation," Eric lamented. Shaking her head and waving him off, "Eric, listen, it all had to happen this way, and I'm definitely better for it. All that matters is that we're here in this space now. "I asked you to talk to see if we could be in each other's lives. When I walked away, I was so angry that you wouldn't do what I wanted you to do. I had an idea of how a woman who's in a relationship should act and respond, and you were the opposite of it. I thought I'd get back at you by walking away and telling you that it was your fault that I walked away. I was so prideful. Once I got over the anger, I realized that I missed you. I picked up my cell to call you so many times, but I didn't make the call. Mostly because I was afraid that you would reject me after walking away," Eric said. He got a little nervous because she listened with an expressionless look on her face. "I will admit, I was angry at you as well, but that was short-lived. I began to look at my actions that led to you walking away. Yes, we can be friends," she replied. He was a little disappointed that she said friends, and he was hoping that his face wasn't expressing how he truly felt. "I can say with certainty, Eric, that I am a different woman, and I'd like you to get to know me for who I am now. I don't think jumping into a relationship is wise right now. I now understand that building a foundation of friendship is what's best for any romantic relationship. He gave her an understanding gaze and agreed to a friendship. On her way home, she called her friends to tell them about her date with Eric. "Our girl has evolved," Maranda joked. "Oh, I have, girls; God has done a lot of healing. My birth parents are ministers in their church, and they connected me with my therapist, who's also a Christian. I stopped seeing my old therapist for one I have now," Veronica explained. "I'm so proud of your progress, sister. Zola encouraged her. "Speaking of progress. How is Jonathan's progress?" Veronica asked Zola. "Yes, he is much better than he was. Sophie and I have spent a lot of time helping. Now, I think I'm going to help him hire a nurse. I think it's time to get back to my life. I feel like I've put everything to the side, including our life with Nick and the girls. I needed to do this, though." Zola replied. "Zola, the fact that you can help him recover after everything that he has put you through speaks of the strength and forgiveness God has placed inside of you." Maranda said. "Yeah, Zee. I'm amazed at you. You, too, have undergone a lot of change in your heart and your mind." Kha'ren said. "You ladies, along with Joshua, have encouraged me to get the healing I need from my past," she went on to say to them. "You deserve to live a life of freedom, my sweet friend." Maranda said, sounding teary. "Look at God. I've been praying for you girls for years. I got in a place where I said, "God, what use is it to be a Christian if I can't influence those closest to me?" Now look at each of you. I've watched you all accept Christ into your hearts, and I'm watching Him heal you from the very things that plagued you and tried to hold you down. What else can I do but praise Him?" There were sniffles on the line. "Randi, you know I don't cry. Look at what you have done!" Veronica exclaimed. They all laughed.

A few days later, Zola and Nick were making dinner in her kitchen. He pulled her into a tight hug. "I'm so glad that we're doing this mundane thing, such as making dinner," Nick said. She laughed and returned the hug. "What's this about?" "I just— we just missed you guys, Zola. You and Sophie are a part of our family, and we noticed when you guys weren't around. The girls and I understood what you had to do, but I will admit, I got a little insecure," Nick replied. She pulled back and looked up at him. "Why would you be insecure, Nick? You know that I love you," she consoled him. He looked away, a little ashamed. "I know. I was afraid that your assisting Jonathan with his recovery would bring you two closer and you'd decide to give him another chance. I thought that you'd go back to him for Sophie. I guess my imagination ran away with me." Nick confessed. She grabbed him by the hands and guided him to the center island

and sat him on a stool. She stood in front of him and looked him in the eyes. "Nick, I need you to understand that I had to do this. Not because Jonathan is Sophie's dad, but I had to pass that test of forgiveness. I know now that helping him meant that I had forgiven him for all that I went through in our marriage. I no longer carry the pain or the hurt from that time. My mom explained that helping him would reveal where I am emotionally, and she was right. I am not in that place anymore, love. I care for Jonathan because he is Sophie's father. You know, she spoke to me about the three of us being around each other these days. She told me that while it was nice to have her parents really getting along, it didn't feel like a family. As a matter of fact, she said she missed the family we now had with you and the girls." He grabbed her and sighed. "I'm so glad you said this. I'll admit that I need to hear it," Nick said to her. "Nick, you have my heart. It's our life that we're building together that I want. Please know that," Zola said. He kissed her, and the girls came in. "Ahhh, come on, you guys. Too much PDA," Alex joked." Zola and Nick both laughed. "Go wash up for dinner; it's almost ready," Zola said to the girls. Sophie and Alex left the room giggling. "Will April be joining us for dinner tonight?" Zola asked him. He released her to check on their meal. "Yes, she should be here soon. She texted not too long ago," Nick said. That evening was filled with laughter and love. Nick was so grateful to have his family back together. He couldn't wait to make this woman his wife.

Three days later, Sophie stayed over at his house with Alex. He called Sophie in the living room, where he was sitting. "Hey, sit for a moment. I want to run something by you." Nick said, gesturing to the seat next to him. "The girls and I are so grateful for you and your mom in our lives. I love when we all get together for dinners or movie nights. It's a joy to support you in your school activities. I would love to make all of this permanent," he said. Sophie looked over at him with a smile spreading across her face. "I want to ask your mother to marry me. I, of course, need your consent too. I know I could never replace your dad's place in your life, and I will never attempt to, but I love you as if you're my own child. I know the girls love you like a sister." Just then, he looked up and found his three daughters standing behind her, smiling. Sophie looked back, smiled, and then tears began to pour down her cheeks. Alex grabbed her and hugged her. "We're finally going to be sisters," she said. Sophie giggled. "So, what do you say, Sophie? Will you allow me to make you and your mom a permanent part of the Gallo family?" Nick asked her. "Yes, of course!" she said, jumping into his embrace. Whispered in his ear, "Thank you." "You got it, kid," Nick replied, chuckling. He told Sophie about his plans to ask her mom to marry him that weekend at his Christmas party. "So, that's why you wouldn't let her help you plan? You know she felt some kind of way about that, right?" Sophie said. He began laughing, shaking his head yes. "How can I help?" she asked. He explained that her grandmother and his mother had done all of the planning. There was nothing to do but keep it a secret and make sure that her mom showed up. That night, he called both his and Zola's moms to ensure everything was in order for the weekend. "I told Sophie that I was going to ask her mom to marry me this weekend," he said. "How did she respond?" Lila asked. "She was delighted. She began to cry," he responded. "Didn't I tell you? My granddaughter is very intuitive and mature for her young age. She sees that you make her mother happy. I can't wait until this weekend. My baby deserves this." Lila said. "This is exactly how I feel about you, my son. You deserve so much happiness. I'm so happy that you and Zola have found each other." Elena said. After his wife died, Nick didn't think he'd ever love again. However, in walked Zola, she captured his heart and changed his life forever.

"Are you still going to be able to make Nick's party on Saturday night? He's proposing to Zola." Kha'ren asked Joshua. He had brought lunch for her. He spread a blanket on the floor of her office and opened a picnic basket for her. He had a spread for her. She was surprised at the effort he put in to eating lunch with her. She would have settled for eating sandwiches as long as they were together. Joshua's artwork was showcased around the country, and he was on tour. Because they didn't see each other the way they wanted, they were very intentional about the time that they had to spend together. "Yes, I can make it. I wouldn't miss it. Zola is the reason we're sitting here right now," he said. She nodded in agreement. She was extremely happy for her best friend and hoped that one day the same could happen for her. "Wow," she said audibly. He looked at her. "What?" She smiled sheepishly. "Just thinking." "About what?" he quizzed her. "I was just thinking about Zola," Kha'ren answered. At least she wasn't lying to him. She just didn't tell him exactly what she was thinking. He smiled, "Right." Changing the subject, "I know your schedule is tight, babe, but are you sure we'll be able to get together for dinner with my friends next week?" she asked. He pushed her hair behind her ear. "Kha'ren, I've taken a week off, so I have the time. My life is busy right now, but I'm making time to be with you and to be with our friends. I love my career, but what we have is so fulfilling to me. So, I will make the time to cultivate our relationship. I want to make sure you are secure in you knowing that it's you that I want. It's us that I want. So, it doesn't matter how busy we both are; our relationship takes precedence. You are a priority for me." Joshua said to her. The sweetest blush spread across her cheeks. He lifted her chin with his pointer finger and kissed her. Kha'ren was grateful beyond words. Never had she experienced this kind of love. This man made her happy.

Zola pulled up at Jonathan's house. She wanted to talk to him about getting a nurse before Sophie got there. She sat in her car thinking of the words. His aunt called her two nights ago and asked about him. She was surprised when she suggested that she get a nurse for him. "Zola, I'm an old woman, but I know the sound of a woman in love. You've met someone." Zola sat quietly, not knowing what to say. "You're happy, and I don't want you helping my nephew to get in the way of that," she went on to say. Zola began to protest, "It really is not a problem. As a matter of fact, this has been good for me. Assisting him these weeks has shown me that I have let go of the past. I've forgiven Jonnie, and I believe a friendship can come out of this." Jonathan's aunt Rebecca sighed, "Darling, he is not where you are. He hadn't told me as much, but I know him because I raised him. He loves you and wants to make up for hurting you." "Wow. Ok. Well, you're right, I have met someone, and it's serious. He has a great relationship with Sophie. I really care about him," Zola admitted. "I knew this, sweetheart. You deserve to be happy. I'm so glad you're over the past. My nephew had his time; now he needs to forgive himself and move forward." Rebecca said. "I think I'll talk to him about getting a nurse." Zola replied.

Zola got out of the SUV and opened the door with the key that he gave her. He came down and met her. "Hey. I didn't know you were coming today. Wasn't Sophie coming today?" Jonathan asked. "Hey, Jonnie. I came over to talk to you. First, how are you feeling today?" replied Zola. He shrugged. "Better, but you know that," Jonathan said. They sat down in his kitchen. Before she could speak, he began to talk. "Zola, I just want to say thank you for helping me. I've been wanting to say that you are a remarkable woman. For you to be here for me after all that we've gone through speaks of your character. In all of these years, you never spoke negatively of me to Sophie. You've always encouraged her to build a relationship with me. I just want you to know that I appreciate you. Also, I love you. I've never stopped loving you. This time, having both of you around simply confirmed my feelings. I know I wasn't a very good husband to you, especially after I became a partner. I'm so sorry for all of that. I feel like asking you to forgive me is moot because it's obvious that you have. Thank you for showing me care and love these weeks. I was hoping that we could spend more time together as a family. I want our family back. I was so foolish and selfish to let it go. I was foolish to let you go. Please give me another chance to show you that I'm not the same man you divorced five years ago." Zola looked at him. "Jonathan, I learned a long time ago to forgive without an apology. I never expected to ever hear one from you, and I thank you. I absolutely forgive you. I forgive us for not making it work. I have to tell you, though, I'm in a rather serious relationship. I came over here to tell you that I want us to talk about getting a nurse in here, if you really need one. I have put my life and my businesses on the back burner so that we can be here for you, but I can't do that any longer," she replied. "A relationship? I didn't know you were in a relationship." Jonathan said, crestfallen. "Listen, Jonnie, I think that this is a new place that you and I are in. We can finally be friends instead of just cordial. We can continue to raise our daughter as friends with no tension. We owe her that. I have always loved you and always will, but I'm happy," Zola said. He grabbed her hands in his and looked at her with tears in his eyes. "I really screwed that one up. I always thought there was time. I never imagined that you would fall in love with someone else. I'm so sorry that I broke our family, Zola." By the time he said this to her, tears were meeting under his chin." She pulled him in for a hug. "Jonnie, all is forgiven. Please forgive yourself for this. That's the only way you're going to be able to move forward and be happy. That is what I want for you. I want you to experience the joys in life. I know you love your career; even when we were married, I always wanted you to see that there was more to life outside of the office." He held her tighter. "Thank you, Zola. Thank you for raising our wonderful daughter. Thank you for building an awesome life for her. Thank you for being an example for her. Most of all, thank you for forgiving me." When they finally pulled away, he told her that he didn't need a nurse but a maid. He explained that he has already started working on cases again. She urged him to take it easy. She attempted to hand his key back, but he told her to keep it.

Chapter 17

On the day of Nick's Christmas party, Zola's friends had scheduled manicures and pedicures. Though she didn't see the need for pedicures because it was cold outside, she got her feet done anyway. They sipped mimosas and laughed. "I've invited Eric to come to the party tonight," Veronica said. The other women gasped. "What is this now? Eric?" Kha'ren said. "Yes, he and I have been in communication. When we met for dinner, we ended up talking for hours. I agreed to be his friend, though I am pretty sure he was getting ready to ask me if we could date again. I told him that I was not the same woman I was when he broke up with me. I told him that it was far more important that he get to know me in a friendship. It is a far better foundation." Veronica replied. "Look at you growing, girl," Maranda said. "Well, you know," Veronica said, smiling. The women threw a barrage of questions at Veronica about her friendship with Eric. Veronica looked over at Zola and asked her about her conversation with Jonathan. "Well, it was just as his aunt Rebecca said. He wanted to get back together. I explained that I had forgiven him, but I was in a committed relationship. I told him that we have the opportunity to give Sophie something that she hadn't had since we divorced, and that's two parents who are friends. He seemed to have understood. I'm so over my feelings for that man. I'm so grateful for where we are, but I will never walk away from the good thing I have with Nick to go back to the past." Zola told her friends. "Good for you, girl. That chapter is finally closed in your life. Now you too can fully move forward," Maranda encouraged. Zola thought about her friend's words and she was right. She genuinely looked forward to her future with Nicolas. He made her so happy. "I'm so happy for us, ladies. We've all found joy," Zola said. Each of the women agreed that "joy" was the word that described where they were in their lives. Veronica reconciled with her past. Kha'ren found forgiveness and peace. Maranda found her true calling, and Zola finally found herself.

 Later that night, Nick insisted on picking her up to take her to the party, but she protested earlier in the day. "You're my date, Zola. Why would we meet there? He asked her. "Because I'm sure you've got some last-minute things to take care of," she replied. "As a matter of fact, I do not. Everything is in order. All we need to do is go and party." Nick said. Zola rolled her eyes. "Alright, Nick." She caved because he was not going to see her side of things. He showed up to pick her up at seven o'clock that evening. Sophie was catching a ride with April, Alex, and Adrienne tonight, so she didn't have to worry about her at least. When she got into Nick's SUV, she kissed him. "You look so beautiful, my love," Nick said. Zola blushed and thanked him. "I look forward to having a good time tonight. This has been an intense few weeks," she said after a while. "Well, I guarantee you a great time tonight," Nick promised. Zola was surprised to see her parents when they arrived at the party. "You invited my mom and dad?" Zola looked up at him. "I invited your whole family. This is also a family event, Zola," Nick responded. She made her rounds, greeting everyone. "Hi Tim. "I'm so glad to see you here tonight," she exclaimed, hugging her brother-in-law. He hugged her back. "Thank you all for having me," he replied. She hugged her sister and then rubbed her swelling belly. She hugged her brother and sister-in-law. "I didn't realize that Nick had invited my entire family." Zola told Richie. He gave her a pensive look. "Why didn't you?" he replied. She slapped his shoulder. "Hush, Richie. He wouldn't let me help him plan the party. "Don't pay your brother any attention, Zola." Dominique, Richie's wife, said. The two women embraced. "You know we never miss an opportunity to get together with the family. Nick's family is great," her sister-in-law said. Zola agreed and moved around the room to greet others. She spotted her friends with their mates. "Hey, everyone. You all are looking great." Zola said to the group standing together. "Nick went all out for this party." Maranda's husband said. "I'm told it gets better and better each year." Zola said as she hugged him. She hugged each of them and made small talk. She spotted her parents in the corner. "Hey, Mama and Daddy. You two look great!" she said. "How's my baby girl tonight? You look beautiful yourself," Richard said to his youngest daughter. "I'm doing well. It's so nice here. Don't you think?" Zola said, hugging her mother. Lila agreed and smiled at her daughter. "You're glowing, my sweet girl," her mother said. Zola touched her cheek. "I am?" Her parents replied yes, in unison. "It's a good thing, though, baby. We're happy to see you so happy." Lila said. Thank you. Zola enjoyed herself at the party, laughing and dancing with Nick, her friends, and her father. The dinner was delightful, she thought. "Thank you, babe. This has been a great night. I'm so glad I get to spend it with you," she said, leaning over to kiss him. He kissed her back. "My pleasure, sweetheart. I've got to give this speech in a little while." Nick said. "Speech? You give a speech each year?" she asked. He nodded and sipped his wine. A few minutes later, Nick went to the front of the room and picked up the mic. He looked around and spotted the girls in the corner giving him the thumbs up. "Ah, excuse me. Can I get everyone's attention?" Nick said. The music was suddenly turned down, and he had the attention of the people in the room. "Thank you, everyone, for coming to celebrate with us. It's been a phenomenal year for the bakery. I look forward to the coming year to enjoy the fruit of all our labor. With that being said, I want to give these to my staff." Nick called each of his staff members up and handed them their bonuses. "Now, I also want to say something to Ms. Zola James. Zola, you are the most beautiful person I know, and I thank you for being in my life. You and Sophie have brought sunshine to the dark and cloudy days of our lives. I would like for you to come up so that I can give you these flowers." She looked around, embarrassed. She walked up to stand in front of him. He handed her the bouquet of roses. She looked down and sniffed the roses when she saw something stuck between them. "Oh, what is that? Let me get that. I don't know how that got in your roses." Nick said. He grabbed her roses and pulled out an engagement box. He smiled down at her and got on one knee. "Zola James, love of my life, my best friend, will you do me the honor of being my wife and spending the rest of your life with me?" he asked her. There were gasps all over the room, but her friends and their families were cheering them on. Zola looked down at Nick with tears flowing down her cheeks. "Nicolas Gallo! What took you so long?" Everyone laughed at her response. "Of course, I'll marry you. I can't wait to spend the rest of my life as your wife." Everyone cheered them on as he slipped the ring on her finger. He stood up, and he kissed her. The cheering continued as people crowded them, giving well-wishes and congratulatory hugs. She noticed her parents' knowing smiles. "So, you all knew about this?" she asked. "Of course, we did, baby girl," her father said, giving her a hug. Zola discovered that his family, her family, and her friends all knew that Nick would propose. Sophie came up to her and hugged her mother. "You knew, too, didn't you?" she asked her. "Yeah, Mama. I knew. Do you know he asked me for your hand in marriage, too?" Sophie asked her. "I'm so glad you said yes, sweet pea." They embraced again.

 On the ride home, Zola began to put the pieces together. "So, this is why you wouldn't let me help out with the planning?" she questioned Nick. "Correct," he replied, giving her a sly smile. She grabbed his hand and kissed it. They decided to spend the night at Zola's house while the girls stayed at Nick's. They snuggled around the fireplace in her living room. There was a comfortable silence between them for a while, until Nick spoke up. "Hey, guess what I found out about Maranda?" She looked up at him quizzically. "What's that?" "She knew Karmen?" Nick said. "Really? How?" she asked him. "Karmen used to come to her cancer support group. Your best friend used to minister to my wife. She would come home talking about the peace the group gave her. When I would ask her if she wanted me to attend with her, she would decline my offer and tell me that it was her journey. I would have never imagined that Maranda was the woman she was talking about. She never spoke her first name, only Mrs. Collier. I found out Maranda's last name while we were planning the engagement party. I'll forever be appreciative of her. She was able to give me insight into Karmen's journey. Though I was with her and took her to all of her appointments, she kept a lot of how she felt away from the girls and me. I suppose she was trying to protect us. There were times when I wished she wouldn't shut us out. Now that I know, I have the missing piece to the puzzle. Finally, I can let this rest. I will always love Karmen, but that life with her is over. God has blessed me with another chance at love, and I'm going to spend the rest of my days letting you know how loved and valuable you are to me, Zola James." Zola was speechless for a moment. She had no idea that Nick's wife was the client that Maranda spoke of. She remembered Maranda shedding tears over her passing away. "You know, we consoled her after Karmen died? Of course, we didn't know who Karmen was. Maranda never gave details about the patients from her groups. She just wept for you and your children." It feels like my life has come full circle, Zola. We were always in each other's periphery. We just didn't know it. Nick said. She sat quietly and snuggled closer to him.

After a few moments, she asked him, "So what date do you want to become my husband?" He chuckled, "Umm, how about tomorrow?"

She wrinkled her nose. "Tomorrow?" He shook his head. "Zola, I would marry you tomorrow if I could, but I know there are many things we need to sort out." "Yes, you are right. Like, what are we going to do about our living situation?" she asked. "I thought about that. I thought we could buy a new house. Karmen and I lived in the house with our girls, and I don't want to bring a new wife into a house that my previous wife lived in," he said. She thanked him silently. "Ok, so that requires us putting our houses on the market," Zola responded. "Mine already is," he told her. She looked at him. "Really?" I didn't see any signs outside in the yard. "That's because I asked her not to put any out until next week," Nick said. "So, you just knew I was going to accept your proposal?" Zola asked him, smiling. Furrowing his brow, "Well, I was praying. I guess you can say that I was walking by faith." She chuckled at his response. She could not believe the journey God had her on. "Ok, so how about a wedding in late mid- to late September next year?" she asked him. "Perfect. Any date works for me, my love," he said. She looked up at him. "I will talk to a realtor this week. Nick, are we really doing this? We're going to merge our lives and become husband and wife?" she asked him. He looked down at her and kissed her. "Yes, we are love." In that moment, Zola realized that it was all worth it. All the situations, heartaches, and lessons were leading her to this moment. She realized that God was leading her to a place of true joy.

www.ingramcontent.com/pod-product-compliance
Lightning Source LLC
Chambersburg PA
CBHW051507050726
47594CB00010B/4008